"THERE'S TROUBLE!"

Manning's eyes flicked to the rearview mirror.

James turned to glance through the back window and spotted the dim points of headlights. A jeep appeared to be closing on them fast. It could only mean police. In other countries they might have stopped, but this time they had to consider the Sudanese police on the opposite side of the fence. A good number of those in uniform were little more than thugs, and out here the Phoenix Force warriors couldn't consider them soldiers on the same side. They would avoid a conflict if at all possible but not at the risk of failing in their mission. Lester Bukatem and his LRA guerillas were a threat that had to be dealt with, and neither Manning nor James would let police officials detain them, friendly or otherwise. Chances were good this meeting would result in their arrest and possible confinement without cause.

"If we stop, we're dead," James said.

"Then I won't stop."

DON PENDLETON'S

STONY

AMERICA'S ULTRA-COVERT INTELLIGENCE AGENCY

MAN®

ARMED RESISTANCE

A GOLD EAGLE BOOK FROM

WORLDWIDE®

TORONTO • NEW YORK • LONDON
AMSTERDAM • PARIS • SYDNEY • HAMBURG
STOCKHOLM • ATHENS • TOKYO • MILAN
MADRID • WARSAW • BUDAPEST • AUCKLAND

Recycling programs
for this product may
not exist in your area.

First edition February 2012

ISBN-13: 978-0-373-80431-3

ARMED RESISTANCE

Special thanks and acknowledgment to
Jon Guenther for his contribution to this work.

Printed in U.S.A.

ARMED RESISTANCE

CHAPTER ONE

South Sudan

Two hundred miles north of the border with Uganda a biting wind swept across the desert, wending its way through the rock formations and echoing like howling spirits.

No matter how much time Samir Taha spent in this environment he never really became accustomed to it. Even after six years spent fighting in the barren and rugged terrain of his homeland, the legends still gnawed at his spirit. For Taha and his men, the wind carried the souls of those who had gone before and fought for liberty and freedom for those in South Sudan.

"You hear them again?" a voice whispered.

"I hear them often," Taha replied, although he didn't look at the man who spoke. He need not look his brother in the eye. Kumar knew better than anyone else the things that troubled him.

"You know I do not believe in the spirits," Kumar said.

"I have never asked you to believe in them, merely respect those of us who do."

"But to what ends?"

"I do not wish to discuss this here and now," Samir said, waving his brother to silence. "Now be still."

Satisfied there would be no further outbursts from

his young and rather impetuous sibling, Samir Taha returned his attention to the camp ahead. Their intelligence had always been good in the past where it concerned those godless bastards who chose to traffic in innocent women and children. It had been difficult to gain support from government officials. Taha wished he could have recruited more men from their own ranks for this mission but General Kiir had refused to provide them. They were a ragtag bunch, to be sure, undisciplined and poorly equipped. Only half of the assault rifles they carried, Kalashnikov variants, were even capable of full auto fire.

A good number of them were semiautomatics—7.62 mm SKS-style rifles smuggled from connections in China or American-made AR-15s chambered to fire .223 cartridges. The remaining soldiers carried pistols and knives, and the ammunition situation was plain abysmal.

Taha had even begged the general to part with a couple of AK-47s but the old man wouldn't hear of it.

"We have no reason to believe your intelligence is good," General Kiir had told him. "If you do this then you do it voluntarily. I cannot risk it as a sanctioned mission."

The general's lack of support infuriated Taha but there wasn't much he could do about it. Although many of the men among them, particularly those who reported directly to Taha, their platoon commander, agreed with Taha, the majority of them didn't want to cross Kiir. Even among the brave fighters of the Sudan People's Liberation Army, who were fighting for independence from North Sudan, there were those who still bartered for position by politicking. Taha had no use for such men and he knew who they were. He had flatly refused some of those who had volunteered to accompany him on his mission, knowing where their loyalties truly lay.

Up ahead, Taha saw the cook fires of his enemy and smelled the roasted meat on which they gorged themselves. Probably most of their food had been stolen from the village they had razed early the previous morning. Most of the men in the village had been slaughtered, their bodies covered with flies and some of their hands—detached by explosives or the heavy rounds of .50-caliber machine guns—mutilated as food for wild dogs and hungry cats. It hadn't taken any imagination for Taha to conclude it was the work of the Lord's Resistance Army.

The very name was vile and brought a sour taste to Taha's mouth every time he thought of it. These men, barbarians whom Taha would not even acknowledge as fellow countrymen, had known their way in this region long enough. If the authorities in the cities and the members of the Sudanese Armed Forces, representing North Sudan, would not lift a finger to protect innocent Sudanese, then Taha would do whatever he could to fight for those incapable of defending themselves. It was what good men did—it was what Christian men did.

"Prepare to sound the signal," Taha ordered his brother.

Kumar said nothing in response; they had practiced this many times and he knew what to do.

In one respect, God had been shining his blessings upon them since the wind would mask their approach. The Lord's Resistance Army would not expect them in the least; their leaders knew of the SPLA's desire to avoid conflict whenever possible. When the fighting grew too bad, that's when the government got involved and sent in armed forces that were well-equipped and well-trained. But those military units were not discerning and their orders were to kill any official combatants irrespective of creed. Somehow, and Taha had never been able to understand it, many more of the men in the Sudan People's Liberation Army had fallen victim to the genocidal policies of the Sudanese Armed Forces than those of the Lord's Resistance Army. It was more than numbers, more than coincidence.

No matter, because Taha no longer feared what another man could do to him—he only feared looking into the eyes of his God and being condemned to eternal hell because of cowardice. He was accountable for the blood of his brothers and he did not want that accounting to be one of shame. So he would bear whatever burdens were laid upon his shoulders in this time and place.

The signal came: a sudden squelch of the radio in his ear. Taha left the cover of the rocks and moved toward the camp perimeter. Many of the sentries were weary and unprepared for the sudden ferocity of Taha's assault. As the men entered the camp, stepping inside the defensive line of men spread across the perimeter, the peaceful solitude of the encampment erupted into chaos. One of the Lord's Resistance Army guards looked Taha in the eye a moment before the warrior leveled his SKS assault rifle and squeezed off three shots. The 7.62 mm rounds cut an ugly pattern in the man's belly and dumped him onto his back.

Taha turned toward his next target only to discover a very young man who could not have been more than fifteen, but the subgun clutched in his fists knew neither age nor restraint. Taha grimaced even as he fired a short burst that blew the young man's head apart. Blood and brain matter erupted from the stump of his neck, some of it landing in a nearby cook fire, and the boy's body followed a moment later.

Taha scooped up the submachine gun, quickly inspected it in the light of the flames now immolating his enemy's small body and realized why its profile had looked so familiar. It was an M-16 A-3 assault rifle, carbine model with stampings from the U.S. military. The markings surprised Taha so much he nearly lost his life with the distraction. Two LRA members rushed him, the muzzles of their weapons leveled in his direction and winking with the first shots. Taha threw himself into the sand and triggered both of his weapons simultaneously. The rounds managed to stop one of the LRA terrorists in his tracks, but the second evaded by jumping to the right.

Unfortunately neither of the men was at a distance that made using his assault weapon practical and they both committed to a grappling match simultaneously. His opponent was younger and much faster, but Taha had strength and experience on his side. Even as the knife blade sang from the man's sheath and swung in for the soft tissue of his belly—the blade glinting wickedly in the light of the fire—Taha managed to get inside the attack. Using a move shown to him once by an American mercenary, Taha twisted the arm and hand in a downward motion while stepping between his opponent's legs. He then twisted in the opposite direction and brought the hand upward while sweeping the outer leg. The force of the sudden reverse in motion effectively dumped his enemy onto the ground, and Taha followed with him. He let his weight do the rest of the work and buried the knife blade into the man's chest to the hilt.

Taha scrambled to his hands and knees, beads of sweat immediately forming across his head and exposed arms, perched over the twitching body of the man. Taha vomited onto him as the fear and adrenaline nearly overtook his system and caused him to pass out. Head swooning and eyes watering, Taha took several deep breaths and in spite of himself got to his feet. He stood unsteadily for a moment before realizing if he didn't recover now he stood the chance of being overcome by additional enemies. Taha searched frantically on the ground until he located his weapons, retrieved them and moved off in search of more men to kill.

Taha made it through the camp in no time and realized that the battle had barely begun before it ended. Taha located Kumar and ordered him to give the signal the group should rally. When they were assembled and a head count was taken, Kumar advised his brother that all were accounted for and only one man was wounded.

"Only one?" Taha repeated.

"They were of no significance, this enemy force," Kumar replied.

Another loyal fighter named Sadiq added, "These were hardly men, my friend. I have fought the dogs of Lakwena before, and these men were untested. They are almost children that were left behind to hold this camp."

None of this made sense to Taha. He looked at Kumar. "A decoy?"

"I have never known them to do anything like this before, my brother."

"Nor have I," Taha said with a vigorous shake of his head. He held up the M-16 A-3 for the men to see. "I also took this off one of the Lakwena fighters. It is American-made and a forgery I seriously doubt."

"Why would Americans equip our sworn blood enemies with weapons to fight us? They will hardly even provide General Kiir with equipment we've requested. Have they switched their allegiance?"

"I do not have an answer, Kumar," Taha said. "But it is not of great importance right now. Begin searches on the remainder of the camp and see if we can find any clues as to the direction they may have gone. Also search the body of every man here. If you find any alive, see if you can revive them enough to question them. I want to know if any of the others have American weapons on them. General Kiir will want to know this and any intelligence that we can take will help us. Let us not return to our leader empty-handed."

With a nod from Taha to signify he had finished giving orders, the men scattered across the camp and began to search the bodies for any information. Taha doubted they would find any—it wasn't like the Lord's Resistance Army to leave behind anything of value.

His unit had learned of the camp from a young girl, a villager who managed to escape notice and waited in the weeds for three days straight, afraid to show herself even after she saw Taha's force arrived at the village. Of course the little girl had been able to tell them absolutely nothing of the size of the force or the weapons they were carrying; such things were not naturally part of a young girl's life and should never have been. Taha had been unable to imagine what that poor, motherless child had witnessed. The Lakwena dogs committed atrocities against the females while the men and boys of the village watched helplessly, tied down to stakes or herded into pens where they had their feet cut off and the wounds cauterized by hot brands so they didn't bleed to death.

Instead they died by infection and dehydration, an

unimaginable death so horrific it made Taha want to be sick again.

As Taha inspected the weapon in his hand once more he wondered if there was a grain of truth to Kumar's accusation. Were the Americans supplying their enemies with guns? It made no sense to him. He knew a few Americans—mercenaries from a paramilitary company who had come to advise General Kiir and bring supplies and equipment. There was no benefit to Americans, military or civilian units, for the fighting to continue among the various factions in Sudan. In fact, quite the opposite since Sudan hosted resources and other valuable commodities of great interest to American companies and their foreign investors. They had always demonstrated a willingness to do what was necessary to resolve the civil strife that threatened stability in the region.

No, it did not make any sense for them to help the Lord's Resistance Army.

There had to be another explanation. He would ask General Kiir to make contact with his friends in the United States. The general had contacts through the CIA operative working out of the capital. These men would know what to do—they would be able to provide answers to this mystery.

And perhaps they would help.

CHAPTER TWO

Stony Man Farm, Virginia

The help would come in the form of the five men who sat awaiting the arrival of Harold Brognola and Barbara Price.

Many briefings had occurred in the confines of the War Room, as well as a good many debriefings following more successful missions than any of those men cared to count. Their presence signaled the results of what just one man can do when he's trying to make a difference. The covert unit at this table, Phoenix Force, had been born from the courage and bravery of the inimitable Mack Bolan. Bolan's war started against the American Mafia but eventually broadened to a fight against worldwide terrorism.

Forged from the spirit and unswerving abilities of Mack "the Executioner" Bolan, the men of Phoenix Force had earned a reputation as one of the finest fighting units in the world. Not even the President of the United States and a good number of his predecessors knew their identities; that was a privilege reserved only for the select few whom this band of brothers trusted with their lives.

Leading the team of warriors was David McCarter, a fox-faced Briton who'd begun his career serving with the SAS. To his left sat Rafael Encizo, whose life had started as a prisoner in the death prisons of Fidel Castro. The lone Canadian was Gary Manning. A former explosives expert with the Royal Canadian Mounted Police, Manning had a penchant for hunting rifles and possessed uncanny knowledge of terrorist groups around the world.

The other two men of Phoenix Force were successors but no less effective in their own rights. Calvin James had been handpicked by the late leader of Phoenix Force, Yakov Katzenelenbogen. A former Navy SEAL and member of a Chicago P.D. SWAT team, James was a human force with which to be reckoned. Finally, the youngest and newest member of the group was Thomas Jefferson Hawkins. Hailing from the Lone Star State and known for his quick wit, Hawkins had served honorably with Delta Force until leaping at the opportunity to join his elite friends.

Together these men had battled and overcome the forces of evil around the globe under the guidance of the most covert special operations agency in the world: Stony Man.

The Phoenix Force warriors greeted the arrival of Brognola and Price with little fanfare. While nobody pointed out the fact the pair was fifteen minutes late for the briefing—something rather unusual for these particular individuals—there was no mistaking the air of anticipation in the room. It hung like an electrically charged cloud above the Phoenix Force warriors, and Hal Brognola, director of the Special Operations Group, immediately noticed it.

"I'm sorry we're behind schedule but it was unavoidable," Brognola said. "I know you're itching for action so we're going to keep this as short and sweet as possible."

"As soon as you're briefed," Price said, "there's a chopper waiting to take you to Andrews. Jack is there now doing the preflight so we'll skip the ceremony."

It seemed as if everyone simultaneously issued a sigh of relief. Not that they would have done anything other than sit patiently while Price laid it out for them in ever-arduous detail. The mission controller was cool and calm under the worst situations, often treating them in a very maternal fashion, although only because of her natural personality; she had no real desire to flutter around them like a mother hen.

"We're sending all of the main details to your portable devices," Price continued as she sat at the table and flipped a strand of the honey-blond hair behind her ear. "You can study those on the flight out."

"Where are we headed, love?" McCarter asked.

"We're sending you for several days of fun-filled adventure in Sudan," Brognola said. "There's a time factor involved here and I want to give you as much time as possible, hence the brevity of this particular meeting."

"Here's the short story," Price said. "Four days ago, a CIA agent in Khartoum received communication from a man named Rahmad Kiir, the general and leader of the Sudan People's Liberation Army. Contact with Kiir isn't apparently that uncommon for the CIA, since they're able to provide a considerable amount of information regarding activities inside the Sudanese government. Those activities are of course the real story about what's happening and not merely the bull hooky they like to feed our embassy. To break it down succinctly, some of Kiir's men were on a mission to rescue villagers who had been taken by members of the Lord's Resistance Army."

"Also known as the Lakwena," Brognola interjected helpfully.

"I thought the LRA was practically obsolete these days," T. J. Hawkins remarked.

"Hardly," Manning said. "Even since al-Bashir was elected president, Sudan still hasn't fully complied with the minimal standards for effective elimination of human trafficking. The situation has been complicated by a civil war between North and South Sudan, which the LRA has exploited."

"That's for sure," Encizo added.

Price nodded. "Sudan is a source country for men, women and children trafficked internally for the purposes of forced labor and sexual exploitation. It's also a transit and destination country for Ethiopian women who are sent abroad as domestic servants. The Lord's Resistance Army is one of the chief entrepreneurs in this business and they harbor a good number of children from both Sudan and Uganda for forced labor, sex slavery and myriad other atrocities. Often they have integrated themselves with militia groups in Darfur and abduct young women and girls for every kind of perversion you can imagine."

Calvin James made a show of cracking his knuckles and said, "Sounds just like the kind of group we specialize in eradicating."

"While I'd love to tell you to go forth and conquer all, I'm afraid that there's a significant U.S. interest in this," Brognola said. "While some of General Kiir's men were hitting this village, they killed a number of LRA terrorists who, as it turns out, were carrying military-grade weapons. Those weapons were stamped with markings naming them as property of the United States Army."

"How do we know they're real?" Manning asked.

"Oh, they're real," Price said. "The serial numbers have already been verified and we have positive photographic identification from our CIA contact. There's just one problem and that's where the President decided it was time to involve Phoenix Force. In fact, even Able Team is going to have a hand in this one."

"I can already see I'm not going to like this," McCarter said.

"You're too ugly to live forever anyway," Hawkins ribbed him.

As the men responded with laughter, Price dimmed the lights and directed their attention to the screen at one end of the War Room. The image of a young, good-looking man in a suit materialized and the room fell quiet.

"Here's complication one," Price said. "This is a case file photo from the dossier of one Jodi Leighton, a CIA case officer who up until two days ago was serving as General Kiir's contact and feeding information back to his higher-ups in Washington. Now Leighton has disappeared along with the evidence recently given to him by Kiir's men."

"Before you ask and because I know you will, we have no idea what happened to Leighton," Brognola said. "He's just disappeared into thin air and his friend and contact who acts as liaison between him and Kiir has been unable to find out anything."

"I hate to bring it up, but have we considered the possibility this chap's gone rogue?" McCarter asked.

"It's not an unfair question but our general feeling is that it's not Leighton's style," Price said. "First of all, the guy didn't have any reason to suddenly pack it in and split. If anything, his efforts here would have won him a commendation and possibly even a ticket out of that place. Naturally when a CIA officer comes into information of this nature it automatically puts him in a dangerous situation. The world of espionage is filled with double agents, deception and betrayal."

"Okay, fine," Encizo said. "But it's also not unlike a CIA spook to simply walk away if they think their identity has been compromised. Six months later they turn up in the Bahamas wearing a Hawaiian shirt and a bad dye job."

"That's true, but we're still not convinced that's the case here," Brognola said. "Tell them about Able Team, Barb."

"And so complication two," Price said. "A few hours ago we called Able Team off of vacation and sent them to Camp Shelby."

"In Mississippi," Hawkins said.

"That's the place," Brognola replied.

"As I mentioned before, we were able to trace the serial numbers of those weapons to determine their authenticity," Price said. "But we were also able to determine the place of origin right on down to the actual armory from which they were stolen. The numbers fell on Camp Shelby and recently the chief Army officer who oversees the S1 facility there, a career supply man by the name of Colonel Jordan Scott, has no explanation."

"Okay, I'm with you guys now," Manning said. "This is no damn coincidence."

"We thought you'd see it our way," Price replied sweetly. "The fact is the appearance of these weapons in Sudan coupled with the disappearance of two high-ranking officials has the Man's skin crawling. The President wants to see action and he wants to see it in the next twenty-four hours. Tops. We have a very short time to accomplish our mission objectives."

"Which are?" McCarter asked.

"Your job is to meet up with Leighton's contact in the Sudanese government," Brognola said. "From there, he will take you to General Kiir's team, who discovered the weapons. We've had a personal request from Kiir and that is to help them retrieve the some fifty women and children who were taken from this camp."

"Begging your pardon here," James said. "I'm not sure I understand why you're sending us to rescue these Sudanese villagers. I mean, I have absolutely no problem doing this but it seems a departure from the normal mission objectives. We typically are asked to run away from the problems internal to countries, avoid any sort of press, as it were. Now you're asking us to do just the opposite? Help me out here."

"Well, first, we've obtained a lot of good information from General Kiir over the years and we've tried to support him every chance we get," Price said. "Second, we believe that if you follow the trail of the Lord's Resistance Army and find the people they've kidnapped, chances are good you will find Leighton, as well. Nothing else makes sense in lieu of the fact that these weapons were found on deceased members of the LRA."

"Not to mention the fact that the Lord's Resistance Army was categorized as a terrorist organization many years ago by U.S. authorities," Brognola added. "If you can take a few of the bastards down while you're at it, I'm sure nobody on this end of the world is going to lose much sleep."

James nodded and with a firm tone replied, "That works for me."

"I assume you'll be coordinating our information

with Ironman and friends?" Encizo asked, referring to Able Team's hot-tempered leader, Carl Lyons.

"Absolutely," Price said. "It will be the status quo and we'll make sure any information they come upon will get into your hands ASAP."

"And what about this Leighton bloke?" McCarter asked. "What happens if we find him dead or, dare I think about it, we don't find him at all? I would think that will pretty much end the trail and kill any further chance of accomplishing mission objectives."

"If you find him dead, then there's a pretty good chance that whoever killed him will have left a trail," Brognola said. "But even if they didn't, the main objective is to retrieve the Sudanese hostages and get those weapons back. Failing that, see to it that they're destroyed. If the United States Army can't use them, we're certainly not going to let a band of terrorists have their way with them."

"The other thing to remember is that you won't be able to trust a soul on this one," Price said.

"I wouldn't have it any other way, love," McCarter replied.

"We have to assume that nobody can be trusted with this outside of our own teams," Brognola said. "Even if you find Leighton alive, until we get some answers from Colonel Scott and can verify the transshipment pipeline that allowed those weapons off the base, let alone out of the country, we have to assume there's treachery on both sides."

"One thing that stumps me is why we weren't alerted earlier that these weapons had gone missing from the armory at Camp Shelby," Hawkins said. "I mean, we're talking about a massive installation, utterly secure with the largest Army reserve unit in the free world stationed there."

"That's part of what Able Team is going to be looking into," Price said. "They'll be carrying credentials identifying them as agents with the Army's Criminal Intelligence Division."

"That's a new one," Encizo observed.

Brognola said, "Since these are military weapons that have gone missing, this would normally fall into their purview. We knew if we sent them posing as members of Homeland Security or the FBI, there was a chance they'd get stonewalled out of the gate."

"At least from this angle the sending of Army CID agents has the dubious distinction of looking like we're trying to keep it inside the family, so to speak," Hawkins observed.

"A very astute observation, T.J.," Price said.

"My mom says I'm smart," Hawkins replied with a cheesy grin.

"Any other questions?" Price said.

"Just one," Manning said. "We know that the situation in Sudan is tumultuous at best. You told us that we basically can't trust anybody over there. What other opposition could we expect to encounter beside that of the Lord's Resistance Army?"

"I wish I had better news but the question is fair all the same," Price said with a deep sigh. "The fact is you're right, there has been an almost constant ethnic and rebel militia going up against some other ethnic and rebel militia since the 1960s. Hundreds of thousands of refugees have been forced out of the country and into the neighboring territories of Ethiopia, Kenya and the DRC. The Sudanese government army hasn't had the resources to combat the widespread terror and violence in the country. These groups aren't just fighting for food and water. In some cases they're filled with religious fervor, as well.

"In fact, the larger part of General Kiir's SPLA fighters are self-proclaimed Christians. They view themselves as men of God and feel it is their solemn duty to protect all citizens of the country. But there are many atrocities committed even among their own groups, something you would not consider all that uncommon in a country filled with this type of strife. Basically, outside of a handful of General Kiir's men you are persona non grata and you will have to rely heavily on the skill of your Sudanese contact."

"I'm surprised they'd even let us into the country," James said.

"They wouldn't and we never intended to bring you in that way," Brognola replied. "Your contact will meet you at the Ugandan capital city of Kampala. You'll fly in posing as oil barons, not an uncommon sight there by any means. He'll then smuggle you over the border into the areas held secure by the SPLA, specifically General Kiir's men."

"Your contact is a man named Kumar," Price said. "General Kiir has assured us that Kumar will conduct your safe passage both into and out of the country."

"Remember, don't take chances," Brognola said. "If the situation gets out of control then do whatever you must to get out of the country alive. That's your top priority if at any point things fall apart. Don't get yourself killed over a few military weapons, men. It's not worth it unless you gain ground and find that it's worth it. Understood?"

The men nodded and mumbled an agreement.

"Then Godspeed, Phoenix Force," Brognola said.

CHAPTER THREE

Camp Shelby, Mississippi

"I should be fishing," Carl Lyons announced.

A military policeman cleared them through the gate with a smart salute.

"Cheer up, Ironman," Hermann Schwarz replied from the backseat of the sedan with the government plates. "We could've been stuck with an assignment someplace where it's cold."

"Or worse," Rosario Blancanales added from behind the wheel. "How would you like to have the mission location Phoenix got?"

Lyons scowled. "We're supposed to be on vacation."

"I'm hungry," Schwarz said. "Wonder what the chow's like here?"

"You've had Army chow plenty of times," Blancanales reminded him. "You never really liked it."

Schwarz looked puzzled. "I didn't?"

Blancanales looked him in the eyes through the rearview mirror and shook his head.

Indeed, both men were quite familiar with Army food. While Schwarz had significantly less experience in the field than his friend, he brought skills that were unusual for a combat veteran. Following a stint in Vietnam as a radio intelligence officer, Schwarz had begun his second tour with Bolan during the Mafia wars after spending only five months at a technical school in East Los Angeles. With his electronic intuition, one that had earned him the name Gadgets, Schwarz was a shoo-in for selection to become part of Stony Man's elite urban counterterrorist unit.

Blancanales had a more distinguished career in the sense of notoriety. A decorated Green Beret, "the Politician" had earned a reputation as an effective member of the pacification programs implemented by the Army during the Vietnam War. He also served as Able Team's medic. Most of the time, Blancanales acted as the team's primary spokesperson due in no small part to his talent at being charming and gregarious.

The team leader was glad to leave these two men to their specific talents. Lyons had first met Bolan when the two men were on opposite sides of the law. Bolan had not spared Lyons's life once, but three times, actually, and it came as quite a surprise when Bolan and Brognola approached him about joining Able Team as their leader—not that he wasn't qualified. The only member of Stony Man's field units who had never served in the Armed Forces, Lyons had been a member of the LAPD SWAT team and a decorated police sergeant. His successful completion of the Ironman competition, coupled with his intense inner strength and physical stature, had earned him the nickname and he wore it well.

"We got a major shit storm in front of us and all you two can think about is food?" Lyons grumbled. "Hopeless, utterly hopeless."

"Well, who peed on your cereal this morning?" Schwarz asked.

"You know he gets like that when he gets hungry,

too," Blancanales said. "He's the boss so he's not really allowed to show his discomfort."

Ignoring the chance offered by his two friends to trade coarse jokes, Lyons said, "What do we know about this General Saroyan?"

"Highly decorated officer," Blancanales cited mechanically. "Came up the hard way, from what I understand. Did tours in both Iraq wars and spent some time with a military intelligence unit following the 9/11 attacks. He's been post commander here at Camp Shelby since 2007. Definitely not the politicking type, which means we can probably assume he'll shoot straight with us."

"He'd better," Schwarz interjected. "The guy doesn't have any choice, especially in light of the fact they decided to slap Army CID credentials on us."

"If he's got nothing to hide then I don't think we'll have to worry about it," Lyons said. "I'm actually more concerned about the disappearance of Colonel Scott. Barb was right when she told us this guy going AWOL and the disappearance of the spook in Khartoum was entirely too proximal to be an accident."

"Well, let's just remember we're not supposed to know anything about Scott unless Saroyan mentions him," Blancanales reminded them. "The Farm got that information from someone inside the administrative ranks. We have to keep our investigation focused on the missing weapons. If Scott's disappearance comes up then maybe we can take an interest, be able to logically tie the two incidents together."

"Sounds like a reasonable plan to me," Lyons said. "The sooner we can get this done the sooner we can get to work and find the bad guys."

"While we're on the subject of bad guys, what do

you two think about Scott's disappearance?" Schwarz asked.

"What do you mean?" Blancanales said.

"Well, I just mean that while his splitting is obviously not coincidental, we don't have any evidence so far that suggests he was taken involuntarily. If we assume he was kidnapped or worse, that would imply whoever's behind smuggling these weapons off this base and out to members of the Lord's Resistance Army would have to be in country. Even if we are able to swing this so that our looking into Scott's disappearance just seems like part of the case, it's a good chance we might walk into a trap."

"You're thinking members of the Lord's Resistance Army might figure someone will come looking for him," Lyons said.

"Exactly."

"It wouldn't be the first time we've walked in with blinders on for the sake of government red tape," Blancanales said. "I think we just have to wait and see what happens."

"Are we there yet?" Lyons asked in an attempt to lighten the conversation a bit.

"I thought I told you to go before we left," Blancanales shot back.

Lyons took the opportunity to give him a light tap in the arm, if there was any such thing from the blond warrior, as Blancanales turned into the parking lot of the base headquarters building. After locating a guest parking spot and asking a short, pert brunette in uniform where they could find the base commander's office, Blancanales and Schwarz made their way dutifully toward the entrance to which she pointed. Lyons straggled just a bit, taking the opportunity to watch her walk away—appreciative of the shapely legs that protruded from the dark green skirt and dipped into black shoes that clopped along the sidewalk in rhythm to her walk.

Shaking himself and realizing his friends had made considerable distance, Lyons jogged after them with just the hint of a smile.

The men found the office of Major General Anthony Saroyan and were shown in by a young sergeant as soon as they arrived. The place was spacious and nicely decorated, many of the pieces on the furniture from the turn of the nineteenth century. There was a fair amount of war memorabilia sitting along the high shelves and a fairly large bookcase occupied another wall. The desk was the only military-issue item in the whole place, and the chairs shown to the Able Team warriors were unusually comfortable.

They were barely seated when a tall, distinguished-looking man in his early fifties entered the room. He had thin hair of a color somewhere between white and gray. The eyes were equally gray but there was no mistaking the intelligence and hard discipline behind them. He was attired in standard Class B uniform, and a bucket-load of medals adorned the left breast of his shirt. The twin stars of his rank rode on dark green epaulettes and glistened in the morning light that streamed through the window.

They rose to attention and saluted in unison. He returned the salute casually, shook hands with each of them in turn and then took a seat behind his desk.

"Gentlemen, this is Command Sergeant Major Shubin," Saroyan said, gesturing to a man who entered right at that point and took a position near the general's desk.

Shubin was considerably shorter than his CO but no

less intense. He wore the identical Class B uniform and nearly as many medals, the only difference being that on his epaulettes were three stripes and three rockers, a star cradled in a leaf centered between the chevrons.

Saroyan continued. "Sergeant Major Shubin is the senior noncommissioned officer on the base, and I've asked him to be a part of this inquiry since the armory here at Camp Shelby falls under his purview along with all of the other S1 depots."

"That's all well and good, sir," Lyons replied, adding the honorific quickly as an afterthought. Damn, he'd almost blown it and he'd barely opened his mouth. "But I assumed that we would be joined by your senior supply officer, as well. We are, after all, talking about a dozen missing assault rifles."

"I'll be candid with you, primarily because you are representatives of the Army's chief law-enforcement division," Saroyan said. "Under most circumstances I would've had Colonel Scott join us. Unfortunately, he had to leave the base quite suddenly. A family emergency—I'm sure you understand."

"I see," Lyons said. He glanced at Shubin and then returned his attention to Saroyan. "Well, I have every confidence the sergeant major here can assist in our investigation."

"Sir," Blancanales interjected, intent on getting the situation into their control as soon as possible. "Being as these weapons have gone missing and Colonel Scott is not present—"

"I know what you're going to say, Chief...?" Saroyan's voice trailed off.

"You'll pardon me, sir," Blancanales said. He made a show of reaching for his credentials.

Seeing they had not demonstrated proper protocol,

Lyons and Schwarz followed suit. They should have presented their identification and orders to investigate to the base commander immediately on arrival, but they knew the oversight would be forgivable under the circumstances. If nothing else, Blancanales was convinced Saroyan didn't know anything about the missing weapons; his choice to not tell them Scott was actually AWOL was little more than courteous. No matter whom they represented, in Saroyan's and Shubin's view the trio were outsiders and would be treated as such where it concerned reputable Army officers until they had proved their trustworthiness.

Once Saroyan made a cursory inspection of their credentials, he sat back and smiled, although Blancanales didn't see much warmth in it.

"Now that we've dispensed with formalities," Saroyan said, "I'd like to follow up on your earlier comment. I've known Colonel Scott for a good many years, gentlemen. As a matter of fact he served as my S1 officer during Operation Iraqi Freedom. He's a man of good reputation, not to mention a United States Army officer and a gentleman. I'm sure his family emergency has nothing to do with the missing weapons."

"Sir, you'll understand if we tell you that it's our responsibility to investigate anything we think may be related to these missing weapons," Lyons said.

"I know your responsibilities, Mr. Irons."

"I think what Chief Irons is actually trying to say," Blancanales cut in, "is that we must consider Colonel Scott's sudden departure as a little untimely. We do need to review all possibilities, of course. However, under the present circumstances will be more than happy to work with Sergeant Major Shubin until we can speak with Colonel Scott."

"I appreciate that, Mr. Rose," Shubin said.

"You must understand, sir, that we *will* have to speak with Colonel Scott before we leave Camp Shelby and return to Washington," Schwarz hastily added.

"Of course, absolutely," Saroyan said. "As I've already told you, gentlemen, you will have the full cooperation of me and my staff and the resources of Camp Shelby at your disposal. We're ready to cooperate with your investigation."

"Thank you," Lyons replied.

Saroyan turned his attention to Shubin. "Sergeant Major, escort these men to their quarters. I'm sure they would like to get cleaned up before heading to the armory and speaking with Lieutenant Jaeger."

"Yes, sir."

"And who's Lieutenant Jaeger, sir?" Lyons said.

"Jaeger's Colonel Scott's XO. He'll be able to answer any questions you have to your satisfaction." Saroyan favored Schwarz with a glance and added, "That is, of course, until Colonel Scott can get back here."

"Exactly how long is Colonel Scott expected to be gone, sir?" Blancanales asked.

Lyons had difficulty repressing a smile. While his tactics were much different in human interactions, there were times the wisdom of his friend shone through. He knew that Blancanales hadn't asked the question because he actually wanted to know when Scott would return; Blancanales wanted to see how Saroyan would dance around the inquiry.

Saroyan replied straight-faced. "I'm not really certain since it was an emergency. I approved a pass of up to seventy-two hours for him if needed, and so I would expect him back here in that time unless he notifies my office prior to that, of course. Will there be anything else?"

"Not at all," Blancanales replied. "Thank you again, sir."

The three men rose, the meeting obviously adjourned, and Shubin escorted them out to the parking lot. They decided to follow him rather than ride in his vehicle so they could discuss the short, if not very strange, meeting with Shubin and Saroyan. Rather than go to their quarters, however, Lyons had insisted Shubin take them straight to the armory depot where the missing weapons had been stored.

"I don't like him," Lyons said when they were alone.

"Who…Saroyan?" Schwarz asked.

"Yeah."

"I don't think he's a bad egg," Blancanales said. "And he doesn't strike me as the type who would get into arms smuggling, especially not with all the checks and balances that are required."

"This was obviously an inside job, Pol," Lyons insisted.

"I don't disagree." Blancanales shook his head. "But at the end of the day I don't think Saroyan had anything to do with it."

"Yeah, but he lied for Scott with that cockamamie story about him having emergency leave," Schwarz said.

"Covering the ass of a trusted officer doesn't automatically qualify the guy for collusion with Sudanese terrorists," Blancanales reminded his friend. "Not to mention the fact that we have no hard evidence to suggest even Colonel Scott's culpable. We're talking about high treason here, committed by more than one Army officer, and I'm not entirely convinced that's the case."

"It wouldn't be the first time somebody inside the U.S. military flipped sides," Lyons said.

"Of course not. But let's consider motives, Ironman, or at least the lack thereof in this case."

Schwarz said, "He's got a point there. There really isn't any evidence to suggest Scott or Saroyan is working with the Lord's Resistance Army."

"I can think of one very good motive," Lyons countered. "Money."

"According to the initial reports we got from the Farm, only twelve weapons were missing," Schwarz said. "The U.S. military property ownership stampings were still on them along with the serial numbers, making them easily tracked, which means that most of the guns could have fetched a price of maybe five hundred dollars each."

"So six grand for the lot, and that's before you pay off customs inspectors, smugglers and anybody else who's due a cut," Blancanales said. He looked at Lyons and replied, "Doesn't seem worth spending the next thirty years at Leavenworth for chump change."

"Okay, so maybe I hadn't thought of that," Lyons admitted.

"You know what strikes me as odd?" Blancanales asked.

"The fact you haven't been on a real date in the last decade?" Schwarz offered.

"Oh…we have a funny guy on our hands," Blancanales said. He continued in a more serious tone. "What really strikes me as odd is why only a dozen guns. Sure, they're military-grade small arms. M-16 A-3 carbines in the hands of trained terrorists or guerrillas can do some significant damage. But you're not going to win a war with them and it seems like an awful lot of effort to go to just for a few guns."

"Especially if you're shipping them to a country where guns are a dime a dozen," Schwarz said.

Lyons had to admit he hadn't considered it and there was no disputing Blancanales's point—no surprises since most of his friend's observations were equally astute. Conflict had been going on for so long in Sudan with the skirmishes and microcosmic civil wars between the various groups, each fighting for its own power and political position, that the arms market had all but consumed the meager resources of the country. Illegal weapons came from every part of the world: Europe, China, parts of Southeast Asia and the Middle East.

And now the United States.

There was certainly no shortage of guns in Sudan. Way more money could be made sending things like food, potable water and nutritional supplements. Medications were also a big game in Sudan. An entire pharmaceutical underground had been established in the country, selling everything from antibiotics to painkillers to experimental drugs. American military personnel getting involved in smuggling weapons out of the United States, even civilians, appeared to create a risk much greater than would prove profitable. It just didn't make any sense.

"Well, whatever's going on," Lyons finally said after a time of silence, "we need to get to the bottom of it so we can get the intelligence to Phoenix Force. David and friends are going to need that information in order to accomplish their mission objectives."

"No argument from me," Schwarz said.

"Agreed," Blancanales added. "I would hate to think

our dragging ass caused them a lot of additional heart-ache. If we—"

Blancanales never got to finish his statement as Schwarz shouted and pointed in the direction of a van hurtling toward the intersection they were approaching from their left. At the speed they were moving it seemed evident they would impact Shubin's car at precisely the moment he reached the middle of the intersection. The cross street had the stop, and from Shubin's speed it appeared the Army noncom hadn't spotted the looming peril.

"That's trouble!" Schwarz cried.

"He doesn't see them, Pol," Lyons said. "We need to get in front of him!"

Blancanales was obviously already in tune with the thoughts of his friend because he'd tromped the accel-erator and whipped the nose of their sedan into the on-coming lane to pass Shubin. As they gained ground, the precious seconds ticking, Blancanales ordered his friends to brace for impact.

And then they smashed headlong into the fender of the van.

CHAPTER FOUR

The crunch of impact and screech of metal tearing fiberglass blasted the ears of the Able Team warriors.

All senses came alive for the trio as their sedan glanced off the van—the torsion created by the forces of the spinning vehicle caused their hearts to bottom out in their stomachs, or at least it felt that way. Blancanales gritted his teeth as he worked the steering wheel to keep some control. Perhaps it hadn't been the best plan they'd ever come up with but at least it hadn't ended in disaster for Shubin. Now all Blancanales had to do was to get the sedan stopped or at least to ditch it in a place that wouldn't put any bystanders at risk. He waited until the sedan spun 180 degrees and then slammed the gearshift into reverse and tromped on the accelerator. The increased speed and sudden change of direction brought them neatly out of the spin that would have occurred had a trained stunt driver not been at the wheel.

Blancanales checked the rearview mirror, found his saving grace in a fire hydrant and jammed on the brakes just before hitting it. The rear bumper collided with the hydrant, shearing off the top portion as the breakaway safety cells locked into place to prevent water from bursting out of the pipe. The valves were not intended to completely block water flow; they merely reduced the amount of water that leaked out and diffused the pressure generated from the hydrant's direct connection to a water main. The result was a bubbling fountain that came aboveground with enough pressure to pool around the vehicle and christen it to a stop.

Lyons took several deep breaths and then barked, "Report status!"

"Nothing broken," Schwarz said from the backseat. "I'm good."

"Pol?" Lyons didn't get an answer and looked in the direction of his friend. Blancanales stared through the windshield and although he seemed unharmed, his skin had blanched somewhat. "Blancanales, snap out of it! Are you okay?"

"I'll need new shorts but I'm good." He waved out the window and added, "I think we're just getting started."

All three watched as the rear doors of the van, now on its side with the front wheels still turning, burst open and armed men staggered out. The scene was almost surreal as if the van was some great creation machine vomiting human offspring. They numbered six in all and appeared to be Caucasians save for one with dark skin and black curly hair. They wore camouflage fatigue pants, black T-shirts and combat boots. Their weapons were mostly SMGs with one or two full-profile assault rifles in the mix. At first they didn't appear hostile toward Able Team or Shubin but that changed quickly enough.

Lyons noticed they were gaining their senses and a few began to sweep the area with the muzzles of their weapons for threats. Shubin had somehow managed to steer his sedan onto a sidewalk and smash into the exterior wall of a PX building. The senior noncom was trying to get his door open, kicking at it while uttering what were probably curses although Lyons couldn't make out any of the words.

"Hostiles. Let's hit it," Lyons said.

The trio went EVA and drew their pistols.

Lyons carried his trusty Colt revolver—this time a .44 Magnum Anaconda with 240-grain jacketed hollowpoints. Blancanales produced his SIG-Sauer P-226 chambered for .357 Magnum. The standard of combat handguns carried by federal law enforcement, Texas Rangers and Navy SEALs, the SIG had proved itself a formidable ally and Blancanales favored it for close-quarters combat. Schwarz had selected a Model 92—a military variant of the Beretta 92-SB—that Stony Man's crackerjack armorer, John "Cowboy" Kissinger, had modified to withstand a hotter 9 mm load and an 18-round magazine.

While the pistols might not have been much good against the autoweapons carried by their enemy, they were effective tools in the hands of these veterans, who weren't shy about demonstrating that fact as they left the sedan and set down a steady stream of fire.

Lyons's handcannon boomed its first report as the Able Team leader took one of the gunners with a clean shot to the head. The heavy slug busted the man's skull open and showered his stunned companions with blood and gray matter. Lyons sighted on the second target but Blancanales beat him to the punch with a double tap from his SIG. Both .357 Magnum rounds cut through the man's breastbone and lodged deep in his lungs. Pink, frothy sputum erupted from his mouth and his weapon flew from numb fingers.

The remaining four realized they had suddenly become targets, their ranks reduced by a third in just seconds. Each man scrambled for cover but realized he was in a poor position for it. They realized the best they could do was split up, each man for himself, and try to keep the heads of the Able Team warriors down while they broke for some kind of shelter from the assault.

"Pol, trunk!" Schwarz shouted as he snapped off three rounds of his own.

Blancanales ceased firing long enough from his position behind the door to reach in and stab at the switch for the trunk release. Schwarz urged his friends to get behind the rear doors, all knowing the thin skin of the fiberglass and metal in the modern sedan wouldn't do much to stop the heavy-caliber rounds. At least the rear doors, both which Schwarz had opened for them, would add additional shielding. Lyons and Blancanales made their dash for the failsafe retreat position even as the enemy began to reach cover and return fire. A maelstrom of rounds peppered the front doors and windshield, a couple tearing through the front doors and exiting the other side in the empty space vacated by the Able Team warriors milliseconds before.

Schwarz reached the trunk, unzipped a long bag and came away with his prize. The M-16 A-3/M-203 sported the classic combination of effective small-arms features. Built with a carbine-style profile, it chambered 5.56 x 45 mm NATO rounds. The tubular style grenade launcher running beneath the foregrips fired a variant of the 40 mm grenades of the grenadier's choosing. Schwarz settled for a high-explosive round this time around, retrieving a satchel of HEs as he ratcheted the breech forward with one hand.

Schwarz popped a shell into the breech, jacked the tube home with a click and flipped the leaf sight into action. He knelt, locked the stock against his shoulder, quick-sighted and squeezed the launcher trigger. The weapon kicked against his shoulder with the force of a 12-gauge shotgun, which paled in comparison to the impact of the blast that came a second later. The shell struck the van center mass and exploded on impact. A fireball erupted from the vehicle, followed by a roiling black cloud of smoke. A secondary explosion signaled the ignition of the gas tank. The blast didn't engulf their enemies but a good number of them were knocked off their feet by the concussion.

Schwarz didn't relent, rocking the tube forward to eject the inert shell and popping a fresh one into the breech.

Blancanales called for Schwarz to surrender his Beretta, which he did reluctantly, but also understanding when his friend gestured in Shubin's direction. He tossed the pistol underhanded and Blancanales caught it one-handed. Schwarz then aimed the grenade launcher and triggered the second 40 mm HE shell. This one he adjusted to land a little farther aft of the van but with no less a devastating effect. Two more of the hostiles died on their feet as the blast separated appendages from torsos and the superheated gases incinerated flesh.

Blancanales used the distraction of the explosion to break cover and beeline for Shubin's sedan. He reached the car unscathed and wrenched on the door with all his might. It came open enough to allow Shubin to squeak out. Blancanales handed the Beretta to the Army noncom and then urged them to get cover behind the sedan. They took no fire during the time, as the enemy had its hands full between the explosions, autofire from Schwarz's M-16 A-3 and the sheer, violent will of Lyons and his Anaconda.

Blancanales and Shubin did manage to pick off a gunner who had adequate protection from Lyons's and Schwarz's position but could not defend his flank. They triggered shots simultaneously, two rounds from Shubin's 9 mm punching into the guy's ribs while Blancanales's .357 clipped his skull enough to tear away the top of his brain. The corpse teetered and then collapsed, twitching a moment before going still.

That left one man who must have realized his opponents had him outgunned because he emerged from cover, threw down his weapons and raised his arms high.

None of the Able Team warriors moved at first, suspecting a potential trick. They could wait it out as long as necessary now that they had the advantages of position and numbers. After some time passed without the appearance of additional hostiles, Lyons broke cover and moved in to secure the prisoner with a pair of plastic riot cuffs sent with him courtesy of Schwarz. Within a few minutes they had the enemy combatant secured. Lyons counted at least five confirmed kills and he suspected at least one or two more never made it out of the van.

The warriors gathered around Shubin's government sedan, a safe distance from the flames and thick, acrid smoke that marked what remained of the enemy vehicle. Their prisoner said nothing—he looked American enough but acted as if either mute or non-English-speaking. Either way, the men of Able Team were careful not to say anything classified around the guy in case he was playing possum, a reflex of their training and experience.

The wail of military police sirens drew nearer by the moment.

Schwarz jerked a thumb at their prisoner and said,

"We can turn sunshine here over to the MPs when they arrive."

"Don't you think we ought to interrogate him?" Shubin asked not without surprise.

"We don't have the facilities or a secure location to keep him on ice until we can get to that," Lyons said. "We need to report back to Washington first."

Shubin expressed confusion.

"This changes things, Sergeant Major," Blancanales explained. "We're on a time-critical mission here. That mission just got bumped up."

Shubin eyed each of the men in turn with skepticism. "There's no way in hell I'm buying you guys are actually with CID. Not even for a second. So who are you... really?"

"What makes you think we're not CID?" Blancanales asked.

"You're kidding, right? I was in the MP Corps for about the first half of my career, then I moved to light infantry. I've met many CID and not one of them would have ever responded the way you guys did. You saw that attack coming, you deterred it—saving my ass in the process by the way, for which I'm real grateful—then took those guys down like you'd done it a thousand times before. I'm guessing you probably have." Shubin jutted his chin toward the M-16 A-3/M-203 slung across Schwarz's shoulder. "And don't tell me that over-and-under is standard CID issue. The sixteen I could see, but no way they issue M-203s to just anybody."

Lyons smiled. "We're the good guys—that's about all we can tell you."

"And I don't suppose you'd be grateful enough to us that we might keep this between ourselves for now?"

Shubin shrugged. "I can keep a secret but I still have

to make a full report to General Saroyan. He'll have questions. Lots of them."

"Yeah," Lyons half said, half grunted. "Can't wait."

"WHAT IN THE holy crapping hell did you guys think you were doing?" Major General Anthony Saroyan's expression bore unchecked apoplexy. "This is a fucking nightmare! I'll have Congressional inquiries running through here for the next goddamn year!"

"Sir," Blancanales began with buttery humility, "if you could just listen—"

"Don't interrupt me, Chief Rose!" Saroyan countered. "I'm the MMFIC on this post, not to mention I outrank all of you! So you'd do well to shut up until you have permission to speak."

Blancanales closed his yap, erring on the side of discretion being the better part of valor. Not that it mattered, because before Saroyan could continue his tirade the phone jingled on his desk for attention. The officer bristled, stopping in midstride the pacing he'd been doing while chewing out the collective asses of the three CID officers. He looked at first as if he might throw the phone across the room, but then appeared to think better of it and swiped up the receiver in one meaty hand.

"Yes?" he barked. A pause and then he looked almost dazed as wrinkles formed in his forehead. "*Who* is on the line?"

A longer pause ensued during which he looked warily at the three men still standing at attention in front of him. He waved at them to indicate they could stand at ease and they complied.

At least the guy wasn't a complete tool, Lyons thought.

"Of course, put him through," Saroyan said.

For the next five minutes Saroyan practically stood at attention himself, saying very little except for an occasional "yes, sir" or "of course, sir" and even one "I understand perfectly, sir." After nearly five minutes Saroyan gently placed the receiver into the cradle, looked over the three warriors and scratched his chin. His previous hardness had melted from his body language and he finally waved Able Team into seats.

"Sit down, boys," Saroyan said. "It would seem that I've been a bit hasty."

"Perfectly understandable, sir," Blancanales said, and Schwarz nodded as if in complete agreement.

Lyons didn't react beyond a smirk.

Saroyan sat and rubbed at his temples, obviously feeling a headache coming on. He said, "Okay, I guess we can cut through the bullshit. You guys obviously aren't CID and from what I just heard it would seem I no longer have any authority over your actions." He looked out the window of his office absently and added, "But I do want to remind you that you're still guests of the United States Army while on this post. I'd prefer you avoid any further firefights or other hostile actions while here."

"It's not like we had a lot of choice," Lyons muttered.

"Ironman," Blancanales cut in easily.

Saroyan looked at the men. "You can understand why this is going to make things very difficult for me. Fortunately, it's Sunday and that means a good number of the civilian DOA and DOD workers are off post. Most permanent party is gone, as well, since this isn't an active training weekend."

"It does help that you maintain the largest Army reservist post in the country," Schwarz agreed.

"It means we can keep this quiet and hopefully the

press won't get wind," Saroyan replied. "Washington has assured me they'll do everything possible to spin this right when it goes public. They're going to call it an accident."

"That might wash for a while but it won't keep long," Lyons said.

"And it'll definitely squeeze our mission objectives against the wall," Schwarz pointed out.

Saroyan cleared his throat. "Perhaps I could help you with that if I knew more about your actual mission here."

"You could start by leveling with us about Colonel Scott," Lyons said.

Saroyan's expression made it apparent he had hoped to avoid that discussion, but at this point they all knew he didn't have a choice. Someone, maybe even the President himself, had just handed the base commander his ass, and maintaining the coy routine wouldn't be a great career move. Lyons could understand the man's position—he didn't give a shit, but he understood.

"Colonel Scott isn't on a family emergency. He's missing and all attempts to reach him have proved unsuccessful." Saroyan reached into the drawer of his desk, withdrew a pack of cigarettes and a lighter and fired one up. Smoking inside a government building was forbidden but being Saroyan was the MMFIC, who was going to argue?

"How long?" Lyons asked.

"Going on forty-eight hours," Shubin answered.

"You've reported him AWOL, I assume?" Blancanales inquired.

Saroyan shook his head as he dragged on the cigarette.

"You're trying to keep it quiet."

"Yes, but I can't hold out much longer," Saroyan replied through a cloud of smoke. "It's my discretion to consider him merely absent from appointed place of duty for up to three days. After that, I have to notify the base provost marshal and Washington that he's AWOL due to his rank and security clearances."

"You should have reported his absence immediately," Lyons said. He raised a hand to ward off any defensive posture.

"But that's spilled milk," Blancanales added quickly to minimize the risk Saroyan would go on the defensive. "So you've leveled with us and we at least owe you that much in return, General. In short, guerrillas in Sudan friendly to U.S. interests stumbled onto a small cache of weapons in the possession of terrorists with the Lord's Resistance Army. The serial numbers of those arms were traced to inventory held in the main armory here on this base."

Saroyan stopped with the cigarette midway to his lips and his eyes went wide.

"Holy shit," Shubin muttered.

"Indeed," Blancanales said with a nod.

"So you think Colonel Scott's disappearance is related," Saroyan said.

"Seems little doubt of that now," Lyons said. "We have some others headed to Sudan now to check out this story personally, since it's a good bet those aren't the only U.S. armaments that might be in the country. Not even every weapon they found had been accounted for."

"So you're suggesting Colonel Scott's in on it."

"We're not suggesting anything of the sort…yet. But there's no doubt his disappearance is more than coincidence. He might be a hostage, maybe even taken by those who were behind what went down this morning."

"Okay, so obviously we've confirmed these weapons are from here at Camp Shelby," Shubin said. "That still doesn't explain how they managed to get them out of the country and into Sudan, never mind getting them off this base."

"It's possible the LRA has a network inside the country," Lyons said.

"And that they've been here for a while, giving them the time and opportunity to build resources," Schwarz added.

"You're suggesting a conspiracy?" Saroyan asked.

"Why's that so hard to believe?" Lyons fired back. "If memory serves, it wasn't that long ago Nadil Hasan opened up with a pistol at the largest military installation in the free world, an act ultimately tied to terrorist conspirators. And he was an American citizen. How implausible is it that foreigners could penetrate this country and set up an arms-smuggling pipeline?"

The room fell silent for a time.

"Would it help if I gave you the address of Colonel Scott's off-post housing?" Saroyan eventually said.

"It's a start," Blancanales said. "You never know what we might find."

"And that's exactly what worries me," Saroyan replied.

CHAPTER FIVE

Kampala, Uganda

It was late afternoon when traffic control cleared Jack Grimaldi to land at the airport and directed him to a private hangar—at least that's what Ugandan air traffic officials called it. A half dozen uniformed security officers with SMGs slung at their sides waited. They wore brown khaki uniforms with utility caps but the weapons made them look more like military troops than police.

As Grimaldi taxied the Stony Man Gulfstream C21 to a halt, McCarter stepped to the main door and disengaged the locks. The engines had barely wound down when the Phoenix Force leader pushed the door out, letting it fall into debarking position. He then stepped aside and gestured for Hawkins to go first since it was Hawkins who could most convincingly act like a Texas oil baron.

As soon as Hawkins's feet hit the tarmac, a man wearing black epaulettes with a circle and diamond on them—the rank insignia for an inspector—stepped forward smartly and extended his hand.

"Good day, sir." The man had very dark skin and an impenetrable expression. "I am Captain Bukenya of the Ugandan Police Force. Please note until I have cleared you that you are not free to leave this area, and that your persons and aircraft are subject to inspection now or at any time that you are in Uganda or its airspace. Before I begin my inspection, have you anything to declare?"

"I have something to declare, all right!" Hawkins said in good-old-boy fashion while pulling a handkerchief from his pocket and wiping his neck. "It is blessed *hot* in this country here and I mean *hot,* boy! We don't get anywhere near this kind of humidity in Texas. You hear what I'm saying?"

Bukenya appeared unaffected and instead directed his men to begin their inspection. They fanned out, two covering Hawkins and his entourage with their weapons held loosely at the ready while three more headed for the plane. The inspector nodded to the remaining officer, who ordered them to line up and patted down each man in turn.

Phoenix Force took the entire parade in stride, confident the more cooperative they acted the quicker they could move past this. The men who went aboard the plane cleared Grimaldi from the cockpit first but the pilot gestured toward McCarter to indicate he had a close eye on them. They had no reason to worry since the armory aboard their plane was well concealed in the fuselage and boasted electronic scanning countermeasures developed by Stony Man's resident cybernetics wizard, Aaron "Bear" Kurtzman. Short of tearing the plane apart, the inspection team wouldn't even know it existed.

The inspection took less than five minutes—something McCarter noted with interest. He wondered if there hadn't been a little influence wielded by the Oval Office but dismissed the idea as quickly. It wouldn't be in their best interest for the U.S. to alert Ugandan officials that Phoenix Force was anything other than who they declared: oil tycoons with a Texas-based petroleum company. The cover seemed adequate considering the large number of such interests in Uganda. The country was a gold mine for trade with U.S. refineries, in particular, and trading continued free of a good many restrictions. Of course the companies that dealt with Uganda paid a premium for that access, so the inspector's relaxed search of their plane had likely been at the behest of his own government.

"Everything seems to be in order," Bukenya said. "Do you need me to arrange some transportation into the city or have you made other arrangements?"

A chocolate-brown omnibus arrived before Hawkins could reply, a young man at the wheel with shiny dark skin. He rolled down the window and in perfect English said, "You Joes call for a driver?"

Hawkins rendered a casual wave and then grinned at Bukenya. "We called ahead so our travel arrangements are made."

"And how long will you be in Uganda, gentlemen?"

"Two days at most," Hawkins said, mostly because he hoped it was the literal truth.

Bukenya slapped the palm of his hand with Hawkins's passport, his eyes narrowing a bit; he looked as if he wanted to say something else but finally he returned the passports to each man in turn and bid them farewell in his native language. Bukenya whirled on his heel, barked at his officers and in a minute they were gone.

As soon as McCarter exchanged pass phrases with the omnibus driver, he struck up a conversation while the Phoenix warriors loaded up their gear and climbed aboard. Within a minute they were away from the airport and headed north out of what passed for the bustle of Kampala.

"Where we headed, mate?"

In spite of the more stilted intervals, Kumar's command of English was good enough that he could be understood. "We can go as far as the border. From there, we will have to go by foot."

"What about our wheels?" Encizo asked from his position in the seat immediately behind Kumar.

The Sudanese freedom fighter glanced in the rearview mirror. "I have a friend who will pick it up and return it to the station here in Kampala."

"We're going to walk from the border?" Hawkins inquired. He let out a whistle and added, "That's a pretty good hike."

"My thoughts exactly," McCarter said. "I don't know how much you know about our mission here but we're sort of short on time, bloke."

"I understand," Kumar replied. "There is another vehicle that will pick us up near Nimule National Park in my country, which shares its southern tip with Uganda. This is an area with large tourism, and lots of vans like this one, so we should not stand out. We will slip across the border under cover of darkness."

"How far to the border?" Hawkins asked.

"I believe…um, maybe eighty kilometers."

"You speak English well," Encizo said. "You had training?"

"Most of the men in our camp are taught English by the U.S. advisers. We are told these men are from language schools and are permitted in the country to help us with reading and writing." He chuckled and added, "But we know they are actually from your CIA."

"Yeah, that's one of the things that has us concerned," McCarter said. "You know anything about our man who disappeared or who might have him?"

"It is not strange, this," Kumar replied. "Americans are always disappearing here. Some just leave and others are killed by wild animals. Some are kidnapped for ransom, perhaps, but not most. Most are tourists and without much money. And they tend to stick to the larger cities. The rest are usually well guarded by police and their own security forces. Your man was known in Khartoum with many friends. I do not think anyone would risk taking him. They fear American retaliation too much these days."

"That's good," Manning muttered. "They should be afraid of that."

"What can you tell us about this Lord's Resistance Army?" McCarter asked.

"They are a knife in our side, this much I swear," Kumar said between clenched teeth. "We have lost many friends and family to these devils. I live now only to serve General Kiir and fight alongside my brothers to defend South Sudan."

McCarter decided not to mention he wasn't particularly interested in hearing the rhetoric. He asked, "Is this the first time you've come across weapons made in the U.S.?"

Kumar nodded. "As far as I know. I've only been allowed into the field in the last year. I work for my brother, Samir, who is leader for our segment. It is actually he who found your guns."

"When can we meet him?" Hawkins inquired.

"We will see him tonight, later…once we have made it over the border. He waits for us on the other side."

McCarter reached into the pocket of his suit coat and withdrew the photograph of Jodi Leighton. The CIA still hadn't heard from their case officer in Khartoum, according to Stony Man's last update. McCarter wasn't entirely sure he agreed with the Farm's theory that if they followed Leighton's trail it would naturally lead them to the weapons. Things weren't always so cut-and-dried in the clandestine services, and McCarter had no reason to believe this would be any different. Still, Kiir's men had way more eyes on the ground than the CIA or Stony Man could hope for; those personal connections were their very best hope to locating the missing agent.

"You ever see this man before?" McCarter said, passing the photograph to Kumar.

The Sudanese fighter took the picture, keeping one hand on the wheel while his eyes bounced between the photograph and the narrow road. He took his time before handing it back to McCarter. "He looks like Joe."

"Joe?" Manning echoed.

"He is with your CIA." Something caused Kumar to chuckle. "We called him Joe because that's what he asked us to call him. He always treated us well, gave us information whenever we asked for it. My brother was not happy when we learned he'd been taken."

That got McCarter's attention. "Taken, you…you telling me that you know what happened to this chap?"

"Of course, that is why General Kiir requested you come. Joe was always fair with us. He never showed disrespect to our cause like so many of the CIA before him. He was a different man, a good man. It's the Lakwena that took him. Most assuredly I tell you this."

"How did they do it?" Encizo inquired.

"Joe would meet one of our people in the city twice a month. He would pass off whatever intelligence he had managed to buy or steal or trade about police movements, and in return we would give him whatever we could learn about the Lakwena."

"Any idea what he'd do with that information?"

"He was working with another agent, a member of one of the British foreign intelligence services, although I am not sure which one. The men were friends, I think. Joe never told us anything about him and we didn't ask. It was when he was supposed to meet this man to trade intelligence that Joe disappeared."

"So you're absolutely certain it was the Lord's Resistance Army responsible for taking him?"

"As certain as I can be, yes."

They rode the rest of the way in silence as McCarter considered this revelation. In all likelihood, if Leighton had been connected with a British foreign intelligence agent it was someone from MI6. Before long, Kumar turned off the highway onto a secondary road that gradually degraded from hardball to dirt and crushed rock, to baked mud with great ruts and divots. Eventually he stopped the vehicle.

"We must walk from here," Kumar said.

McCarter ordered the team to go EVA, unload the vehicle and wipe it down for prints before questioning Kumar on their next move. It wasn't that he mistrusted the guy as much as he wanted to know what they could expect to face out there. "Hoofing it across this kind of terrain at night isn't exactly what we had planned, mate. We're not equipped for a hike."

"This is not a problem," Kumar replied. "There is clothing in one of the bags for all of you, and I think you'll find that it all fits. General Kiir was notified ahead of time of your arrival, so we planned all of this. You'll find boots and fatigues, and drop bags for the clothes you are wearing. They may stay with this vehicle and all of your belongings will be delivered to Khartoum, where we were informed you would make your exit."

"What about the rental?" James asked.

"We have friends here," Kumar said. "Do not worry, gentlemen. They will pick it up and return it to the rental company."

"How far do we have to go?" McCarter asked.

"Samir is less than three kilometers, on the other side of the border. We are now a half kilometer this side of my country, so we should be able to pass under cover of darkness without raising attention."

"What if we encounter border patrols?"

Kumar laughed. "We have much greater worries than the border patrol. While there is a ceasefire between my people and the government of my country, we know that they still hire the Lakwena at times to do their dirty work. The patrols of these fighters, many of them barely men, are vigilant and familiar with the borderlands. They will be vigilant and they will not attack with warning, neither will they take prisoners. The ones who raped my sister and killed by mother and father are led by a man named Bukatem, Lester Bukatem. He has many who answer to him and he is feared in these parts."

"Lester?" McCarter interjected. "That doesn't sound much like an African name."

"Many of the people here who end up in the refugee camps take on English or American names in the hope their real identities aren't discovered," Gary Manning pointed out. "These people live under constant surveillance or are perpetually targeted by the Lord's Resistance Army. I'd venture a guess that this Bukatem was conscripted as a child and brainwashed to fight for the LRA during the 1990s, when the conflicts were still in full swing."

Kumar nodded. "That is right. In fact, we were raised

in the same village as this man. My older brother once called him friend. Now he is our enemy and if we ever make contact with him, I can guarantee he will experience a slow and dishonorable death."

"Let me be clear with you, bloke," McCarter said. "There's no room in our mission here for your personal vendettas. We appreciate the help, but if you plan on using us to seek vengeance on this Lester wanker you'd best just put the idea out of your mind. We're here to do two things—find out what happened to the man you call Joe and shut down the weapons pipeline to the LRA from the States. That's it."

Kumar didn't look offended but when he replied his voice took on an edge. "I intend only to help you, American. There is no reason to tell me what my duties are. But you should know that my people must first swear fealty to our own because they are defenseless and God demands we protect the innocent."

This was something with which McCarter could empathize and he nodded in acknowledgment. They understood each other.

As soon as the group had changed into their fatigues and stored their gear, they set out single file. Encizo took point. They didn't know what they would encounter and it wouldn't do for Kumar, the only one who really knew where to go and was intimate with all sides of this fight, to buy the farm for that very reason. Hence, McCarter put Kumar between him and Encizo, and the remaining Phoenix Force warriors followed, each careful to put at least ten yards between each man.

A steady rain had begun to fall, only making more precarious their already treacherous journey through the mountainous jungle terrain that made up the border between South Sudan and Uganda. For each man to know where the one in front of him was, since the cloud cover had suppressed what little moonlight might have illuminated the trail, the Phoenix warriors wore small LEDs that clipped to the backs of the military webbing that held their side arms and canteens. A long-life watch battery powered the dim light that glowed in a suffused red, just enough for a follower to see but virtually undetectable from observers at the front or side of the team. Each man carried a spare in his pocket, as well, in the event that his primary gave out.

McCarter hoped they wouldn't be there that long.

As they traveled, his keen senses staying attuned to their surroundings, the Briton began to wonder what they were walking into. He didn't mistrust Kumar— hell, the chap seemed cooperative and decent enough— but he couldn't figure how Bukatem, or anyone in the LRA, would have known Leighton worked for the CIA. Not unless somebody told Bukatem. McCarter hated to think Leighton might have been betrayed by this mysterious British agent, who was most likely attached to either SAS or MI6. McCarter didn't want to believe a countryman would betray a fellow agent but he also knew the rules were much different in the world of espionage.

In either case, the mission had suddenly become more complex. McCarter didn't like complicated; the Phoenix Force leader liked simple. In fact the bloodier simple it was, the better. Unfortunately it didn't appear things were going to get simpler.

After more than three hours of traveling, the entire crew drenched and worn down, McCarter was about to call for them to stop and rest when the staccato of autofire resounded from somewhere ahead of their position. McCarter couldn't be sure of the distance, since sounds were difficult to judge in the dense foliage of the jungle, not to mention the dark. The reports of weapons were especially deceptive because they bounced off obstacles like trees and boulders, and were suppressed by the canopy of intertwined branches overhead. These factors usually made them closer than they sounded.

McCarter signaled the others to form on Kumar's position and then moved forward to converse with Encizo.

"How far ahead, you think?" he asked the Cuban.

"Maybe fifty yards," Encizo replied. "Hard to tell."

"That's about what I figured."

"Sounds like quite a firefight, too."

"Stand fast," McCarter ordered. Encizo nodded and the Briton returned to Kumar. "We anywhere near our rendezvous point?"

"Very near," Kumar replied with an anxious nod.

"Okay, it sounds like your brother may have hit some trouble."

"I would agree."

"We're going to help him but we'll do it my way. Understood?"

Kumar mumbled something McCarter deemed as affirmation.

McCarter turned his attention to Hawkins and James. "You two swing around on the west side and see if you can flank the fire zone, but don't engage until you get my signal."

"And what's that?" James asked.

McCarter grinned wickedly. "You'll bloody well know it when you hear it. Go."

The pair moved off and McCarter tugged Manning's shoulder to indicate he should stick close to Kumar. "Give us ten seconds, then follow on our position. Make sure you keep your fields of fire away from Hawk and Cal."

Manning nodded.

McCarter turned and moved back to Encizo's side. He reached to his belt and held up one of the M-69 fragmentation grenades that had been procured for his team by Kumar's contacts in Uganda. "We'll go in using the Old Fifty-One. You ready?"

Encizo nodded his understanding of McCarter's plan. The technique dated back to the Korean War, a reference to when Korean forces attacked U.N. command positions that were manned by numerically superior forces. Because the Koreans wanted to ensure success, they attacked the positions using gongs and cymbals so as to disorient the enemy. McCarter planned the same thing, only using something more conventional and spectacular.

They set off and traveled about the distance Encizo estimated before they saw the first evidence of the firefight in the form of muzzle-flashes. From what McCarter could observe, it looked like a small skirmish. It was still too dark to determine what lay ahead, friend or foe, but McCarter wasn't planning to lob the grenade into the center of the fray with reckless abandon. His solution would prove more elegant.

McCarter waved his fist to indicate Manning and Kumar should hold position where they were at—about fifteen yards to the rear—before he yanked the pin and tossed the grenade toward the east, far outside the perimeter of the fire zone. Three seconds ticked off before the hand bomb exploded.

And with that, Phoenix Force moved in to engage the enemy—whoever it might be.

CHAPTER SIX

David McCarter had been right: as soon as Hawkins and James heard the grenade explode, they weren't in any doubt the show had opened.

"Sounds like an Old Fifty-One," Hawkins whispered as he put the MP-5 he carried into battery.

James did the same with his M-16 A-3 carbine and replied, "Tally ho."

The pair stepped from the jungle brush behind which they were concealed and met the first enemy gunners head-on. James wondered a moment how they could tell the bad guys from Kumar's people but then he remembered that the LRA generally wore uniforms since they considered themselves an organized military force, while the SPLA dressed in whatever rags they could acquire. The green dungaree-style fatigues worn by the four men they encountered, coupled with the nasty silhouettes of Kalashnikov variants, served as positive identification.

The LRA fighters were surprised and while they responded with incredible speed, it couldn't match the battle-tested skills of the Phoenix Force veterans. James leveled his M-16 A-3 and triggered a short burst that lifted the nearest target off his feet and dumped him into the wet grass with a sloppy thump. The 5.56 mm rounds from James's weapon ripped holes in the man's chest. The second gunner tried to swing the muzzle of his weapon to bear, but James had angled away from his original position and triggered a burst on the run. These also found their mark, stitching a bloody pattern across the man's midsection. His eyes widened with shock and he triggered an ineffective burst of his own reflexively before staggering forward and dropping his now useless weapon. James finished with a second volley that blew off the top of the terrorist's head.

T. J. Hawkins dispatched his first opponent with the sweep of a muzzle in corkscrew fashion. The 9 mm rounds weren't as high-velocity as those from James's weapon but they were no less effective. The slugs drilled through the man's body and dumped him face-first in the wet muck of the jungle floor. The remaining LRA terrorist managed to get a short burst off before Hawkins cut him down with a fusillade that left a near-perfect vertical pattern from crotch to throat. The man produced a gargled scream as blood erupted from his mouth, the 9 mm buzzers rupturing his lungs.

The men of Phoenix Force swung their weapons in every direction but no further threats appeared, and they finally relaxed a moment to catch their breaths from the encounter.

One lucky round had hit Hawkins in the forearm, taking a small chunk of flesh with it. Hawkins didn't immediately notice. It wasn't until James pointed it out that the area began to burn like a dog bite. Calvin James, who doubled as the team medic, immediately whipped a medi-pouch from the small supply bag he carried, ripped the top away with his teeth and slapped it on the wound.

"Ouch! Shit, Cal, take it easy there," Hawkins snapped.

"Don't be a sissy," James said as he wrapped the

pouch with the attached elastic bandage and tied it off with a hasty knot.

"I thought you medical people were supposed to have some compassion."

"Compassion won't keep you from bleeding out."

"Dandy of you to point that out," Hawkins replied drolly.

THE REVERBERATIONS from the explosion had barely subsided when McCarter and Encizo burst through the underbrush and engaged the enemy.

The first LRA fighter, identifiable by the fatigues and gold epaulettes, was still preoccupied with the spectacular light show in the distance. That hesitation cost him his life as he detected Encizo's approach much too late to respond effectively. The Cuban leveled his MP-5 sub-gun and triggered a short controlled burst that ripped through the man's guts and spun him into a tree. He smacked the trunk head-on and fell stiffly onto his back.

McCarter took the next two with a weapon he'd not utilized in some years, an Ingram M-10 machine pistol. While no longer as popular as it had once been, the Ingram suited McCarter in a close-quarters situation due to its accuracy at shorter ranges and its stopping power. The weapon stuttered, McCarter holding it tight and low as it spit death at a rate of nearly 1200 rounds per minute. Of course, McCarter didn't need nearly that many since the .45 ACP slugs, one of the two native calibers for the M-10, proved more than effective.

The first LRA terrorist caught a 4-round burst dead-center, the slugs blowing golf-ball-size holes out his back. The second took two rounds to the pelvis, which left smashed bone and cartilage in their wake. The man screamed and dropped his weapon, the scream cut short by two more rounds that entered below his jaw at an angle and blew off the top of his skull, generating a grisly spray of blood and gray matter.

McCarter and Encizo pressed forward even before the last body hit the ground. A couple of rounds buzzed over their heads but it sounded as if most of the fighting had abated. The warriors pushed through more brush and entered a clearing where they spotted eight men, three of them on the ground motionless and a fourth cradled in the arms of another. Blood dribbled from the man's mouth, visible only because another man had a flashlight on him.

The remaining men gathered around the pair turned toward McCarter and Encizo, raising their weapons in preparation to engage. McCarter heard a shout a heartbeat before something brushed past his arm. He looked to see Kumar throw himself in front of the Phoenix Force warriors and raise his hands.

"Wait! It is me. I have brought the Americans!"

The men waited a moment longer and then lowered their weapons. Kumar nodded at McCarter and then rushed to the man who knelt with the wounded one cradled in his arms. A brief conversation took place between them and each clamped the shoulder of the other. The man between them, blood continuing to ooze from the corners of his mouth, coughed and smiled at Kumar. Slowly, then, the light started to leave his eyes and less than thirty seconds later his body slumped in the arms of his comrade with a finality McCarter had seen too many times.

Gary Manning sidled alongside McCarter at about the same time as James and Hawkins appeared from the brush on the opposite side.

"What's going on?" Manning inquired.

"I'm not sure but I think this was our rendezvous party," McCarter said.

"Looks like they were ambushed before we could get here," Encizo added.

"Well then, we're bloody well lucky because if we'd met any earlier we would have been hit right along with these blokes."

The men who had been ambushed were, in fact, Kumar's people. He introduced the man who had been cradling the wounded SPLA fighter as his brother, Samir Taha. They shook hands in turn and then Taha ordered his men to secure the perimeter, searching the bodies for intelligence while they guarded the party from further attack.

"We thank you for coming when you did," Taha said.

"I'm sorry we couldn't get here sooner," McCarter replied. He gestured toward James. "This here is Calvin. He's a medic. Any of you hurt?"

"None that are still alive," Taha replied as his eyes flicked to the dead body at his feet.

McCarter frowned. "How do you think the LRA knew you were here?"

"I do not know."

"How about a guess?" Encizo pressed.

Taha looked at him with a haunted expression. "I do not guess, sir."

"Okay, never mind that," McCarter said with irritation. "We just bloody well need to worry about getting out of here. What about our man? Your brother seems to think that maybe this Bukatem bloke might have taken him. Do you believe that?"

"Our people in Khartoum have confirmed it. But we do not know the location of Bukatem's base of operations or even if your man is still alive. We only know they are operating deep inside of our country. We do not know where. And General Kiir will not provide additional men to help in our search."

McCarter smiled. "Well, let's just see if we can't help you with that."

IT WAS DARK and musty and smelled of death.

Jodi Leighton had been in places like this, mostly during his early training at Camp Lejeune, North Carolina, as a U.S. Marine recruit, again during his urban terrain training facility prior to his assignment to Khartoum and then later at Langley during his tenure as a CIA operative trainee. But that had only been training; this was real life and he doubted he'd be going home alive at the end of the day.

Leighton had known the risks. Hell, he'd known the risk he was taking just agreeing to this assignment. It's not as if he'd ever intended this to happen; neither had he expected to fall in love with British agent Kendra Hansom. A long-legged brunette and simply beautiful, she'd stolen his heart the first time he'd met her in that skanky little bar near Khartoum's city buildings. Leighton wasn't sure what had become of his British Secret Intelligence Service companion but he tried to keep his thoughts confined to their little trysts and secret meetings.

Of course, it hadn't been easy to keep the affair a secret. He'd told his case superior, who chose to look the other way and declared plausible deniability if word got out. Leighton wondered if Kendra had spoken to any of her own SIS superiors about it. She'd always seemed like the straitlaced kind who followed orders, for the service of Her Majesty, and all that other patriotic rot for which some Britons were known. But there was also something entirely seductive about Kendra, something forbidden—in legal jargon he might have called his affair with her fruit of the poisonous tree. Such relationships were strictly forbidden, something Leighton's supervisor had reminded him about when advising he'd completely deny knowledge if the affair came to light with his superiors.

Not that any of this mattered.

Leighton had accepted he was going to die and there wasn't a whole hell of a lot he could do about it. The mess he'd made getting involved with Kendra didn't even come close to the one he'd made allowing Lester Bukatem to capture him. They had already tortured him, in a manner of speaking, although Bukatem hadn't personally participated in the torture, nor had they asked him any questions. Not yet, anyway. Leighton suspected before long that they would and that's when the real suffering would begin. It was times like these Leighton wondered why they didn't issue an agent some kind of suicide remedy, like the old cyanide capsules, and he knew his ordeal had started to take its toll because he chuckled out loud at the cliché of this thinking.

It was nice to hope that someone might actually come after him, but Leighton knew there wouldn't be any rescue this time. Bukatem had a base of operations in the middle of nowhere, which in this country was basically the equivalent of being in the middle of nowhere that was in the middle of nowhere…and so forth. Sudan had turned out to be a very poor country with little to offer.

Still, Leighton had always done his job the best he knew how. He'd made connections in Khartoum with agents from other secret foreign services—British and

Israeli and Russian were just a few—along with establishing ties to the local chieftains. While the government of North Sudan maintained that it was in control, the SPLA still acted as a major influence in the region and protected its citizens as best it could from the guerrilla unit led by Bukatem.

Leighton had first learned the SPLA called the Lord's Resistance Army by the name Lakwena his first couple of days in country. It was one little-known piece of valuable information his predecessor had left him. That was just before he got piss-drunk and tossed out of the sixth-story window of a club in downtown Frankfurt while in transit to the States, where he was to be debriefed before retiring. Somebody had decided to "retire" him early and some insiders even speculated he'd met his demise by doing something in Khartoum that displeased the unknown third party.

Leighton's heart and breathing quickened a moment when he thought he heard the approach of his captors, but after a minute he relaxed some when they didn't show. *Cripes, man, don't get worked into a tizzy,* he thought. *They'll get to you soon enough.*

Leighton heard the whisking aside of a tent flap, sensed the entry of at least one person and possibly more. He tried to get a feel for how many were actually inside the tent—they had removed the blindfold at one point and punished him with bright lights pointing at him from every angle—but he couldn't count the footfalls. His ears had started ringing from the long-term silence he'd experienced, washed out only by the steady drone of what could only be a distant generator.

Leighton felt the knot of the blindfold that had been digging into his head loosen and then someone ripped it away and lights replaced the darkness once again.

Leighton squinted, attempted to discern the blurry silhouettes of two human figures in front of him, but the change from deep darkness to harsh light made it impossible, a matter that became worse as the strain caused his eyes to tear.

Then came the blow to his jaw, a blow hard enough to split his lip on incisors and rock his head in an awkward direction. A second blow followed, this time from the other side, and somewhere over the thud of leather against bare skin. His. Nausea rolled straight to his gut, and Leighton thought he felt a tooth loosen up. Probably his jaw had cracked under the impact of that last blow.

"Enough!" barked a voice with an Afrikaans accent. "I believe our guest is awake now."

Leighton couldn't see more than the darkened shape of the speaker but he didn't really need to, to know he was dealing with Lester Bukatem. The LRA guerrilla leader had been well-educated, according to intelligence reports, and his cultured accent bore that out. Leighton could think of no other member of this LRA unit, and he was certain it *was* the LRA that had captured him, with a leader that well-spoken. Not to mention that the man had bothered to speak English at all; that meant he knew Leighton was an American. Only Bukatem would have that kind of information. The CIA guy had to wonder where Bukatem would have come into such information. Had his British counterpart betrayed him? Leighton didn't want to think so but he also realized he had to consider the possibility. Maybe he'd fucked up after all.

"Mr. Leighton, it is a pleasure to finally make your acquaintance," Bukatem said. "You and your predecessor have proved somewhat meddlesome in the affairs of my people, if not worthy adversaries. For this reason I shall permit you to die quickly."

Weak and in pain, Leighton still managed to find his voice. "That's big of you."

"A man in your position cannot afford to mock me, American," Bukatem said. "Although it does mean you still have a bit of fight left in you. That's good. It will make my next task more…shall we say, entertaining?"

Leighton smiled and ignored the pain that came with it. "Say what you want, asshole. But I don't know anything and I'm not telling you anything."

"Oh, if I'm certain of anything it's that you'll talk, Mr. Leighton. I'm a patient man. But I can assure you that the sooner you answer my questions, the faster I'll kill you. Should you force me to prolong my inquiry, this will be a difficult engagement for you. I promise."

"Promises, promises."

Leighton couldn't see much but he did make out what appeared to be a nod from Bukatem's silhouette. A moment later someone raised his legs and he could feel the heat from the spotlights as they were placed much closer to him. Then his legs were forced into some kind of container filled with water; Leighton heard the slosh as his feet hit the surface and his shoes and socks were immediately saturated.

"You going to give me a bath?" Leighton snickered. "I've never been treated so well by the bad guys."

"Your flippancy annoys me, Mr. Leighton," Bukatem replied. "It's little more than false bravado and something I can assure you'll come to regret in a moment."

"Oh yeah? Well—"

Leighton never finished the sentence as excruciating pain lanced from his groin, traveled up his chest and set the very tips of his hairs on fire. So it felt that way. Leighton couldn't be sure but he thought he let out a scream and still it seemed like that would've been impossible because he vomited unproductively. Mostly the bile burned his throat in the aftermath of the shock and he experienced more cramps and dry heaves than anything else. The cycle was repeated a second time, then a third, and on the fourth Leighton thought he would pass out.

The CIA man realized they were applying some type of electric shock to his body—hence his feet in the water—but it was probably connected to an independent power source since he didn't notice any flicker in the lights that practically seared his face. Their proximity, coupled with the electric shock, made it feel as if Bukatem's men had set his body on fire.

"What?" Bukatem's voice seemed to reverberate inside his head, as if listening to the man speak under water. "Nothing to say now? I'm disappointed, Mr. Leighton. I thought you would definitely conjure a response to this newest form of interrogation!"

Another series of two jolts, these more painful than the first, followed Bukatem's taunting.

"What do you have to say to that?" Bukatem continued. "Do you understand now that I can generate this pain as long as I choose? You see, Mr. Leighton, I invented this technique. The food and water we gave you contains a special concoction of my own design. This prepares your body for what follows, and intensifies the pain. Oh, do not worry…there won't be any permanent damage. But you can rest assured that within an hour you will beg me to kill you."

Another jolt came and Leighton wasn't prepared for it this time. He bit his tongue and immediately tasted the salty, coppery blood from it. To some degree he re-

gretted being so cocky but there wasn't much he could
do about it now. Not that it would've mattered. Bukatem would have employed this torture no matter what
Leighton told him or what questions he answered. He
could have sold his mother, his whole damn country
down the river, and Bukatem wouldn't have faltered for
a moment. This had been planned, coldly, calculatingly,
decisively from the beginning.

"Now, American…let's begin to discuss your recent
activities in Khartoum," Bukatem said.

CHAPTER SEVEN

An estimated fifty-two thousand people lived in Hattiesburg, Mississippi. The city bordered the northern edge of Camp Shelby and like any military town it provided adequate housing needs to officers and other select personnel who chose to live off post. U.S. military billets were great for single enlisted men, permanent party and the like, but they weren't decent fare for a family man like Colonel Jordan Scott. The Scotts had acquired a split-level townhome in a peaceful neighborhood on the west side of Hattiesburg off I-59.

Sunset had passed by the time Able Team cruised through the neighborhood in their military sedan, a loaner from the HQ Company motor pool. Flashing a badge at a middle-aged woman in a jogging suit—the figure that filled it out could get a guy to thinking— bought Rosario Blancanales the information he needed regarding the Scotts. Lyons now watched the front door and windows of the house through binoculars as Blancanales picked his teeth with a pocketknife and stared down the street. Schwarz sat in back, snoring loud enough that it started to grind on the nerves of his two comrades.

Lyons lowered the binocs. "What do you think about that woman's story regarding the van?"

"Sounds like pay dirt, you ask me," Blancanales replied with a shrug.

Lyons shook his head. "A van matching the description of the one that hit us is parked out front of Scott's house the day before yesterday, but she doesn't remember seeing anybody inside? Something feels wrong about it."

"What?"

"It's too convenient," Lyons replied as he lifted the binoculars to his eyes. "Good fortune rarely drops right into our lap. I don't like it."

"Maybe whoever's behind this weapons smuggling doesn't know anybody's on to them."

"After the assault they launched against us this morning?" Lyons reminded his friend.

"Okay, you got me there."

"What are you two grumbling about now?" Schwarz muttered from the back. "Can't you see I'm trying to get my beauty rest?"

Blancanales tipped his head so he could make out Schwarz's shadow in the rearview mirror. "A hundred years of uninterrupted slumber couldn't help you, amigo."

"Hold up," Lyons cut in. "Vehicle coming. Looks like a van."

The warriors were parked far enough away that the sweep of the vehicle's lights didn't illuminate their faces. They waited silent and unmoving, wondering if the van would continue past the Scott residence, but no such luck—the van turned sharply into the driveway and the headlights winked out.

"Now, this is interesting," Blancanales said evenly. "Looks like some more of our friends."

"What's the play, Ironman?" Schwarz asked.

Lyons thought through it with a measure of debate.

"Should we take them?" Schwarz asked, wide-awake now.

"I don't want to jump the gun," Lyons replied. "If they risked coming back to Scott's residence for a reason and we hit them early, we might not find out why. We should wait it out and see what they do."

"What if Scott's inside the residence?" Blancanales inquired. "Or his wife and kids?"

"We've been watching the place for the last two hours," Lyons pointed out. "There hasn't been any movement. I don't think anybody's there. The fact they've played their hand gives us all the more reason to wait."

"Agreed."

Blancanales followed that with a sigh, but Lyons didn't try to question it. He understood they were anxious to get answers and he was, too. The irony was that his partners were usually the reserved ones and typically had to hold their leader back. But something in Lyons's gut told him that if they engaged the enemy too soon, not only would they attract a lot of unwanted attention but it stood to reason a firefight would end in a bunch of dead terrorists; that wouldn't put them any closer to finding out what had happened to Jordan Scott. It might also precipitate Scott's death if he was operating as an unwilling accomplice or being coerced to cooperate.

For all Able Team knew, Scott and his family were now hostages. If whoever was behind this weapons-smuggling ring figured government agents were on to them, they might simply kill Scott and his family, cut their losses and flee. In that scenario, it would be damn near impossible to track them. Part of Phoenix Force's success in Sudan depended on Able Team getting to the

bottom of whatever the hell was happening at this end
of the pipeline, and Carl Lyons had no intention of letting them down.

The shadowy figures silhouetted in the streetlamp,
six in all, exited the van and moved up the drive in
leapfrog formation. They traversed their course with
the practiced efficiency of professionals. Lyons noted
this and filed it away. The enemy had been trained well,
something the Able Team warriors had agreed upon following their first encounter at Camp Shelby. The questions they'd directed to the one in custody had revealed
nothing. Their prisoner had been resolute, silent, unwilling to share information of any kind. Lyons had
proposed applying more direct methods of information
extraction, but being he was under the protective custody of military police they didn't think it wise to devi-
ate from standard operating procedures.

Able Team had enough problems without adding
"torture" to the equation.

Even a search by Stony Man hadn't pulled anything
up on their prisoner, and that had Lyons on edge. Obviously they were dealing with some sort of black-ops
unit, which didn't concern him nearly as much as the
fact they had managed to implement such an operation inside the United States undetected. Since 9/11, the
FBI, in concert with other units attached to Homeland
Security, had done a crack job in detecting these types
of threats and neutralizing them before they became
a problem. They had apparently missed the boat this
time. That was okay; a situation like this was exactly
why the special operations group at Stony Man Farm
existed. Lyons and the rest prided themselves on doing
the job nobody else could do, faith that had been placed
in them by Brognola and the rest, and Lyons had never

questioned their reasons for existing. Of course, they had a consummate role model in the hardened and relentless personage of Mack Bolan.

Lyons scratched his chin and watched with interest as the enemy unit moved out of view. "Okay, we've waited long enough." He turned to Blancanales. "You stay here and be ready if they try to bolt. Gadgets and I will take out the wheelman first. Let's see what taking away their mobility will do."

"Roger that," Blancanales said.

"Here." Schwarz passed an AA-12 shotgun to Lyons from the backseat as the Able Team leader double-checked his Colt Anaconda .44 Magnum revolver before holstering it in shoulder rigging.

Lyons took the weapon and quickly inspected it in the dim light, the weapon forestock gleaming with a light coat of fresh oil. Originally designed as the Atchisson Assault Shotgun, the manufacturing patent of this newer model had been turned over to Military Police Systems, Inc. It included an 8-shell box magazine—also capable of sporting a high-capacity drum magazine for vehicle mounting—with a cyclic rate of 300 rounds per minute. The model had been modified by Stony Man's elite armorer, John "Cowboy" Kissinger, with a 12.6-inch barrel, nearly a half inch shy of the military-grade version. The shells were a preferred mix of No. 12 lead and double-0. The weapon also sported antipersonnel capabilities by chambering a special Frag-12 round stabilized by a 19 mm fin that distributed fragmentation using a small charge of RDX explosive.

Schwarz procured his own preferred weapon, the M-16 A-4 with an M-203 grenade launcher. While they weren't expecting to utilize high explosives, the versatility made Blancanales more comfortable. This model included the latest standard Picatinny rail to which Kissinger had mounted an SCP-7552 military sight system manufactured by EOTech. Powered by standard batteries, the sight had the ability to superimpose an aiming dot on the target, speeding target acquisition to tenths of a second and increasing first-hit probability under the most adverse conditions, such as night or inclement weather.

"All set?" Lyons asked. After a grunt of assent from Schwarz, he added, "Let's do it."

Lyons and Schwarz went EVA, keeping their weapons low and tight as they made a beeline across the street and moved up the sidewalk. The two were afforded quite a bit of concealment from the array of trees that lined the front yards of the bedroom community. They continued toward the van with one providing cover while the other advanced, moving in concert that came from years of experience and training.

The pair overtook the van in less than two minutes, coming alongside the driver's side undetected. Schwarz held back as Lyons moved to the window, which was cracked. A cloud of smoke gusted from the gap and the odor of cigarettes assaulted Lyons's senses. The Able Team warrior looked back with a nod at Schwarz and then reached gingerly toward the door handle and eased it outward. When the latch clicked with detachment Lyons whipped the door open fully, reached in and hauled the smoking driver out of his seat.

The man's cigarette flew from his mouth and struck the pavement in a shower of sparks a moment after its owner landed prone, skinning his hands as he struck the concrete with a dull thud. A muffled *whumpf* escaped his lips as the air left his lungs and Lyons helped the effort by stamping a boot between his shoulder blades.

The guy fought for air as Lyons jammed the shotgun against the base of his skull. Schwarz moved forward and snapped a pair of thick plastic riot cuffs on the man's wrists. Schwarz applied a chokehold, blocking air and blood flow to the man's head and within ten seconds the guy was out cold.

Lyons made a quick inspection of the interior and spotted a radio positioned in the console between the pair of captain chairs. A small red light indicated the radio was on—the driver had probably been alert to receive any transmissions from the team that had converged on the house. He considered taking the radio with him but ultimately dismissed the notion. If they decided to head for the house and were suddenly radioed by a team member inside, the transmission might be heard and used to pinpoint their position.

Schwarz and Lyons headed up the drive, Schwarz keeping his weapon high while Lyons proceeded in a crouch. They made good time and eventually reached a trio of concrete steps that led to a side door. Lyons nodded and Schwarz went up the stairs and tested the door. The storm door was locked, something that could have only been done from the inside—the enemy had gained access some other way, probably through the back.

They held their position and considered their options.

"Should we split up?" Schwarz whispered.

Lyons shook his head. "Too risky. And if we try to go through the back, they might have a sentry."

"In which case the jig is up," Schwarz replied.

"What about through the front?"

"If the doors are locked like here, it'll be noisy."

"Noisy?" Lyons appeared to brighten. "That sounds like exactly what we need."

"You're thinking a distraction."

Lyons nodded. "Got any whiz-bangs with you?"

Schwarz did a quick check of the grenade satchel at his side, confirmed the presence of two 40 mm flash-bang rounds and nodded at his friend. They'd done this kind of thing before: make a lot of noise and give the enemy reason to react, then spring the trap on their flank before they knew what hit them. To be effective, however, it would take a third party and getting Blancanales up there in short order might alert their quarry. The plan also stood the risk of hurting any innocent bystanders inside although Lyons considered such a risk negligible. It was the best they had.

"Go around back and aim for a first-floor window," Lyons said. "Give thirty seconds to get into position and then send it on."

Schwarz nodded and Lyons left their position, skirting the house in the direction of the front porch while Schwarz made his way to the rear.

As he went, Lyons activated the throat mike transmitter and ordered Blancanales to be ready to bring their wheels in a hurry. Chances were good the distraction would make the enemy congregate toward the front in the hope of making it to the van. This would allow him to pin them down until Blancanales and Schwarz could join him and shore up the defense. It would take cracker-jack timing and Lyons could only hope the ruse worked.

SCHWARZ PRIMED the M-203 with the 40 mm flash-bang, eased the tube forward and pushed until he heard the soft click indicating the hammer was locked in place.

He reached the back and peered around the corner, watchful for movement before proceeding to a hedge and taking up a position that afforded the widest field of fire. He understood Lyons's plan relied on a lot of assumptions, the main one being that the flash-bang coming through the back would push their enemies toward a natural desire to exit from the front. There were a lot of variables, too many to make Schwarz comfortable, but he trusted his friend implicitly—Lyons hadn't let him down yet.

Schwarz waited until he heard the simple two-click burst from Lyons's transmitter.

He took a deep breath, leveled the M-203 until he had acquisition of what looked like a kitchen window in his leaf sight and then squeezed the trigger. The weapon stock bucked against his shoulder with the kick of a 12-gauge shotgun. Flame belched from the muzzle of the M-203 as the grenade sailed through the window, smashing glass in its path before landing inside. Unlike the high-explosive rounds, the flash-bang had a timer delay and did not explode on impact. A heartbeat elapsed and then the grenade went, its effects evidenced by bright flashes and the whip-crack report that shattered another two windows.

Schwarz was already loading a second grenade even as he detected commotion inside and heard men shouting. He couldn't make out what they were saying but it didn't sound like English. Not that it mattered. They had one objective and that was to either track their enemies to their origins or take them down. Schwarz hoped for the first option since the latter would spell certain doom for Jordan Scott and his family.

Schwarz waited another ten seconds and then fired the second flash-bang, this time immediately following on its trail as the grenade traversed a similar path to the first. Schwarz had reached a rear corner of the house when the grenade popped, and he could feel the vibration through the outside wall against his back.

Lyons's voice suddenly came strong over the VOX. "It worked. Both of you get up here *now!*"

Schwarz didn't think a second about it, instead turned and headed toward the rear door. He found it ajar and slipped inside, confident that their plan had worked and he would take the enemy combatants by surprise.

The plan worked just as they had discussed. Schwarz came through the kitchen and heard the first reports of autofire coming from the front of the house. Their adversaries had obviously engaged Lyons, although it was more probable Lyons had engaged them, a thought that brought a smile to Schwarz's lips.

Schwarz primed the M-16 A-4 and moved in the direction of the firing. To the average man it would have seemed absurd to move toward the enemy fire. Like his companions, however, Schwarz could be considered anything but ordinary—a fact his partners in Able Team were never remiss to bring up whenever the opportunity presented itself.

The only sound audible above the weapons reports was the hammering in Schwarz's ears as his nervous system went into overtime. The battle had been joined, reached a point of no return. They were committed to the plan now no matter what the odds.

And Hermann Schwarz was prepared to go all the way.

CHAPTER EIGHT

As Lyons and Schwarz guessed, the enemy had clustered at the front of the Scott home in the aftermath of Able Team's ruse.

They may have been trained but they bought into the trick and Schwarz planned to take full advantage of their tactical blunder. He came through the kitchen doorway that led to the front of the house with his over-and-under held low. The first of their mysterious enemies clothed in black fatigues turned toward the Able Team warrior, but Schwarz easily had the drop on him. Despite this, the man swung the muzzle of his weapon toward target acquisition. Schwarz blew him away for his trouble, punching holes in his chest with a short burst of 5.56 mm NATO tumblers. The impact lifted him off his feet and he slammed through the heavy glass of a coffee table in the center of the living room.

Two more terrorist gunners split off and angled in opposite directions, knowing Schwarz couldn't take them both. Schwarz knelt and swept the muzzle of the M-16 A-4 toward the most viable target moving along the left flank. A volley of autofire cut the man off at the knees and he continued moving, propelled by the force of his forward motion, until his face contacted the edge of the short wall that ran just outside stairs leading to the second floor. Schwarz rolled to cover behind a heavy leather sofa just as the other terrorist gunner flanking his right side fired at the position he'd occupied a moment before. A maelstrom of SMG fire chewed into the hardwood floors, scattering splinters in all directions. With no time to acquire his target at that range, Schwarz whipped his Beretta M-92 from shoulder leather, leveled the pistol and fired two shots. The first round tore through the fleshy part of his enemy's neck and the second struck him full in the face, splitting his skull apart and dumping him onto the floor.

The echo of the gunshots died away but no further threats appeared. This puzzled Schwarz as they had witnessed at least a half-dozen terrorists exit the van. Where the hell were the rest?

Schwarz got his answer a moment later when the unmistakable boom of a shotgun reached his ears. Lyons! Schwarz regained his feet and turned toward the front door. In the gloom he realized it was open just a crack. The remaining opposition had obviously beat a hasty exit and stumbled right into Lyons's open arms.

Schwarz sprinted for the door to help his friend.

CARL LYONS had waited patiently for his friend's signal.

Schwarz delivered the grenade just as planned but the enemy hadn't completely played into their hands. Only an estimated half of the terrorist force actually left the house, and only a moment after they emerged onto the front porch did Lyons hear the sounds of combat coming from inside the residence. Lyons watched a moment as the three figures descended the steps and moved furtively toward the van, the wicked outline of weapons held ready in their hands. Lyons had taken position behind the cover of the van and as the men came nearer he leveled the shotgun and shouted for his enemies to freeze and lay down their arms. Naturally, the terrorists didn't listen and Lyons had to duck behind the rear of the van to avoid being ventilated by a storm of hot lead. Rounds ricocheted off the driveway and punched through the flimsy body of the van, ripping chunks of plastic and metal framework away. A fiery pain seared through Lyons's leg as fragments from a round caught him in the fleshy part of his calf. The Able Team leader dropped and rolled away from the assault, cursing at his stupidity.

This wasn't going down the way he'd planned.

Lyons came to his feet behind a thick line of shrubs. It wouldn't provide much in the way of cover but it would afford concealment. Lyons tracked the shotgun on the nearest moving target and squeezed off a blast. The AA-12 made short work of the terrorist gunner, blowing out part of his hip. The man spun with the impact, his scream of pain drowned by the reports of return fire. Fortunately the enemy didn't have Lyons's position spotted well and they were far and wide of his location.

Lyons turned at the sound of squealing tires and spotted Blancanales as he whipped the government sedan into motion, bumping over the curb and driving straight up the lawn to the right of where Lyons waited. The Able Team leader grinned at his comrade's ingenuity, returning his attention to the task at hand. Lyons sent two more blasts of heavy shot to keep heads down and then beelined toward the cover of the sedan. It wasn't much more effective than the shrubbery, he knew, but at least it put a little more between him and the enemy fire.

In the wake of battle, he could see the terrorists heading for their van. Well, they wouldn't get far without keys, which Lyons had thought to pocket earlier. The roar of the van engine surprised him and he watched rather helplessly as tires smoked under the van and it began to move in reverse.

"Ironman to Gadgets," Lyons said into the mike. "Where away?"

"Still inside," came Schwarz's reply.

"You clear?"

"Yeah."

"We're out front. Double-time, it looks like they're going to rabbit."

"How—?" Schwarz began but he obviously cut the transmission short, realizing now wasn't time to play twenty questions.

As the van backed out of the lot and the driver dropped the stick into Drive, the still-open side door revealed two terrorist gunners who began to lay down fire on the sedan. Blancanales got clear of the driver's seat and leveled a Belgian FNC. Built on the reliability of the original FN FAL, the FNC was a 5.56 mm marvel of modern weapons manufacture and remained a favorite of the Stony Man teams. It was tough, reliable and versatile, all features that made it ideal under almost any conditions. Blancanales held steady as he triggered the weapon from the hip, spraying the side of the van with NATO stingers. Several rounds caught one of the terrorists center mass and pushed him back into the deep darkness of the van.

That seemed to neutralize any immediate threat, and as the van rocketed from the scene Lyons turned to see Schwarz sprinting toward the sedan. The trio climbed inside and barely had the doors closed before Blancanales backed out of his angled position, slammed the wheel hard left and hit the street from the drive to avoid a bottom-out. Now wouldn't be the time to trash their only vehicle.

Schwarz produced a gust of air from the backseat. "Well, that didn't quite go how we'd hoped."

Lyons didn't reply, instead reaching to feel the damage to his calf through clenched teeth.

Blancanales noticed Lyons's movements in his peripheral vision but didn't take his eyes from the road. "You hit?"

"Flesh wound."

Schwarz reached to a medi-pouch on his belt and came away with a bulky dressing pouch. He tore away the seal with his teeth, keeping one hand on the M-16 A-4 to protect accidental discharge from the jostling, and passed the dressing to his friend. Lyons grabbed it with a hiss of thanks and packed the wound.

"How serious?" Schwarz asked.

"Not sure," Lyons replied as he wrapped the attached bandages. "It feels like a through-and-through, but I don't think any major vessels were hit so at least I won't bleed to death."

"Maybe we need to regroup, Ironman," Blancanales said through a grimace.

"No way…you stay on these assholes! If they have Scott or his family and we lose them now, the show's over!"

Blancanales and Schwarz may not have liked hearing that but they knew Lyons was correct. Chances were good from what they'd witnessed so far that Scott was an unwilling participant to the gun-smuggling operation. The Sudanese terrorists had clearly been operating within the country for some time, and Able Team's only chance of stopping them would be finding the source of their operation—getting them where they lived and schemed. Otherwise, they would just pack it up and move somewhere else, and the hunt would have to start over. Phoenix Force had put themselves in harm's way, and none of the Able Team warriors planned to let them down while they still had breath in their lungs.

The van's taillights were barely visible but it didn't seem they were gaining ground.

The driver had slowed and his driving implied he thought he'd shaken Able Team. At that time of night traffic was thin and losing them wouldn't be easy. Schwarz had an idea and tuned the channel of their VOX system to the police emergency broadcast channel. He called up a dispatcher and gave them information, calmly delivering a description of the van and advising they were federal agents in pursuit of armed terrorists and that law enforcement wasn't to attempt pursuit unless requested specifically to do so. The call would go out to not only local police but any county sheriff units in the area and the Mississippi State Police.

"That ought to keep the cops at arm's length," Schwarz said with a grin as he clicked off the radio.

"They're heading south," Blancanales announced as the van swerved across two lanes and headed for an entrance ramp marking Old Highway 49.

Lyons whipped out his cell phone and dialed the direct access code to Stony Man.

Aaron "Bear" Kurtzman answered midway through the first ring. "Talk to me, Ironman."

"We're shadowing our Sudanese friends," Lyons said without fanfare. "They're heading out of Hattiesburg, south on Old Highway 49. We need satellite up if we can get it, Bear."

"It'll take time, boss," Kurtzman said. "Which I'm assuming is something you don't have."

"You assume right. Can you pull up a map of the area?"

"Already done. What do you need?"

"There has to be some reason they've chosen this route," Lyons said. "Look around that area given the direction we're headed and list me off some probable targets."

"It's pretty much a mix of urban and rural," Kurtzman said, the sound of keys clacking in the background. "Wait! Got a good possible here. There's a small airport near there—Bobby L. Chain Municipal."

"Any scheduled flight plans?"

"Checking. Wait, one."

Lyons tried not to let the splitting pain that materialized behind his eyes overcome his waning patience. His leg throbbed with each pump of his adrenaline-rich blood, which echoed the splitting thump behind the migraine. He felt nauseated but not as if he would pass out, although he could tell blood from his wound had started to seep through the bandage. He couldn't believe he'd been ill-prepared to mass an offensive against a numerically superior force without a better plan of action if it all went to hell, which he'd half expected it would. So far their Sudanese counterparts hadn't shown any fear to join a conflict if it came down to it.

Kurtzman came back on. "Ironman, I just got off the horn with the tower. They have a departure flight, small twin-engine craft, in the next twenty minutes. They've already received their clearance for takeoff once they've boarded their passengers."

"Destination?"

"New Orleans."

Lyons considered that a moment. He couldn't see any reason they would be operating that far from Camp

Shelby, unless… "Unless they have a port operation out of there," he guessed.

"Come again?"

"That has to be where they're headed," Lyons said. "Okay, let Hal know we think the funnel point might be out of New Orleans. We'll need backup supplies there as soon as possible. And have a medic meet us at this Bobby L. Chain."

Kurtzman's balk was audible. "Who's hurt?"

"I am but I'll live. Maybe local law enforcement can head them off in New Orleans if we don't stop them here. Tell Hal we think that's where Scott might be, too."

"Wilco," Kurtzman said. "Anything else?"

"Yeah, reach out to Charlie Mott. See if he's available for a standby."

"Roger that," Kurtzman said. "Good luck, Ironman."

Lyons grunted an acknowledgment before clicking off. "Cripes, Pol, can't this thing go any faster?"

"Doing the best I can, Ironman, but we're pitting a V6 against a V8 and they had the jump on us."

"Then it's best we back off some, keep a good distance."

"What?"

"Do it," Lyons ordered. "We need to go into observation mode. There's an airport near here and I'm betting that's where they're going. We try another suckhead play like the one before, we might risk making civilians dead, as well. There's a plane waiting for takeoff at a nearby airport and I think it's for them."

"We can't let that plane take off, Ironman," Schwarz said.

"I don't think we have a choice," Lyons countered.

"We try to stop them and we may end up doing exactly what we don't want to do."

"You aren't actually suggesting we hold back," Blancanales said.

"I am," Lyons replied. "I'm also not feeling so good and if we have to go another round with them I could end up being as worthless to you as tits on a bull."

Blancanales sighed but took his foot off the accelerator some. "I don't like it, but you're in charge."

"Yeah," Lyons growled. "Lucky me."

TWO MEDICS ATTENDED to Carl Lyons's leg in the back of an ambulance, and although they had recommended transport to the nearest medical facility, he declined. As suspected, the fragments from the ricochet had gone clean through the wound and although it had bled some it hadn't turned out as dramatic or bad as Lyons had imagined. Besides, there wasn't much they could do for a hole in his leg. Sutures were out of the question and antibiotics were pointless since Able Team had a combat medical kit that included prefilled ampoules of high-dose penicillin, which they had already administered to him under medical oversight.

Harold Brognola had contacted Lyons as soon as he received word of their encounter. He'd been briefing the President the first time they called, and Price had taken the evening off to get some well-deserved rest.

"You did what you had to," Brognola told Lyons. "It's a lot to balance."

"I appreciate the confidence," Lyons said. "Although there's no guarantee we'll be able to pick up their trail in New Orleans. I'm concerned I may have dumped our only lead."

"We've got feelers and contacts out in every part of the city. We expect to have some intelligence soon."

"Something weird about this," Lyons said.

"What do you mean by 'weird'?"

"I mean weird." The Able Team leader nodded acknowledgment to the medics as he swung his legs over the side of the stretcher and bailed from the back of their ambulance. It wouldn't do to have the paramedics eavesdropping on government secrets. When he was out of earshot Lyons continued, "I hadn't expected them to return to the Scott home."

"I thought that's why you were sitting on it in the first place?"

"We were sitting on it in the hopes of catching Colonel Scott red-handed or verifying his family was all right. Now it would seem they're in real trouble. What I can't figure is why armed gunrunners would return to the scene. These weren't ordinary terrorists, Hal. They were well-trained and well-equipped. And they fought like they had something at stake."

"How so?"

"The driver we sacked before engaging them. They shot him dead before they left—shot one of their own who was tied and unconscious."

"That does seem a little on the strange side, even for extremists like the LRA. But it's not what I would call completely out of character."

"Not for a group that had something to hide."

"You believe they figured he might talk."

Lyons sighed. "Right. At least I think so. Aw hell, I don't know what to think anymore. I'm tired and beat up as hell and now I'm pissed off."

Brognola couldn't resist a chuckle at Lyons's expense. "You were itching for action."

"Not the kind I had in mind, Hal." Lyons switched gears. "What's Charlie Mott's status?"

"He'll be there within the hour. We got extremely lucky on that count. He just so happened to be operating a charter out of Texas. As soon as Bear reached out to him, he contacted us and got airborne."

"Maybe our luck will hold out."

"Maybe so."

"All right, Hal, we'll wait for him to get here and then head straight to New Orleans. You'll call us when you have something?"

"As soon as I have something."

"Understood. Out here."

Lyons disconnected the call and ran one hand through his blond hair. It had started to grow thin over the years and parts of it were beginning to show more gray-white than the maize tone of his youth. The sun had bleached some of it out but Lyons knew he wasn't getting younger. He wondered how much longer he could keep it up, this hard-and-fast lifestyle. Turning back the clock wasn't something that even he could do. One day he'd be too slow or go right when he should have gone left, or just be in the wrong place at the wrong time.

And that would be that.

"Yo, Ironman," Blancanales said, lumbering up to his friend. He looked at the bulky dressing and said, "All patched up?"

"Yeah, I'm fine. Where's Gadgets?"

"He's talking to the boys in the tower, getting a look at the flight plan filed and information on the plane."

"I'm sure it was chartered and they probably forged any identification."

"Probably, but it's something. And it will confirm if we're on the right trail."

As if on cue, Schwarz joined his colleagues on the tarmac.

Lyons looked expectant. "Well?"

"It was definitely them," Schwarz said. "No question about it. They filed a flight plan for New Orleans and they were in a real hurry when they arrived, according to the tower guys. We going after them?"

Lyons nodded. "Just got off the phone with Hal. Charlie Mott was apparently close, so we should be headed that way soon. Hal and Bear have all ears to the ground. With luck we can get a line on these guys and shut them down quick."

"Looking for swift resolution?" Blancanales asked.

Lyons pointed to his leg and said, "Nope. Just some good old-fashioned payback."

CHAPTER NINE

Jonglei Region, South Sudan

The sun dangled at high noon by the time Phoenix Force and their allies reached the Sudanese encampment near the White Nile River a few klicks north of Juba. It had been some time since McCarter and his men had visited Sudan. It was nothing short of a miracle that they hadn't been intercepted by either Sudanese police officials, military or rival guerrilla groups traveling along the only vehicle-worthy roadway north into Juba from the Sudan-Uganda border.

Their SPLA escorts seemed to know what they were doing, and McCarter observed Taha ran a pretty tight ship. In some respects, it didn't surprise the Briton all that much. Having served with the SAS a number of years before his recruitment into Stony Man, McCarter had worked among others like Taha and his men. These were warriors born out of necessity, men who lived with the horrors and tragedies of a life filled with bloodshed and violence. Many times they didn't know where their next meals were coming from, let alone the bloody bullet that could end it all.

And there were soldiers in other armies who cried abuse if they didn't get three hots and a cot every day—clearly they needed to spend some time with Taha's crew. McCarter couldn't pay anything but the deepest respects toward them, if not for their creed then at least for their tenacity and discipline. Without taking sides, McCarter imagined the atrocities committed by Taha's men on occasion probably paled in comparison to those of the LRA.

As they climbed from the old jeepney utility vehicle, McCarter looked around the camp and said, "Where's General Kiir?"

"He is not here," Taha replied, not without some surprise in his tone. "This is a forward observation camp. General Kiir is quartered much closer to Bor."

"Seems like a pretty large territory to cover," Encizo remarked. "This location must be at least, what…150 miles from there?"

"Slightly less," Taha replied. "We have learned that this is as far north as the Lakwena can afford to operate without meeting resistance. As long as we can hold them here, we stand some chance of limiting the damage they do. Were it not for the refugees crossing the border, it would be more difficult."

The Phoenix Force warriors all knew the truth of Taha's statement. Refugees crossed the border by the hundreds and thousands every year. They were displaced from their homes and culture, willing to risk even death to reach the camps nestled safely in Ethiopia and Kenya, and Uganda to a lesser degree. This influx of poor and needy kept the LRA busy near the border since even they didn't have a limitless pool of fighters from which to draw, and many of their conscriptions came directly from those refugee populations.

"But that is another matter. My brother tells me—" Taha glanced at Kumar, who merely nodded at his sibling in way of acknowledgment "—that you believe if you find your missing man from the CIA that you can also recover the weapons smuggled into the country. We believe it is Bukatem who holds this man, but it may not be possible to find him in time. Bukatem and his command party move quite often to evade detainment."

"We have ways of finding him," McCarter said. He turned to the rest of the Phoenix Force team. "Why don't you blokes get the gear off-loaded, and then have Kumar show you where you can eat and clean up."

Taha nodded at Kumar and inclined his head to indicate he should do as McCarter suggested. The two leaders then moved off to Taha's command tent. McCarter would take time later to get some chow and attend his own gear, but for the moment he wanted to speak to Taha alone. He trusted the others but he also knew that as the team leader it was his job to pump Taha for any intelligence the man might possess and come up with a plan the rest of them could execute. He wanted them to be prepared to move out a moment's notice and, the way he saw it, bantering strategy wasn't the best use of their time.

Once inside the command tent McCarter said, "I'll level with you, mate, since our CIA man's cover is obviously blown. The man we're searching for is named Leighton." McCarter spelled it. "He took over as case officer in Khartoum a few years ago, and our higher-ups think he might have learned about this smuggling operation, which is why the LRA snatched him up."

"I hate to bear you bad news, but if your CIA man was taken under Bukatem's orders, there is a very good chance he's already dead," Taha said.

McCarter shook it off. "Doesn't matter if he's dead or alive. It's only important we find out who took him. The timing of this thing's just too neat. Think about it. You discover U.S. arms have been smuggled into your country and then not two days later the CIA case officer in Khartoum disappears. My people think if we find Leighton, dead or not, we'll find the head of the smuggling ring."

"And once you have found this head, what is your intention?"

"We'll bloody well chop it off."

Taha seemed to think on McCarter's words and then nodded. "There is only one of two places I believe Bukatem would have taken this man of yours. The first is a base maybe ten kilometers outside of Khartoum. It's a small encampment, one that I believe he thinks we know nothing of. The other is much closer here, a main base of operations that is heavily guarded."

"So you don't think he'd have him somewhere inside the city."

"It is too dangerous."

"This main base you're talking about, what sort of odds would we be up against if we attempted to get inside?"

"This is not easy to say," Taha replied. "None of our men have ever successfully made it out alive once inside, and that's not due to lack of trying."

"So since nobody's come out alive, you're not sure of the layout of the place or its fortifications."

"Correct."

"Bloody hell," McCarter said as he rapped his knuckles against a large table in the center of the tent.

Taha gestured to an aide nearby and the man nodded. The aide turned to a tall, narrow, gray metal cabinet and withdrew a large rolled paper with a waxy overlay. The aide deployed the poster-size paper onto the table with a flick of his wrists. It contained a topographical map of the operational areas of the entire country in great detail. McCarter leaned over it with interest as Taha pointed out key locations.

"We are here," the SPLA leader said. He pointed to an area just outside of Khartoum. "This point marks the small base I told you about." He pointed to a second area and added, "This is the location of Bukatem's main encampment. At least that's its last known location to us."

McCarter nodded. "This is quite a good map. In fact, I think this just might help us out a lot, mate."

"In what way?"

McCarter gestured to the vertical and horizontal grid lines along the edge. "These are the latitudinal and longitudinal marks of the area, right? With that kind of information my people can pinpoint those areas by satellite and provide us with just about everything we need to know. Personnel movement, equipment, terrain…the whole bloody lot. And we could probably have the information inside an hour."

"It would seem that you have more influential connections than even General Kiir made known to me, my friend," Taha said with expressed admiration. "It excited me when we learned of the fact we'd be working with a specialized team of Americans. Although you would seem to be almost a foreign legion of operatives, as your accent betrays your British origins and I think one of the other men is Cuban or Mexican, no?"

"Naturally, I can't confirm or deny it," McCarter said. "But you're obviously experienced enough to know we're more than we might appear on the surface."

Taha nodded and waved it away. "It is of no importance beyond the fact that I believe we can trust you."

"Trust is all we've got left," McCarter said.

"I think it best we await a reply from your government before deciding how to proceed."

"That's fine by me, mate," McCarter said. "But before I do I was wondering if you could tell me something. This Lester Bukatem bloke…what's his angle? Why would he risk smuggling weapons into this country all the way from the United States?"

"I do not understand, I think," Taha said.

"I'm just trying to figure out why he'd risk this much for American arms when he could obviously acquire them from other locations. It seems like he's taking a big risk, that's all."

"It is to be noted, what you say. Unfortunately, I do not have an answer for you. But this is the way of men like Bukatem. I do not understand why he would turn against his own people, plundering the poor and raping its women. Who knows why men do what they do, eh?"

"Yeah," McCarter said. "Who knows?"

"YOU'RE GOING TO BE up against quite a bit," Barbara Price announced, directing her voice toward the supersensitive microphones arrayed throughout the briefing room at Stony Man Farm's Annex facility.

She sat at the table as electronic data scrolled tickertape fashion along the bottom of the satellite photographs displayed on a mammoth screen at the opposite end of the table. Upon receiving McCarter's call and obtaining the coordinates, Price had immediately turned the information over to Kurtzman's team with orders to get rolling. It hadn't taken Kurtzman long to return a boatload of intelligence about the two locations in question. In the case of the major encampment close to the SPLA base camp where McCarter and the team were holding, the news wasn't good.

"We estimate there's a significant amount of equipment at this location," Price continued. "Everything from underground generators to vehicles."

"Armor?" McCarter's voice interjected.

"Without a doubt," Kurtzman said. "We've also seen buildings, mostly metal prefabs although it looks like there might be one or two stick-built. The place is also surrounded with what looks like cyclone fencing."

"How many ways in or out?" McCarter inquired.

"Just one," Price said. "It's heavily guarded and there isn't much traffic. Very little movement during the day and absolutely none at night, and infrared signatures indicate there are a score of roving patrols. It's not all that large as operational bases go, but it appears to be well locked down. In fact, I don't think I've seen tighter security in a base of this kind."

"There's a good chance that's where the weapons are being cached, then," McCarter said.

"That could well be, David, but we must also assume their contacts inside the States aren't the LRA's only supplier," Price pointed out.

"What are you getting at, love?"

"I'm trying to say that a place like this won't have only U.S. suppliers. There are bound to be other contributors with an interest in keeping this thing going. War's still a good business for those who can supply arms. It means not only political control but also cash. The arms black market has always thrived in countries with long-standing conflicts like Sudan. Who could forget Somalia or Kosovo, or the fighting that's been going on right there for generations?"

"You think this goes deeper than the LRA," McCarter said.

"I believe it might," Price replied. "We don't have any evidence of that, mind you, only a working theory. But we happen to believe it's a pretty good one and there's no way the LRA could continue operating effectively in Sudan without a steady supply of arms and equipment."

"Our contacts here suggested it might be officials in Khartoum who're actually keeping this war going. It looks like maybe even Leighton was working on this theory, possibly had some proof someone high up was supplying weapons and intelligence to both bloody sides."

"Well, that would explain why the LRA grabbed him up," Kurtzman said.

"Speaking of that, what have you learned about this Bukatem wanker?"

"Oh, he's a real gem," Kurtzman answered. "It would seem that a lot of intelligence has been collected about him by a number of foreign agencies, as well as our own government. Why they've never been able to catch him is a mystery but he's undoubtedly one of the most elusive of his kind. They even tried to bring him in a couple of times for peace talks but he always refused."

Price added, "It's not clear exactly when he took over as leader of the Lord's Resistance Army but the circumstances are well-known. He apparently succeeded leadership after arranging for the death of their previous head. Since that time he's instituted a reign of terror across Sudan and along the border regions, and doubled LRA membership."

"Conscripted against their will from what we know," McCarter said.

"This isn't going to be easy, David. In many cases you'll be up against fighters who are reticent, at best, certainly untrained and only interested in survival."

"I understand. We'll do our best to minimize contact. I wish we could acquire some air support. My arse has taken a real beating over the terrain here, and it's slow going as you can imagine. But we'll stay on mission by locating Leighton, if he's still alive, and finding the remaining weapons. Maybe if we can destroy their supplies and arms, that will take the fight out of Bukatem and minimize bloodshed."

"Especially your own blood," Kurtzman pointed out.

"There's also something else," Price continued. "Some months ago, Leighton's handler filed a report with his superiors at CIA headquarters. Leighton had apparently taken up intimate relations with a member of British intelligence named Kendra Hansom."

"Name doesn't ring any bells," McCarter said.

"We gathered almost nothing on her, despite a very thorough search," Price said. "Leighton thought his supervisor had kept the entire affair a secret, but we all know there's really no such thing in covert ops. Leighton's handler reported it anyway, probably trying to cover his own ass after the debacle that occurred with the agent in place before Leighton."

"You think Hansom might be an alternate source of intelligence on Bukatem if we can't locate Leighton," McCarter concluded.

"Possibly. There's also a chance she might have some idea of where Bukatem might have taken Leighton. Naturally, the SIS wouldn't authorize her to mount any sort of official rescue mission. That's not to suggest she might not do it on her own, which means if we can connect you with her, she might be willing to work with you."

"Where can we find her?"

Price looked at Kurtzman and winked. "Bear's working on that even as we speak, although I'm sure you realize it'll take time. The only information we have on her movements is what Leighton's handler provided to us. At present, he's on leave but Hal's working that angle. It's not as if Her Majesty keeps us regularly informed on the movement of their agents, so we're sort of feeling around in the dark here."

"I can appreciate that, love. I'm sure you're doing your best. What about Bukatem's contacts there in the States? Do you think he's getting supporters from inside the U.S. military?"

"We haven't discounted that possibility. Able Team ran into trouble at Camp Shelby shortly after their arrival. It's possible Colonel Scott is an unwilling accomplice, perhaps operating under duress. Able Team thinks it's possible that Sudanese operatives are inside the country and have threatened Scott's family in some way. Carl and crew are checking it out as we speak."

"If they learn anything that could be of value to us, let me know. Or if you get a line on this Kendra gal."

"Will do. Good luck, David."

After the Phoenix Force leader disconnected, Price's eyes met Kurtzman's and she sighed. He knew what she was thinking. They didn't have anything solid here to give the field teams. They were groping around, grasping at straws and making uninformed guesses. Guesswork wasn't something either of them was very comfortable with. Their warriors needed solid intelligence and Stony Man hadn't done a very good job of providing that so far. It wasn't just a matter of professional pride—it could also put lives at risk.

"Don't worry, Barb," Kurtzman said unbidden, his massive hand covered her slender forearm. "We'll get something solid soon and then our boys can do what they do best."

"I know," Price whispered. "I just hope we don't get the information too late."

CHAPTER TEN

Khartoum, North Sudan

Kendra Hansom was worried.

Where the hell was he? She glanced surreptitiously at her watch again and tried to keep her face impassive—not that anyone could see it behind the burka. While a good number of the traditions in Sudan were long-abandoned, wearing the local dress and covering her face did have its advantages, particularly in the espionage business. She hoped her body language didn't betray her apprehension.

She sat in a small café along Barlaman Avenue. An outside observer might have viewed the place like any number of big-city streets in America, with its tan tenement buildings and single-story commercial shops. A two-lane hardball surface made up the street, and crushed gravel laden with sand provided parking for the shops. Some of the buildings were darkened hulks that left no doubt they were long abandoned. The walks in front of them were dirty and cluttered with disuse, the windows boarded or just open to the air.

Most of the sandy side streets were forbidden to vehicles and boasted only foot traffic. Pedestrians were everywhere and very few vehicles occupied the roads day or night. It wasn't a mecca of prosperity but it didn't necessarily imply the widespread poverty of lore. Hansom had been in places, including some on London's West Side, that made Khartoum look downright touristy. She had come to like the country in many respects, as well as its people. They enjoyed a peaceful, civil life for the most part—not daring to venture into the rugged countryside where violence and perdition awaited the unwary.

Khartoum wouldn't have been her first choice for an assignment, but her forbidden tryst with Jodi Leighton had changed all that. Unlike her lover, Hansom had elected not to report her personal indiscretions to her superiors. There were strict rules about involvement with members of another intelligence agency, even the agency of an ally, and her SIS handlers wouldn't have been nearly as forgiving. She wondered if that wasn't partly due to the fact she was female, but Hansom had to wonder what they expected a woman alone in a male-dominated country to do with her natural urges.

As she'd once confided to Jodi, "I like sex and I bloody well like it with white men whenever possible."

Her statement had surprised him but she didn't deign to explain it. She wasn't a prejudiced witch but she had her own preferences just like everybody else. Those urges were especially strong now but she'd start looking somewhere else soon for her satisfaction if Jodi didn't get his arse in gear. The man was nearly an hour late!

Hansom checked her watch again and then noticed the entrance of a plainly dressed black man. He was tall, thin and made a poor attempt to look like a native. Hansom tried to pretend that she hadn't noticed him but in her peripheral vision she saw him glance in her direction and then approach. Hansom dropped her left hand to the concealed pocket in her plain black dress. By not wearing pants she could avoid hassles by the police so she didn't figure the guy to be an undercover cop. The way he moved told of professional training and as she looked directly at him she figured him for an American.

Jodi had told her he wasn't the only CIA operative in the country and that he had an out-of-country handler, as well as an agent inside—what he called a mirror—whom he'd never met. Hansom wondered if this was the mysterious mirror, an agent of equal qualifications who operated as a sort of insurance policy for the official case officer assigned to the area. The man came close but he didn't sit or even look at her.

As his eyes took in the half-full café in a manner suggesting he was looking for anybody but her, he muttered, "If you're Kendra, wait five minutes and then follow me outside and go to Alley Kilo."

He looked around the room a moment longer before turning, making a show of a huff and leaving.

Hansom chewed her lower lip as she considered this. He had to be CIA because only an intelligence agent, unless really good, would know about the letter references to unnamed side streets. It had long been habit for covert ops to divide foreign cities into grids and map those grids using phonetic alphabets. It made it easier to navigate and mitigated the risks of specific locations being overheard in conversations. The fact the man had said "kilo" indicated his strong knowledge of the military's radio alphabet, and further that use of the word indicated he was American. It also meant he knew Hansom was an operative who would understand the reference and provide a means of authentication.

Hansom made her decision, waited the full five minutes and then rose and left the café. She turned in the opposite direction of Kilo and strode down the crushed-gravel walkway. After two blocks, she turned and crossed the street, ventured another block to make sure she hadn't picked up a tail and then headed back toward Kilo.

The man waited there, one hand in the pocket of his slacks while the other held the cigarette at which he puffed. Hansom wasn't sure she liked the guy's nervous attitude but he saw her and now she was committed. If she turned away he was sure to follow and that could get them both in hot water. Whoever he was, Hansom suspected his appearance had something to do with Jodi; every fiber of her being screamed that something bad had happened to Jodi.

Hansom checked her flank before stopping to speak with him.

"Not a very private place for a meeting."

"When you hear what I have to say, you'll probably realize it doesn't much matter. Your cover's been blown and so has Joe's."

"I don't know what you're talking about."

"Come on, Kendra, let's not play that game." He took a last drag from the nub of the smoke and then crushed it out underfoot. "Someone grabbed up your boyfriend and I got the shit job of finding you to tell you about it."

Hansom braced herself for the answer. "Is he dead?"

"Dunno," the man said. "Probably, but it's unconfirmed. For right now he's been listed as MIA."

"You're his mirror?"

"Yeah. Lucky me, huh?"

Hansom took it in and tried to calm her voice as she lowered the mask of the burka. "Any chance it's a mistake? Maybe he's gone to ground for a bit."

The man shook his head. "I wish it were that easy. If he planned to do something like that he would have checked in with our handler, and if he couldn't he would have at least reached out to me."

"Maybe there wasn't time."

"Goddammit, lady, stop acting like a little girl. This isn't tiddledywinks we're playing. The guy's been in-country awhile now. He didn't check in and he's disappeared. What does that tell you?"

Hansom wanted to lash out at the man but she bit it back. She had reacted irrationally. This was the business and despite her feelings for the man she knew only as Jodi—he'd never explained why everyone else he knew called him Joe—there were inherent risks in the espionage game. Personal feelings weren't allowed to get in the way. The most disconcerting thing about it was this man was right. If Jodi had been compromised then it stood to reason her cover may have been shot to shit, as well.

"What are you doing to find him?"

The man expressed indifference. "What are we doing? What would you have us do, lady? In case you hadn't noticed it's not like we got a bus full of spooks around with nothing to do."

Something in her eyes must have triggered a reaction because the man's expression changed and his tone softened.

"Look," he said, "I know you cared about him."

"I still care about him. You're talking like he's dead."

"I'm just being realistic. The fact is we don't have the resources to go scouting about the country looking for him. I wish it were different but it isn't. Now my handler's given me instructions and I plan to follow them, but I wouldn't get your hopes up."

"If you can't go look for him, maybe I will," Hansom said.

"I'm afraid not."

"Pardon me?"

The man's eyes shifted toward the ground a moment as he muttered, "My handler said he's going to reach out to your superiors." He looked her in the eye and continued. "I wasn't supposed to tell you, but I don't give a shit. I'm not happy with the way the higher-ups are handling this but there isn't a lot I can do about it. I have a few connections. I plan to reach out to them and see what I can see. But what we don't need is some SIS-type going off half-cocked on an unsanctioned search-and-rescue mission."

"I appreciate that," Hansom said.

"Beside the fact you might get in the way and inadvertently get yourself killed."

"Getting myself killed is my business."

"Look, I'm not your superior but I am Joe's friend. And I'm telling you what I would do in your situation is look for extraction and look for it early. Get out of the country while you still can."

Sure, she thought. *But not until I find Jodi.*

THE PHOENIX FORCE warriors were ranged around the map table, watchful as McCarter briefed them.

He could tell they were itching for action but jumping the gun wouldn't do any good. At least they wouldn't be fighting alone. While Taha's men were a meager force in comparison to Lester Bukatem's numerically superior resources in manpower and equipment, the SPLA had experience and they knew the area much better than Phoenix Force. Coupled with Phoenix Force's technical advantage—constant satellite communication with Stony Man and hard intelligence on the mission target—McCarter felt confident they could get quicker results.

"Our other advantage," McCarter continued in earnest, "is that these bloody terrorists don't know where we're at or what we have planned."

"Unless Leighton's already told them," T. J. Hawkins pointed out. "The guy won't last forever, even with his training. We're more than thirty-six hours into this. There's a good chance he's already talked."

"Or he's dead," Manning said.

"Maybe so, but we can't play what-if," Encizo said. He looked at McCarter. "What's your plan?"

McCarter gestured to the map coordinates of the base location pinpointed by Stony Man's elite satellite surveillance systems. "According to Bear, this base is well-stocked. There are a number of outbuildings there, along with munitions and fuel-storage areas. There's also a fighting force on the ground but we don't have exact numbers. We're estimating a strength of maybe twenty terrorists, but no more than fifty."

Manning whistled. "That's going to be a tall order."

"Sure, but it's not what's got me worried most. The largest tactical problem is that while this compound isn't necessarily as tough as others we've encountered, it's spread across a large area. Probably to mitigate damages in the event of an air assault. That will make it tougher to navigate without high-altitude support, particularly in the dark."

"You will also have much ground to cover," Taha said, a corner of his mouth quirking in a smile. "Or we will. It will require us to conduct a building-by-building search if we're to find your man."

"No chance we could get Eagle in a chopper, huh?" James asked in reference to Stony Man's ace pilot, Jack Grimaldi.

"The government's rated this entire region a no-fly

zone," McCarter replied. "We'd have to pull strings at the diplomatic levels and that would take more time than we have."

"Or Leighton has for that matter," Manning said.

"I wish we had bloody more to go on, boys, but this is what they've handed us and we have to deliver. Not only for Leighton's sake but also for Taha and his men here."

"We're fine." Taha waved it away. "My men are strong and have much experience fighting. Most of Lester Bukatem's people are little more than children. We will be victorious."

McCarter saw several of the men look at Taha in surprise but he didn't say anything to them—a look was enough that he expected no replies. Judgment wasn't their business and, anyway, they weren't in the same category as Taha, a man who had lost many members of his family and had been fighting this war for years. In truth, the SPLA had gained little ground and not by any fault of their own. It wasn't for want of effort or resolve. Men like Lester Bukatem had always thrived by exploiting the poor and unfortunate, and McCarter, for one, would be happy to put him down and keep him down.

Personally, if he could.

"Anything else?" he asked.

Silence followed and he nodded that they should make their preparations. There were still some hours until nightfall, but they would begin their trek before dusk. They had close to ten miles to cover over the Sudanese wilderness and only part of that could be by vehicle. The base had been made inaccessible for good reasons. While McCarter would have preferred to attack at dawn they didn't have such luxuries. Taha could only commit five of his own to the force, as the rest were on a vital mission passed down by Kiir.

While the rest of the Phoenix Force warriors went about preparations, Encizo requested a sidebar with McCarter who had stepped away from the headquarters tent for a smoke.

"What's up?" the Briton asked.

"I understand Taha won't be coming with us," Encizo replied.

"Right. He's taking a group on some other errand. Orders from up top from what he said."

"So Kumar's going to be our guide."

"Is there a problem?"

"Not really a problem," Encizo said. He lowered his voice. "I don't mean to snub our benefactors but my Spidey sense tells me something's not right. I'm not sure I trust Kumar."

"He does strike me as a bit of a squirrely bugger," McCarter agreed.

"You noticed it, too."

"What's eating you, Rafe?"

"Nothing. I'm just thinking it seemed awfully easy for us to get this far. Could be coincidence but we all feel the same way about coincidences. He seemed well-connected for being a junior troop among his brother's men. It also sounded as if he had an inside pipeline straight to someone in Kiir's ranks, and that doesn't bode right for a young and inexperienced type like him."

McCarter shrugged. "Seemed pretty good in a fight."

"Maybe." Encizo sucked air through his teeth and added, "But if it's all the same to you, I think I'd like to keep a close eye on him."

"I have no problem with that. Probably be a good

idea for us to keep an eye on everyone going along on this little expedition. I wasn't keen on taking them at all. I'd rather work this just among our own. It removes the complications of what you're proposing. But Taha insisted and he made a good argument for why we should take some of his men. We have to consider the possibility there's an informer in the unit given that our rendezvous point with Taha was compromised."

"Fair enough." Encizo turned and McCarter called after him.

"Thanks for bringing this to me, Rafe."

Encizo nodded and was gone.

McCarter turned his attention to the surrounding jungle foliage. The calls of untold fauna echoed from their depths, almost as if mocking him. He tried to shake it off but had to admit that Encizo's instincts were typically spot-on; chances were good his friend was right. Maybe there was a traitor among Taha's unit and maybe there wasn't, but at least taking the unit along would allow the team to keep an eye on them. If someone working for Bukatem was among the company, the chance of that individual finding an opportunity to warn the LRA leader of the attack would be scant.

One thing McCarter had done after the rendezvous location got made was ask Kurtzman to monitor any transmissions coming from their AO. An informer would have to find some way of communicating with Bukatem and the only practical means was by shortwave radio or satellite phone, either of which Stony Man's technical powerhouses would be able to detect. If anything came up, Kurtzman had promised to alert the Phoenix Force leader immediately. For now that was the best McCarter could expect.

The rest of it was up to him and his comrades.

McCarter detected movement and turned to see Kumar approach him. The young man smiled when their eyes met and McCarter nodded in acknowledgment. He'd seen the guy fight, certainly, and he considered the young man a formidable adversary. There weren't any of the telltale signs he'd expected but Mc-Carter had lived this long not underestimating anyone, ally or foe, and he didn't plan to start now.

"Our men are prepared," Kumar said. "We only await your word."

"We've got a few hours yet. They can relax," Mc-Carter said.

"We have learned never to let down our guard, *sadeek.*"

McCarter grunted at that: the Arabic word for "friend" happened to be something he knew—just about the only word he knew in that language. "I imagine it's tough to get a good night's sleep about here."

"To sleep can mean to sleep forever in my country," Kumar said.

He put his hand to his chest and opened his mouth as if to say more, but McCarter immediately saw his eyes fall on the breast pocket of McCarter's fatigues. He smiled and reached inside to withdraw a pack of Player's cigarettes. He offered one and Kumar happily accepted. It's what he'd wanted really but the kid had too much in the way of manners to come right out and ask.

McCarter offered a light and in a cloud of smoke Kumar nodded thanks.

They stood and looked at the dense surroundings without speaking to each other. McCarter figured Kumar only sought the comfort of company. It was a common thing among fellow combatants. He wasn't going to worry about it. If Kumar was a traitor he'd make his move deftly, without anyone around to see. That's what cowards did and Kumar didn't strike Mc-Carter as a coward.

He would know with certainty soon enough.

CHAPTER ELEVEN

Lester Bukatem listened with interest as one of his aides reported updates on the efforts of their connections in Bor.

Bukatem would have preferred to be there to personally oversee the operation but his face was too well-known and prevented him from moving freely around the city. Many of the Sudanese dogs considered him a devil, a godless one who cared only for his own prurient interests, and in a way they were correct. What Bukatem desired more than anything, though, was power— unlimited power to do as he saw fit and to build an army that would become unstoppable.

General Kiir's men had offered a degree of resistance to this point that Bukatem had to admit he hadn't expected. Kiir was savvy and knew how to leverage his contacts among the power brokers throughout Sudan. He'd begged to solicit arms and supplies from anyone who would listen to his pleadings, including certain officials in the Sudanese government who operated anonymously. Bukatem had just as many connections from the same cesspool within the man's own government, connections who had a vested interest in seeing Bukatem victorious over his enemies. It was easy to exploit the tensions between North and South Sudan.

Bukatem probably would have succeeded in destroying the remnants of Kiir's army but other governments, larger and more influential governments, had managed to run interference. One of those has been the United States, and for Bukatem America remained his single greatest enemy and the one he most hated. Some Americans considered him a religious fanatic while others thought him simply mad, and Bukatem was content to let them keep guessing. His desire to be an enigma—perhaps something of a legend in certain parts—allowed him the luxury of maintaining a posture of mystique.

Above all, however, was the recent reduction of his arms supply inside America. Some of Kiir's men had surprised one of his many encampments caching weapons destined for frontline positions in the southern part of the country. Bukatem held no illusions he would ever conquer Sudan—at least not in the strictest sense of the word. He did believe that he was destined to rule some large part of it, though, and with a fresh trail of refugees to provide a nearly limitless supply of manpower, he might very well realize his dream sooner than expected.

Yet no man could undermine his enemies without a strong battle plan founded on sound military strategy. These two particulars trumped all else in the game of war and Bukatem had proved adept at wielding them to suit whatever ends he envisioned. He also commanded strict obedience of his conscripts and fierce loyalty from his men. Bukatem had learned to do this by not acting as had his predecessor. Many had accused him of murdering the former LRA leader, Jendayi Mukony, something Bukatem had never denied but not openly discussed with anyone, not even his wife. The freedom fighter hadn't talked of how he slipped into Mukony's tent one night and cut his throat from ear to ear, then dragged the body to the river and let the White Nile's residents do the rest.

Mukony had been weak, trusting his subordinates and taking them into his confidences. Such was not the mark of a true leader. The great leaders believed that only distance and summary rule were the allies of those with the will and means to exploit them and Bukatem ranked himself among such subscribers. Disobedience carried a death sentence and incompetence meant exile and shame, lifting all failures to become targets of public ridicule. Yet Bukatem could not tolerate dissension among his subjects, particularly the fighting men of their movement.

Bukatem's second-in-command, Kato Kamoga, entered the tent with a strained expression. Bukatem interrupted one of the field commanders giving the report by telling him to get lost. The man looked uncertain but immediately saluted before turning and leaving the tent. A cloud of blue-gray smoke clung eerily around Kamoga's head from the massive cigar clenched in one corner of his mouth. The man smoked like a fiend but Bukatem did not mind—Kamoga had proved himself a ruthless soldier and skilled combatant, not to mention he had tactical training as a former officer in the Uganda People's Defense Force.

"You look troubled, my friend," Bukatem said. He rose from his chair and walked to a nearby table lined with canteens. He took a drink from one of them; the water was refreshing but flat and tasteless from the chemicals used to purify it.

"We have a problem."

"There are never problems," Bukatem chided him. "Only opportunities."

"Then you'll forgive me when I say that this opportunity comes in the form of American special operatives."

Bukatem whirled on his heel. "Where?"

"From what our spies have learned, they are operating both in the United States and locally. They may already be on their way here to the base."

This news gave Bukatem pause, although he would never have told anyone it caught him by surprise. Another tenet of leadership was to act as if such things had been expected, that a plan had already been set in motion to counter contingencies such as these. He figured that the Americans would eventually discover the operation in their own country and they would have to dissolve the group and reassemble in some other location once they found a new supply line from which to draw. Of course, he had plenty of backup sources—some of them as primary as the Americans—including equipment from Russia, Iraq and a sister gunrunning ring in Turkey.

"CIA?" he asked Kamoga.

"I don't believe so."

"They must be a special American military unit then, perhaps Delta Force or Navy SEALs."

"Or possibly they are from a covert group of which we know nothing about. I don't need to remind you that there are such groups operating in America that even their own people don't know exist. They usually operate under cover identities of some official agency within the U.S. but they do not actually belong to those organizations."

"Whoever they are it's of no significant consequence," Bukatem said with a wave. "I expected the Americans might try something like this when we learned that Kiir's men overran our transfer encampment and discovered the weapons. What of our man inside Taha's camp? What can he tell us?"

"We've had no contact since his last check-in when he told us of the rendezvous with parties unknown."

"And you now believe they were meeting the Americans?"

"I think it's likely." When Bukatem didn't reply, Kamoga said, "What are your orders?"

"Since there are American Special Forces in this country, we can only assume they know about this location and further that they will attempt to overrun it."

"Should we move the American?"

"What is his status?"

Kamoga appeared to think on it before replying, "His resistance to our methods is considerable. He's obviously been well-trained by his CIA masters. However, I do think he will break before long. Your techniques are peculiar but effective, and I have no doubts we'll acquire the information we seek once we've applied them a bit more."

"Then as long as he is not dead or has not answered us, he still remains a valuable asset. I think you are right, however—we should move him to the alternate location. See that it's done. Immediately."

"Yes, sir."

"Is there something else?"

Kamoga looked hesitant to broach the subject and Bukatem felt impatience growing. One of the side effects of maintaining strict discipline among the men was their reticence to deliver what they deemed to be bad news. Bukatem had attempted to break them of this but they still seemed to hesitate and it irritated him more than the news itself. On some level he couldn't blame them as they were fearful of reprisal, yet Bukatem's punishments—while severe and final—were fair and he did not believe in scourging a man unless there were compelling reasons.

"Go on, Kato," Bukatem said. "What is it?"

"I've been told that a number of our men in Mississippi were killed in action," he said. "There is a second unit allegedly attached to the U.S. military, although I doubt that is really their allegiance, which repelled an assault planned against one of the base leaders."

"The diversion they tried to create." Bukatem slammed his fist into his palm. "I told Daudi it wouldn't work!"

Daudi Muwanga had been in charge of the American unit since the establishment of Bukatem's plan to smuggle weapons out of the U.S. Since that time, Muwanga had done a less than adequate job. On a number of occasions Bukatem had considered removing him but relented under Kamoga's advice. He understood the reasons—Muwanga was Kamoga's brother-in-law and the two had fought alongside each other in numerous campaigns—but that didn't mean Bukatem's patience wasn't worn with Muwanga's less than stellar record. Muwanga was a pragmatist but not a visionary, and any good leader needed to be both. Bukatem had sensed him unequal to the task. Only the fact their supplies from America had been steady and of adequate quality had stayed Bukatem's hand. But this was the last straw.

"I want you to select a new man to take charge of the operation there. And I want to hear no further protests. The subject is closed. We cannot afford to lose our foothold in America. It has taken us too long to get all of our people in place and we must protect that asset as if our very lives depend on it, mostly because they do. Is that clear?"

"Yes, sir," Kamoga said, but Bukatem could tell from the man's expression he wasn't happy about it. "And what of the Americans here?"

"Put together two units, ten men each should do. Send one on long-range patrol and the other to Bor."

"Don't we risk exposure putting men in Bor?"

"We would if these Americans knew what they were looking for, but I believe they are grasping at air. Even with the help of that accursed, meddling Taha they cannot be terribly effective without intelligence. I would be interested to learn how they got into the country undetected, however. It was by no official channels—of this much I can assure you. Do you think that you could discover this?"

"I will give it my best efforts."

"Good. Everything is coming together, my friend. Before too long we shall taste the delights of victory. And our enemies will taste the vengeance of God."

KENDRA HANSOM finished the inventory on her get bag, sealed it, slung it over her shoulder and left the apartment. She'd paid up through the end of the month so nobody would miss her for the next few weeks. She'd donned a pair of khaki fatigue pants and black tank top, and wore her dress and burka over that. Once she got out of the city she would change clothes.

The next task would be finding decent transportation. There were cabs or buses, the select few women were allowed to ride, that could take her as far as the city limits and maybe into one of the nearby suburbs. Beyond that, public transit vehicles stayed to the main roads that were heavily patrolled by Sudanese police. She couldn't purchase or lease a vehicle, at least not one that could handle off-road trails, so she was left with only one option.

Hansom found the rental place that specialized in off-road vehicles. It was nearing 2200 hours and the place was long closed for the day. A pair of small cutters got her past the cheap wire fencing that surrounded the lot. She moved slowly among the vehicles, careful to search for one that would serve her purpose and thankful the moon had disappeared behind a bank of low clouds. Thunder rumbled in the darkness, a signal of the impending rain. Monsoon season had arrived just a week before and she had to find a suitable vehicle soon before she got caught in hammering downpours that blazed across the Sudanese landscape.

An early-model Jeep caught her eye and within a minute she'd gained access. As she snapped away the ignition panel and fumbled in the dark for the ignition wires, she thanked her instructors at Fort Monckton for teaching her how to do this—although she'd never really thought a need would come for it and especially not under these conditions. She smiled as she thought of all the James Bond movies and how a British espionage agent's life was anything but the glitz and glamor portrayed by those films. In this world, bullets were as real as the dangers she'd faced.

Two minutes went by and she finally got the leads connected. A stout knife in the ignition and a crank of the engine with pedal to the floor got the bloody thing started. In a short time she was on a side road, she couldn't even remember its name, that led out of the city and into the rugged Sudanese country. Hansom called up from memory the maps she'd studied carefully before Her Majesty had sent her to this hellhole. She'd gleaned enough intelligence to know that there was only one group capable of doing something like this to Jodi.

When she thought of the Lord's Resistance Army, the name of Lester Bukatem was the first that came to mind. Bukatem was a cold-blooded bastard who led an army of cold-blooded bastards. They claimed to fight for God but their actions could hardly be deemed Christian from the viewpoint of any decent humanitarian. Being raised in a devout Catholic family, Hansom had to wonder what possessed such men to proclaim themselves the arbiters of God's will and purveyors of holy law while they committed the worst atrocities one human being could against another.

What rot! It was bloody pointless to consider this as a contributing factor to her mission. Hansom cared about only one thing and that was finding the man with whom she'd shared her most intimate moments. It occurred to her that her actions would most likely prompt her superiors at Vauxhall Cross to declare her in rogue status and withdraw any support. Maybe Commander Brighton would see his way past her indiscretion once he heard from the CIA; maybe he wouldn't. Either way Hansom didn't really give a damn.

Hansom kept to the main roads until a good ten miles outside of Khartoum before killing her headlights and turning onto a rough road—really more of a trail—that led into no-man's-land. Some of the trails were heavily patrolled but Hansom had it on good authority this one rarely saw official oversight. Anyway, it didn't matter. If police or a Sudanese military patrol attempted to stop her she would resist with everything she had, which wasn't much. The Browning L-9A1 rode in her pocket, and her get bag held the components for a carbine version of an SA-80.

It would be enough against a couple of opponents but if they threw any considerable resources against her she would probably not survive the encounter.

She continued with deft precision across the rough trail and killed the interior lights to give her as much of a night-vision advantage as possible. She had a particular target in mind, a small camp that nobody else knew was there save for her superior officers. Officially known as Checkpoint Omega, it was here she could gather additional equipment and intelligence before heading deep into the bush. The British government had used it as a safe haven for their agents, a place of last resort in the event something went terribly long and an agent might have to wait out an extraction effort.

For now it would serve Hansom's purposes. She could only hope and pray it wouldn't be too late for Jodi.

Clouds clung to the Sudanese sky like wet wool, obscuring moon and stars.

Rain had started falling, increasing with intensity as the squad of heavily armed men slogged through the boggy jungle floor. The humidity played equally cruel tricks on them and the sweat that soaked their fatigues chafed at their skin.

Still they moved without complaint or conversation, each alert to potential enemies that might observe them even as they moved closer to their target.

David McCarter considered his men and couldn't help but compare them to the motley crew handpicked by Taha to accompany them. He was glad to have Encizo and Hawkins along with him, but he wished the whole of Phoenix Force had been there. He understood the need to assign James and Manning to head for the alternate base location pinpointed by Stony

Man, though, and they could make do for a time. Given Encizo's concerns regarding a potential traitor among them, McCarter hadn't given the order to send the two men until the last moment, and then he didn't feel a need to explain their absence to Kumar and his men. Not even Taha had known about the change, since his departure preceded that of McCarter's team.

At least Taha had left clear instructions that McCarter was in charge and that they should obey his orders as they would those of himself or General Kiir.

This seemed to suit Kumar just fine; the young man was respectful of McCarter's superior experience. Kumar was almost conciliatory, in fact, offering to let his men take point and constantly check their every move first with the Phoenix Force leader. McCarter had only permitted their team to take two radio sets, one packed by Encizo and the other by one of Kumar's men, Halan, whom McCarter picked randomly. McCarter also ensured that the Sudanese radioman kept enough distance from them that both radios weren't compromised in an ambush but not so far he wasn't in sight at all times.

One of the point men raised his hand and the squad halted.

Kumar moved forward to the point position, conversed briefly with him and then made his way to McCarter's side.

"We are close," he said.

"How close?" McCarter asked.

"Twenty meters, no more."

McCarter nodded and checked his watch. The luminous red-orange hands revealed it was just shy of midnight. There hadn't been time to train for this op, so most of McCarter's instructions had been relayed to each man during their trek. McCarter nodded in self-affirmation and then ordered Kumar to take up his assigned position. He turned and gestured at Hawkins.

Hawkins slung his MP-5 barrel down, and then reached into a cargo pocket and withdrew a small cylindrical object. He popped it into the tubular chamber of a Czech-made RV-85 flare launcher passed to him by one of Kumar's men. The warrior double-checked the load, then angled it high and aimed toward an opening in the overhanging foliage. The device popped like a cap gun and the 26.5 mm flare soared high above. The men surged forward as the flare ignited and lit the sky with a bright flash.

The operation had begun.

CHAPTER TWELVE

New Orleans, Louisiana

Daudi Muwanga closed the computer screen displaying the encoded email and sat back in his chair, furrowing a troubled brow. The news hadn't been good, although he'd expected it to come so his orders weren't any surprise. Not that he intended to obey them. Muwanga had never recognized Lester Bukatem's authority and he wasn't about to start now. It was by design his brother-in-law had managed to get him assigned to this post. They had worked too long and hard in America, far away from their homes and families.

Muwanga would die before bowing to Bukatem's wishes.

The covert operatives posing as agents with the U.S. Army were an interesting development, enough that Muwanga had felt obligated to report their encounter to Bukatem. But he had no obligations beyond that, other than to complete his mission. As long as they continued to supply their brothers with weapons, Muwanga saw no reason for Bukatem to complain.

Anyway, it didn't matter at this juncture. According to the men who returned from their mission in Hattiesburg a few hours before, any covert operation they had at the Army base would soon be exposed. His men had sworn they lost the American agents but Muwanga wasn't convinced. These men had demonstrated time and again their resolve and ferocity under fire. They would not give up so easily. In fact, Muwanga had no doubt they were already in New Orleans, which meant he would have to step up their operations and get the remaining weapons out of the country. They could not leave such value behind, even if they thought the mission lost. That's exactly the kind of ammunition Bukatem would seek against Muwanga and only prove himself right and Muwanga wrong.

Muwanga had no intention of abandoning his mission here until it was complete, because to do so would also be an abandonment of his men and the cause of God. He couldn't have that on his conscience.

"Pakim!"

Muwanga's lieutenant burst into the room of their rented house only a moment after being called. He was young and inexperienced, but equally efficient and loyal. Muwanga had never trusted too many of his own kind, another reason Bukatem had been reticent to assign him this mission. Bukatem's faithlessness angered Muwanga in a great many respects because Muwanga had never done anything to earn it. For over a year now they had been faithfully smuggling U.S. small-arms shipments out of America to support their holy cause. How dare a man who had advanced to the top of their ranks by betrayal and murder question Daudi Muwanga!

Pakim saluted. "Yes, sir!"

"Do we have any further information on the American agents?"

"Our men are watching the major transportation hubs as you requested, sir, and there is no sign of them. But…" His voice drifted.

"But what?"

"We are spread very thin, sir. We've had considerable losses and I didn't dare send more men than we could absolutely spare."

"You made a correct decision, then. It would seem that our efforts are futile in that light. I'd recommend you contact them and advise they are to return here at once. We have operations we must get under way with our last shipment, which is doubly large. We shall need every man we have."

"Yes, sir."

"Once you've completed assembling the team, I want you to head for Camp Shelby. We have one last shipment to retrieve before we leave this country. I will meet you at the usual rendezvous point twelve hours from now. First I must go to our headquarters and close off loose ends. Dismissed."

When Pakim departed, Muwanga rose from his desk and proceeded to a hideaway recessed into the wall and concealed by a bookshelf. He disengaged the locking mechanism and pulled out the hinged shelf to reveal the contents of the steel-lined recess: a passport, fifteen thousand dollars in U.S. currency, small bills, along with twice that denomination in Euros. He wouldn't be able to return to Africa directly once they had completed their task. His only alternative would be to get out of the country and head to Germany or the Czech Republic. There he would wait for a few months until he could build a new identity and return to Uganda.

What Muwanga wouldn't do is give up on his mission or his men. They'd had to kill one of their own—his team had told him the man was too far gone to salvage and the team leader had ordered him killed so he didn't fall into enemy hands—when they were ambushed at the home of the American colonel. One of their men was still being held prisoner at Camp Shelby, and no matter what, Muwanga had no intention of leaving him behind. Abandonment was not in his code and he didn't give a damn what Bukatem thought of that. There were no "acceptable losses" to Muwanga as long as he had the breath in him to do something about them.

Muwanga emptied the contents and pocketed the U.S. currency while stuffing the rest into an attaché. Their battle plan was in place. First they would meet at a nearby planning location on the outskirts of New Orleans. Once his men understood the order of their operations he would then have Colonel Scott eliminated. They hadn't been able to find the man's family so there wasn't much leverage they could use. Scott hadn't resisted the torture, really, which had surprised Muwanga. Scott had proved very useful when the appropriate pressures were applied. At first simple bribes had been effective to solicit Scott's cooperation but over time Muwanga had noticed the man becoming cocky, demanding more money for his continued cooperation.

Muwanga had acted conciliatory at first but after Bukatem continued to complain about the increased cost Muwanga finally had to take drastic measures. This final shipment was too important to leave behind, no matter what his colleagues thought of it. Besides, Lester Bukatem wasn't the grand warlord or military genius he wanted his ranks to think he was. The man had never been much more than an underling before his rise to power and he boasted about the experience of Muwanga or many others, including Kamoga.

Bah! What did it matter? Muwanga chided himself. *Why let such things preoccupy me?*

Muwanga closed the bookshelf, sealed the attaché

case and left their small office storefront bound for their tactical retreat. Pakim awaited him in his personally owned vehicle, an early-model compact Muwanga had purchased while posing as a student at a local community college.

Once they'd accomplished their mission, he would leave the country, and when the time was right he'd return to face whatever consequences awaited him. That's assuming Bukatem didn't get himself killed first. Muwanga didn't wish to see the death of any of his brothers; they were all fighting for the glory of God.

But for Lester Bukatem, Muwanga could make an exception.

AARON KURTZMAN already had the audiovisual linkup established to the powerful Stony Man data processing servers when Price and Brognola arrived. Comprised of a massive array of servers with a satellite-integrated network, the technology at the Annex would have put systems at the CIA and Department of Defense to shame. Only the NSA boasted as robust and complex a system as Stony Man's, and many of those systems were shared by the Annex hookups, making Stony Man's computer processing power second to none.

"Talk to me," Hal Brognola said as he and Price took seats at the massive briefing table in the Annex.

"Given the information we obtained from Ironman," Kurtzman began, tapping a few keys, "here's what we've come up with. It's still a working theory but it's something."

"It's more than we had before," Price remarked with evident exhaustion.

"Right." Kurtzman hit one more key with pomp, and the black-and-white still of a dirty, worn and thin face appeared on the high-resolution screen. "Meet Daudi Muwanga, a Ugandan army veteran and now suspected member of the Lord's Resistance Army. About eighteen months ago, Muwanga came to the U.S. under a false identity as a college student. His term of exchange was six months, during which he attended a community college in New Orleans. Address of record was supposedly in Jefferson Parish."

"What happened to him?" Price interjected.

"Dropped off the radar," Kurtzman said with a shrug of his broad shoulders. "Hasn't been heard from or seen since. Most people that were questioned by ICE about his status said he was a pleasant enough man, highly intelligent, and that they would never have suspected him of being a terrorist sympathizer."

"That's the most dangerous kind," Brognola interjected.

"Any idea of his whereabouts?" Price asked.

"Well, I wouldn't have had the first clue, but given what we know about Bukatem's connection with someone here in the States it's a good bet Muwanga's still operating somewhere out of New Orleans. We think he may have an entire team working there now, funneled in one or two at a time over the past year."

"There would seem to be plenty of evidence to that effect," Price said. "Could you track down a probable location by running a complex pattern algorithm on his movements?"

Kurtzman smiled. "Already working on it, my dear, and I think I'm close to finding just that."

"Keep on it, Bear," Brognola said.

"As soon as you have something solid, you'll want to get it passed on to Able Team," Price added. "It sounds like they're going to need us to pull out all the stops on this one."

"I'll do my best."

Price smiled. "That'll be more than enough, I'm sure."

"Meanwhile, I have some promising news," Brognola said. "I got back a couple of hours ago from speaking with the President. He's finally managed to convince the authorities in both North and South Sudan that we're on their side, thanks to some very good haggling skills. We apparently owe our American ambassador a hand up, as I understand he's been keeping close tabs on several of the CIA case officers assigned there.

"It never ceased to amaze me how much the bureaucracy there chooses to look the other way. There are at least a dozen countries with covert operatives there and yet not a single one of them has been caught, much less detained or questioned."

"It's not so surprising if you think about it," Price replied. "The infighting there was going on when I was still with NSA. The government's always had its hands full dealing with myriad factions that have come through there, each one rising with a different name but all being little more than variations on a theme. With the operation of guerrilla units from Uganda and the influx of Egyptian terrorists hiding there, Sudan has become a big center for terrorist activities. That's kept the government too busy to worry about a few spies. Especially with recent efforts to divide the country into North Sudan and South Sudan."

"Maybe so, but they sure do wield a big sword when it comes to politicking," Brognola said. "Up until this afternoon, the entire country had been declared a no-fly zone with the exception of very stringent commercial air traffic in and out of Khartoum and Sudanese military. We've now managed to get approval to let Jack fly within specified areas. They had some conditions, however."

"Which were?"

"One, our people would have to be escorted wherever they went. The government of North Sudan has promised to give us a representative from their 144th Counter-Terrorism Unit, part of the Ninth Airborne. They've been pretty effective in combating the terrorism, according to Ambassador Hamakam."

"McCarter's not going to like that, methinks," Kurtzman said.

Brognola grunted. "I'm pretty sure that McCarter isn't going to have any choice in the matter if he wants to be able to get around quickly and unmolested. We have assurances the counterterrorism representative will only be there to assist and observe. They've promised no outside interference provided our people confine their activities to striking *pure* hostile targets."

"What's that supposed to mean?" Price asked.

Brognola raised his hands, palms upturned. "Beats me. That was my question, as well, and the Man was very noncommittal in his response."

"Well, at least air support will help them work more quickly and efficiently," Price said.

"Indeed," Kurtzman agreed.

"With this development, do you have a new mission plan in mind?" Brognola asked Price.

"Hunt's working on that piece of it as we speak," Price said. "According to McCarter, one of Kiir's key team leaders, Samir Taha, sent McCarter and his team with Taha's brother to check out the encampment we spotted via our satellite linkups. That operation is probably under way right now. As soon as they check in we can let him know that we've bartered for the fly-zone clearance and have Jack extract them from wherever they're located."

"Sounds good. Then what?"

"Well, although McCarter didn't have any ideas about where Taha was going, we do suspect that the SPLA sees the presence of Phoenix Force as an opportunity to step up their operations against known LRA encampments. It's always been General Kiir's belief that if he could keep the LRA busy with short, surgical strikes, that would choke off the potential supply lines and hamper their ability to procure additional firepower.

"It's a sound strategy, when you look at it. Unlike conventional warfare between countries, the success or failure of the prevailing forces looking to liberate the masses from oppression comes down to who has the most bodies and how many of those bodies carry small arms. Our profile on Kiir agrees with that of the CIA and NSA in that the general's a realist. He knows this war can't be won going up against the government, at least not as long as the LRA has a foothold on key territories within the country.

"More refugees are being recruited—" Price made quotation signs with her fingers "—every day and Bukatem is building a veritable army of conscripts. For him, it's a holy war…of a sort."

"But only as long as it serves his purposes," Brognola concluded.

"Right."

The head Fed sighed as he reached into the breast pocket of his coat, withdrew a roll of antacids and popped three in his mouth. He chewed with a grim expression. "I think if Bukatem is allowed to succeed that his war could very quickly turn from religious to political. Why he's searching for power inside of Sudan instead of his own country, I'll never understand. It's never been our policy to interfere in the political affairs of other countries, and particularly not in civil wars, unless it threatens the stability and peace of this nation."

"But we can't ignore the fact that Lester Bukatem is using U.S. weapons to fund his own private war and oppress refugees," Price said.

"Correct. And now it seems clear he's kidnapped or coerced U.S. military personnel," Brognola said. "I'm not arguing the moral or ethical implications of this. We're bound by executive order to do something and we're going to do it, with or without Kiir's cooperation."

"You think he's hiding something?" Kurtzman asked.

"I think it's possible. I'm not particularly keen on the idea of this Taha withholding information from Mc-Carter when our boys are in there risking their own necks to help them, even if in an unofficial capacity. It smells rotten."

"It *is* rotten," Price said. "But at least they'll have our full support here and the more intelligence we can give them, the better their chances of finding Bukatem's force and the weapons."

"And Jodi Leighton," Kurtzman added.

"Indeed," Price said.

"Whatever we do, we'd better do it quickly. I want a full court press on this until we get some solid leads. What are your other thoughts as far as strategy, Barb?"

Price fingered strands of her honey-blond hair behind her ear as she said, "I think we should focus most of our energies toward locating Daudi Muwanga's center of operations. If Able Team can get to him and shut this pipeline down on the inside, that will remove some of the urgency for Phoenix Force. They're battling some very inhospitable conditions at best right now, not to mention they've had to split up their team to maximize the coverage."

"So you believe Muwanga's our man," Brognola said.

"Absolutely no doubt in my mind," she replied. She looked at Kurtzman and said, "I trust Bear's intelligence implicitly and, coupled with my own intuition, the timing has to be more than coincidence."

"Yeah, I don't believe in coincidences like that, either." Brognola brushed absently at his thinning hair. "Okay, let's go with that plan. It sounds solid. We need to find out everything we can about Muwanga and hand Able Team a probable target as quickly as possible. Charlie Mott was about five hours out and that was more than ninety minutes ago. I imagine he'll have Able Team in New Orleans by late afternoon."

"And Phoenix Force?" Price said.

"Wait for them to make contact," he said. "As soon as they do, let them know about Grimaldi and their escort from the 144th CTU. Advise that the North Sudan government's agreed to look the other way for twelve hours. If they don't have the situation well in hand by that time, the 144th CTU will take charge of the operation and their primary mission objectives will be timely extraction from the country by whatever means possible. Emphasize I want them all alive and well."

Price smiled. "Understood."

"They're also to find and salvage Jodi Leighton if they can, but that's a secondary concern. He still has some of his own people in Khartoum, but I imagine if we can't find him, they're not going to put for much effort. They can't risk their intelligence foothold in-country by pissing off the government."

"It does seem professional charity only extends so far in places like Sudan," Kurtzman commented.

Brognola nodded slowly. "Indeed it does, Bear."

CHAPTER THIRTEEN

Jonglei Region, South Sudan

Gary Manning drove the pickup like a madman while Calvin James kept a vigil for the occasional road hazard.

Neither of them had rejoiced at McCarter's decision to split up Phoenix Force but they knew it had been practical and necessary. Time wasn't a luxury on this particular mission, as was the case on most of their missions. They had two targets a good distance from each other, and without any sort of air transportation McCarter's plan made sense. Even at this rate it would take them more than twenty hours to reach the target and that was under ideal driving conditions. Monsoon rains hammered the roof so loudly they couldn't hear each other unless they shouted—that didn't constitute "ideal" in any sense of the word.

What bothered the pair more was they had no idea what to expect. McCarter had made it clear they were on a scouting mission and only if fate dealt them a trump card were they to engage enemy forces. And then they were only to do so if they located Leighton's position with surety and could successfully rescue him. If that didn't pan out, they were to return to the Juba encampment and await the arrival of their teammates.

Fortunately the 1990s pickup—a former rental commandeered by General Kiir and given to Taha's unit as a command vehicle—was filled with fuel cans so they wouldn't have to stop in any populated areas. They didn't encounter many vehicles as they went, and they passed those they did without incident. They reached the outskirts of Bor and picked up the main road leading into the city just after midnight. Since neither of them read Arabic, they could only determine their position by miles covered save for the road map downloaded by Kurtzman to their digital pads.

Eventually the rains died some and the men relaxed.

"What time do you think we'll reach target?" James asked.

Manning shrugged. "Barring any delays, I'd guess around 0100 hours."

They had departed the region north of Juba just minutes before their friends had, and the one hundred miles they had to cover made their drive bearable. The difference in the States was they didn't have to worry about police patrols or military interdiction teams. The decades-long fighting that had afflicted this region made uninterrupted travel difficult. There were checkpoints along every artery in and out of most major cities. Somehow they'd managed to avoid these but James didn't think their luck could hold out much longer.

The other problem was strictly logistical. They didn't have much to go on relative to the base that might or might not be occupied by Bukatem. For all they knew, the base might be deserted or occupied by independent guerrillas. There were a few who had taken up arms in defense of what little resources they could scrounge, which was understandable since wholesale murder seemed to be the order of the day from men like Lester Bukatem. Those with the will and arms to resist could not be discerning, and neither James nor Manning would blame them for blowing away any armed strangers on sight.

Hence they planned to heed McCarter's order to avoid conflict at any costs, something that was easier said than done in a hostile zone like Sudan.

"There's trouble," Manning said as his eyes flicked to the rearview mirror.

James turned to glance through the back window and spotted the dim points of jeep headlights that appeared to be closing on them fast. It could only mean police. In other countries they might have stopped but this time they had to consider the Sudanese police on opposite sides of the fence. A goodly number of those bearing the uniform were little more than thugs and out here the Phoenix Force warriors could not consider them soldiers on the same side. They would avoid a conflict if at all possible but not at the risk of failing in their mission. Lester Bukatem and his LRA guerillas were a threat that had to be dealt with, and neither Manning nor James would let police officials detain them, friendly or otherwise. Chances were good this meeting would result in their arrest and possible confinement without cause.

"If we stop, we're dead," James said.

"Then I won't stop."

The vehicle started to gain and its outlines got sharper as it got close. It was definitely a military-grade jeep. Manning dropped the stick into overdrive and stepped on the gas. Before long they were topping ninety miles per hour and it appeared they might outdistance their pursuers. The police were driving a vehicle inferior in speed and James began to hope they might avoid a conflict after all. The rains had ceased but the roads were still slick with water.

"Any more speed, we'll hydroplane," Manning said.

"That'd be bad," James replied.

"Yeah."

Another minute passed, the pickup doing a decent job of outdistancing their pursuers. James considered it might not have been a police vehicle but the materialization of a dim, flashing blue light a half mile ahead squashed his hopes.

"Roadblock," James said.

"Hang on!" Manning coaxed everything he could from the pickup.

They didn't hear anything, but the flash of muzzles from behind the line of vehicles told them everything they needed to know. It had become a matter of survival now. One thing they couldn't beat was a radio, and before long the highway would be replete with police and military units with only one purpose—finding and killing them. Manning gave no indication of slowing and James reached beneath his windbreaker for the M-92 Beretta 9 mm snug in shoulder leather. James cranked the window, stuck his pistol out and snapped off two rounds well over their heads. He knew the chances of hitting anyone at those speeds—even on their direct approach vector—were slim to none.

The autofire raked the road, sparks left by their trail, or buzzed the air around the pickup. None of the rounds struck their vehicle that James could tell and he wondered if maybe the police were only firing warning shots first. It didn't matter either way because Manning clearly had no intention of stopping to find out. He bore down on their position and at the last minute steadily decelerated and then left the road and buzzed past the simple three-vehicle roadblock.

In the blue flashes James could barely make out the

stunned looks on the faces of several of the officers. The Sudanese police were obviously unaccustomed to such blatant defiance. Their dumbfounded expressions were a blur but enough to elicit a chuckle from James.

"It doesn't look like they were expecting you to do that at all."

Manning's eyes flicked to his side mirror as he replied, "Agreed, although I don't think it's going to take them long to recover and give chase. We need to get off this road for a bit until some of the heat's off. Suggestions?"

James reached for the data pad inside his breast pocket and accessed the road map. After taking a minute to review it he said, "There's an access control road that runs past what looks like a radio tower. It's a little out of the way but it joins up with another road that will bring us back to the highway on the north side of the city."

"Fine," Manning said. "Unless it's some sort of military communications post, it's a good bet nobody will be there at this hour. We should be able to pass it unnoticed."

"And it would serve as a good landmark to keep us oriented," James said. "I don't mind saying I'd prefer to avoid getting lost out here, if you know what I mean."

"I can't argue with that, brother."

Manning turned off at the road James indicated and before long they were headed toward the radio tower site. The road was narrow and although not paved it seemed in good repair, so they made decent time. With luck, the police wouldn't look for them this far east and as James had indicated, this road would eventually circle back to the highway. They would probably hit a number of small villages or towns along the way, which might prove useful. Some native garb and adornments for their pickup might make them less conspicuous.

"I don't get something," Manning said.

"What's that?"

"Rafe was worried about Bukatem having a spy inside Taha's unit."

"And?"

"Well, it just makes me wonder why they didn't grab Leighton before now. The guy's been in-country for more than a year and he's been helping the SPLA almost since he arrived. Why wait until the weapons are discovered before snatching him up?"

"Maybe they didn't want to draw attention."

"That's exactly what doesn't make sense. Think about it, Cal. They had someone providing information to them from inside the SPLA. They know about Leighton but they choose not to do anything about it until Taha's men discovered the weapons after the LRA razed that village. Doesn't that seem a little strange?"

"It's odd, I'll grant you."

"Well, one way or another I think it's an important thing to remember," Manning said. "Something tells me that before long we'll have an answer to all our questions."

"Yeah," James muttered. "Me, too."

THE RAIN had subsided by the time Kendra Hansom reached Checkpoint Omega.

She maneuvered deep into the underbrush where she left the shelter of her vehicle and continued on foot for another two hundred yards. She found the camp just as she'd been told. It was comprised of a small bunker dug into the jungle floor, the entrance camouflaged by dense foliage that had nearly grown to the point of preventing admittance. Only the small homing signal emitted to a rotating 800 MHz frequency transmitted to her cellular phone allowed her to find it at all.

She got through the heavy wooden door and walked down the sloping path that ran about ten yards at a forty-five-degree angle when she reached a second, inner door. This one was constructed from steel rods reinforced with lightweight Kevlar. It had a tumbler lock combination and it took Hansom three tries before she finally got it right. The humidity was oppressive, and trickles of perspiration dotted her neck and forehead.

Once she had the door open, Hansom got inside and used a penlight to locate the array of battery-powered lanterns. She clicked the circular switch set into the top of one and the fluorescent light flickered to life. It didn't provide a lot of illumination but enough she could easily see. Shelves lined one dirt wall reinforced with 8x8 uprights and MDF wall panels. Crude shelves protruded from the walls and supported rows of military ration packs and other basic staples. In one corner there even stood a portable toilet. Hansom yanked an empty rucksack from one of the shelves and immediately filled it with enough rations for a week, as well as spare batteries, a combat medical kit and water purification tablets. She cinched the stuffed rucksack and slung it across her shoulder, then turned her attention to the other wall.

The lamp cast sheen on the grease paper wrapped around a rack of weapons. Beneath the first one Hansom found an L-85 A-1, a full-profile companion to her SA-80. The weapon chambered 5.56 x 45 mm NATO rounds, a can of which Hansom found on a pallet to the left of the rack. She slung the weapon across her free shoulder and then unwrapped an MP-5K, the H&K

9 mm machine pistol. A box of ammo was available for this, as well.

Hansom realized if she tried to take anything else she'd have to make two trips, and she didn't want to take the chance of discovery. Keep moving, that's what her instructors had taught her. Hansom started to extinguish the lantern, then thought better of it and slung it to a free strap on the rucksack before clicking the switch to the off position. She didn't know where she might need it and several remained behind in the event someone else needed them. That somebody else would likely be her successor since she couldn't be sure she'd leave the country alive. Even if she managed to find Jodi alive, they would still have to get back to Khartoum and then, only then, would she know her status with Her Majesty's service.

"Don't think about it, Kendra," she said to herself.

Hansom secured the bunker and made her way back to her vehicle. She had just finished loading the supplies when the sound of an engine whining in the distance was carried by the breeze that swayed the massive leaves far above her head. At first she thought her ears were playing tricks on her but Hansom realized in short order that she'd heard it correctly. A vehicle! On the road she'd been traveling. Hansom considered it too much of a coincidence. It sounded like the vehicle was moving slowly, the echo of its engine rising and falling. A patrol, most likely, but Hansom wondered what she could have possibly done to alert the Sudanese police. She'd been traveling more than two hours and hadn't encountered a soul. Now the bloody police were on her? Worse, it might be LRA or a freelance mercenary team.

Either way, Hansom wasn't about to let her mission end before it barely got started.

She closed and secured the back hatch of the Jeep by leaning her weight against it, and then advanced to the front and brought the SA-80 carbine into play. She checked the load and then put the weapon in battery. Hansom stopped and listened but the winding engine noises were fading. Her heart hammered in her ears, making it difficult to hear. She swallowed hard and took a couple of deep breaths. She had to stay calm; if panic set in it would be all over before it got started.

Hansom waited until she couldn't hear the engine anymore and then climbed behind the wheel of the Jeep and started it. She clenched her teeth as she put the clutch to the floor, dropped it immediately into second and wound her way back along a different path in the direction of the road. When she reached the edge of the woods she paused, climbed from the Jeep and stood behind the cover of a tree as she checked the road in both directions.

Not a sound.

Hansom returned to the Jeep, put it into gear and swung onto the road and headed in the opposite direction she surmised the vehicle had been traveling. She made perhaps a mile before two pairs of headlights winked on from the wood line and the military jeeps pulled onto the road, blocking her way. Hansom cursed and reached for the SA-80 even as she performed a U-turn by swinging off the road to give her room. The right tire hit some kind of rut and bounced her out of her seat, causing her to strike her head against the roof. Thankfully it was a soft-top.

Hansom careened onto the road, the Jeep fishtailing as the tires sought purchase on the slick sand and gravel. Some points were lined with limestone or shale or laterite, all of which were slick in the damp climate. It wasn't long before she had gained speed and she checked her rearview for sight of pursuers. She didn't see any. It was a trap and even before she saw the vehicle she knew it would be there.

Hansom squealed in outrage with shock as the windshield of the Jeep seemed to disintegrate under the hammer of autofire. Being older and constructed from whatever spare materials the rental agency could find, the windshield wasn't safety glass and it succumbed to the merciless assault. Hansom swerved to the slick shoulder to keep the blinding headlights out of her eyes and triggered the SA-80, sweeping the muzzle in the gaping, jagged hole of what remained of the windshield. Her fire found its mark, shattering the headlights, which winked out under her salvo. Hansom thought she saw one of the Sudanese troops buckle under the fire and she bit her lip at the involuntary taking of life.

There was no turning back now.

A fresh outburst of gunfire struck her vehicle, the *tink-tink-tink* of the rounds deafening as they struck the metal frame. Hansom clenched her teeth and hoped one of those rounds didn't find their mark. That would put an end to her crusade real quick. Luck or something else held and she managed to bypass the roadblock, although the back corner of her vehicle slammed into the rear panel of one of the military vehicles and she heard the bumper tear away with a screech of metal. Hansom righted her Jeep, saving it from a full-on crash with a tree and managed to gain the rough roadway.

She put the accelerator near to the floorboard, checking the rearview mirror for signs of pursuit. It would take them some time to regroup and get into their vehicles, and she planned to use that to her advantage. She could easily lose them in the uncharted roads and trails scattered throughout the region. The wind howled and roared through the cab and Hansom could only thank her luck it wasn't cold, although the damp air could play enough havoc on her equipment and weapons.

A new mode of transportation would be in order as soon as she could find it.

Hansom proceeded three miles before turning onto a paved road, killing her lights and checking that it was deserted before she advanced carefully. A half mile down the road she turned them on and realized that only one was actually illuminated—the other must have been hit. One light out would definitely attract attention, and as if the gods had heard her thoughts the moonlight cut through the dissipating clouds and she killed the one working headlight altogether.

Hansom searched her memory and approximated her position. According to the latest intelligence reports from London, assuming they could be trusted, the LRA had a compound approximately eighty miles from her location. She could make that long before dawn arrived, assuming she didn't run into any more patrols. If Jodi was anywhere, if he was still alive, it would be at that base the LRA thought nobody knew anything about. Hansom forced her thoughts on a more positive outcome. Jodi was alive and she was going to find him.

Or die trying.

CHAPTER FOURTEEN

Accompanied by Hawkins and Encizo, McCarter hit the perimeter of the encampment just as the starburst round exploded.

Shadows flickered in the wake of the flare as the trio advanced. Resistance appeared in the form of two sentries armed with assault rifles who swung their weapons to bear, but the Phoenix Force warriors had them dead to rights. Encizo held his MP-5 tight and low as he squeezed the trigger. The weapon chattered and a trio of 9 mm Parabellum rounds caught the first target in the chest, lifting him off his feet and dumping him in the mud with a splat. Hawkins got the second one with a sweeping burst from his M-16 A-3. The rounds buzzed across the terrorist's stomach and chest, punching small holes in his front torso but leaving decent-size exit wounds.

Movement in McCarter's peripheral vision caused him to turn as another pair of LRA terrorists rounded the corner of a squat outbuilding. They were running full speed, their weapons held with reckless disregard for combat preparedness—it looked more as if they simply wanted to escape. McCarter had other plans. Even as he took in their young faces with regret he swung his FN FAL battle rifle to his shoulder and squeezed the trigger. A volley of 7.62 mm rounds cut them off, the initial few punching through the guts of the first man. The terrorist rolled several times, carried forward by his momentum, and then lay still. Another round caught the second LRA fighter square in the head and cleaved his skull as effectively as a machete, exploding it under the high-velocity impact before he crumpled to the ground.

Reports from other weapons echoed in the night as light from the flare began to die out.

It seemed Kumar's men had encountered some resistance of their own. McCarter turned to his friends, who quickly frisked the enemy troops for identification or intelligence. They came up empty-handed and McCarter gestured to give up and begin the search. The men broke off and headed for the first building while McCarter turned in the direction of the sounds of continued fighting.

The Briton trotted along the perimeter, turning his ankle a bit at one point as he navigated the uneven terrain. He would've preferred to do this some other way but he knew that wasn't going to happen. They'd gone into this thing with a minimal amount of intelligence and absolutely no idea whether they'd find Leighton. If the CIA man wasn't found here, McCarter could only hope Manning and James had better luck.

McCarter quickly located Kumar's team, who'd been pinned down by a number of unknown terrorists dug into a fortified position. It looked as if they had dug foxholes deep enough to stand in and this impressed McCarter. Not that it mattered, since the foxholes wouldn't do much to protect them from what came next. McCarter reached to the cylindrical object dangling from his LBE harness and unclipped it. Its normally bright red body had been painted over to conceal the ordnance type, but McCarter knew it well.

The AN-M14 TH3 weighed about thirty-two ounces, more than half that weight being an incendiary thermate mixture. A modern-day equivalent to the white phosphorous grenades used during the Vietnam War, the TH3 in the grenade turned to molten iron at temperatures of approximately 4000 degrees Fahrenheit and burned on oxygen. Not even water could put them out as the LRA terrorists firing from their fighting positions were about to learn the hard way. McCarter yanked the pin and tossed the grenade with all his might. He then dashed toward Kumar's position and shouted for the men to grab any cover they could find. When the grenade went, it showered the area like a searing fire bomb and produced blood-curdling screams as it did its merciless work.

While not all of their opponents succumbed to the incendiary effects, the shouts of agony provided enough distraction that McCarter, Kumar and his men were able to leave the tree line and overrun the enemy position in seconds. Many of the LRA terrorists who'd survived the grenade were gunned down by Kumar's men on the run. Only one of the SPLA fighters was brought down by an LRA terrorist before several of his comrades riddled their hated enemy with bullets. McCarter grimaced at the wasted ammunition but he understood their fury.

The men fanned out as the battle died and began searching the buildings under Kumar's orders.

McCarter raised a radio to his lips. "Fire Team Alpha, report."

A moment passed before Encizo's voice replied, "No go, boss. We have one building left but it's not looking good."

"Keep me posted. Team Leader, out."

McCarter cursed as he clipped the radio to his harness. As he was afraid, they'd been duped once more and without reason. The paltry resistance they encountered left McCarter without any doubts that someone had been warned of their arrival. Lester Bukatem was keeping one or maybe even two steps ahead of Phoenix Force and McCarter didn't have the first clue how. Kumar's teams returned one by one and reported the same as Encizo and Hawkins, the latter showing up a minute behind them.

"Place is empty of any personnel," Hawkins said.

"Maybe they moved him," Kumar said.

McCarter squinted into the darkness. "If he was here at all, which has me wondering how Bukatem knew we were coming."

"I don't understand."

"It's real simple, mate," McCarter said, scrutinizing Kumar. "Either he was never here, which means our intelligence was bad, or they got wind of our mission and buggered out. Either way we're left with diddly-squat. And chances are good our man's sleeping with the bloody worms now."

"Nothing like looking on the bright side," Hawkins said.

"I'll save that for the liberals. I'm a pragmatist."

McCarter noticed Encizo's absence now. "Where's Rafe?"

Hawkins jerked his head in the direction from which he'd come. "He's checking out the equipment."

"What did he find?"

"Beside a weapons cache there's at least a dozen drums of diesel, those thirty-gallon types, and two full-size utility jeeps that I think are Soviet-army vintage."

That got McCarter's attention. "Anything else?"

"I didn't see much else but I'm sure if it's out there, Rafe will find it."

"I'm sure you're right," the Cuban's voice resounded from the darkness. Encizo was a veteran of many jungle settings, so neither of his teammates had even heard his stealthy approach.

"What else?" McCarter asked.

"You're not going to believe it," Encizo said. "I could barely believe it myself. They've got an armored personnel carrier hidden here. Took me a little bit of time to identify it in the dark, but after closer inspection there's no doubt in my mind. It's an old M113-A1 APC, used throughout the U.S. Army during the eighties and nineties."

McCarter swiped at the oily droplets of sweat that were making his neck itch. How he hated the bloody jungle environment. "This doesn't make sense. How the hell are they getting this stuff inside the country?"

"That's a very good question."

"I do not understand this," Kumar said. "Why does this matter?"

"Oh, it matters," Hawkins said.

"Moving small arms is child's play in a place like Sudan," McCarter explained. "My granny could do it with her eyes closed, actually, but smuggling heavy equipment and military vehicles into this area takes something much larger."

"Not to mention what it would take to get them out of the country," Hawkins said.

"Although it's not as tough as we would apparently think," Encizo said. "They've somehow managed to get equipment out of the States but I'd imagine that's because exports aren't watched nearly as carefully as imports. Customs is spread thin as it is, and with American military presence spread across the world right now we're lucky we catch as much as we do."

"He's right," McCarter said. "There's way more going on here than we originally suspected."

"What are you saying?" Kumar asked.

McCarter sighed. "We're saying that your people might have bloody well bit off more than you can chew. Lester Bukatem has an army and he's getting the funds and supplies to equip them for something."

"Something big," Hawkins added.

"Yeah, but what?"

"A full military coup seems a little unrealistic," Encizo said. "Bukatem wouldn't have anything to gain by attempting to overthrow the government of North Sudan. And no matter how many poorly trained refugees he arms with rifles and pistols or how many armored vehicles he acquires, he still couldn't come close to going up against the SAF."

On that point they could all agree. The Sudanese Armed Forces, directed by authorities in North Sudan, numbered over 125,000 members with a full navy, air force and land-based military. While they had recently dissolved a portion of the Joint Integrated Units that combined the SPLA and SAF into a single fighting force, the LRA was still no match for them. The JITs hadn't proved all that effective in combating the terrorist actions of the LRA or other armed groups simply due to the random and scattered efforts of their operations and underlying friction between North and South Sudan. Given the country's geography alone, such infighting had proved problematic for a military structure designed more to prevent external attack than quell the ongoing civil war.

To complicate matters, the Popular Defense Force

had among its ranks a large number of Muslims who aligned themselves with the New Islamic Front. This had been the tip of the spear insofar as keeping the religious fervor at a full boil. While the LRA declared itself a Christian organization waging holy war, the Sudan People's Liberation Army was mostly geopolitically motivated. The SPLA was poised to become the official army of the entire South Sudan but lacked a decent defensive strategy and equipment.

"I agree that a military coup is unlikely," McCarter said. "But a regional war for land and resources wouldn't be at all out of the realm of satisfying Bukatem's goals. The guy's a power-monger, plain and bloody simple. He's interested only in building up enough of a fighting force and equipping them so that he can march across this territory without a thought, and the locals won't be able to offer much in the way of opposition. Particularly not if he's recruiting and stealing as he goes."

"And he's not shown one moment's hesitation about slaughtering combatants and noncombatants alike to achieve those ends," Hawkins pointed out.

"Exactly, mate."

"So what do you think is his true objective?" Encizo asked.

McCarter scratched his chin and then looked at Kumar. "I think our friend here is better informed to make that decision than we are."

"My brother has always believed that in order for our enemies to win, they must take Bor. Not only is it the capital of the Jonglei state but it is also the birthplace of our movement."

"Bukatem's looking for a cultural defeat, as well as a military one," Encizo said.

"It would seem that way," McCarter agreed. "Guess it would also make sense given our intelligence says that's where Bukatem may be holding our man; at an alternate location somewhere inside the city. Kumar, how many people are in Bor?"

"I believe it is over two hundred thousand," Kumar said. "But probably more since the treaty that separated us from the north."

"Well, this is one stash that won't help him," McCarter said. "Kumar, tell your people to raze everything. Burn this place to the ground and don't leave anything."

"But there is much here we can use," Kumar said.

"Take only what your people can carry, but no U.S. equipment or arms. I don't want them falling into the wrong hands. Everything else has to be destroyed save for the utility vehicles and jeeps. We'll take care of disabling the APC. Understood?"

Kumar nodded and left to relay McCarter's orders to his men.

"You believe that guy?" Hawkins asked his friends.

McCarter looked at Encizo. "I'm beginning to wonder if your suspicions about him aren't spot on. I had the heebie-jeebies the entire bloody time we were storming this place. Wasn't sure if I'd get stabbed in the back the moment it was turned or what."

"Didn't mean to worry you," Encizo said.

"Not worried, just cautious," McCarter replied as he produced the sat phone and connected to Stony Man's secure communication system.

Barbara Price came on the line immediately. "Is that you, David?"

"Indeed it is, love."

"Sit rep, please."

McCarter began to run down the events of the past

few hours and included details of what they found. He also posited their theories about Bukatem's operation being in Bor.

Price listened until he finished and then said, "It would seem that way. We think that perhaps Taha's secret mission might have been to Bor."

"Why wouldn't they tell us?"

"I'm not sure," Price said. "Hal's convinced that if General Kiir's holding anything back it's because he doesn't see telling us as in his best interests."

"So what now?"

"Well, I have some good news for a change. Jack's been cleared to operate inside the country. We've already arranged for a chopper provided by the SAF and we're going to send him your coordinates. He should be extracting you within the next hour, so find a decent clearing because he'll be coming in hot and in the dark. Also he'll have an escort so mind your p's and q's."

"Understood."

"Once you're airborne, you can head directly to Bor and pursue your theory."

"I'm sure Gary and Cal will appreciate that," Mc-Carter said. "You might want to ring their bell. I haven't heard anything and they should have checked in by now."

"It's possible they were intercepted. My understanding from Hal in his talk with the Man was that SAF patrols were beefed up along with local police units. There's still a relatively new border between the north and south sides of Sudan, and the fighting's apparently very intense in the DMZ in particular."

"We'll try to avoid that area."

"I'd think so," Price said with a chuckle. "Okay, we'll try to make contact with the dynamic duo and get some sort of status up or down. We'll have something by your next check-in."

"Roger. Out here."

McCarter gave his teammates a recap of the conversation.

"We've finally got clearance for air support," Hawkins said. "That is good news indeed. My feet are killing me."

"Don't be a wuss," Encizo snapped.

Hawkins stuck his tongue out at the Cuban.

"Cut the clowning," McCarter said. "We've still got two missing men out there and until we know what's happened to them mum's the word on our operational strategy. Agreed?"

The pair nodded and McCarter swiped at a fresh sheen of sweat. The first flames began to appear from a nearby outbuilding, licking at the window frames and fed by the fresh air. It was almost poetic, McCarter thought, that the first stage of Lester Bukatem's empire would fall under the quenching fires of justice. And before it was all through, the rest of his murdering fascists would end the same way.

In a funeral pyre.

CHAPTER FIFTEEN

New Orleans, Louisiana

It was late afternoon by the time Able Team arrived at the private airport in New Orleans.

The Able Team warriors prepared their weapons for transfer while Charlie Mott taxied to a small hangar. During their forty-minute flight, Schwarz had attended to the task of cleaning and checking weapons, and then reloading. He'd also loaded additional magazines. Lyons elected to trade his automatic shotgun for an MP-5 SD-6. Coupled with the one Blancanales carried, their enemies were in for a firestorm. Schwarz had retained his M-16 A-4, and all three warriors had their pistols tucked in shoulder holsters. Additionally, Blancanales and Schwarz were carrying satchels filled with C-4 explosives.

A special van, arranged by one of many of Stony Man's local contacts, awaited the Able Team warriors. Mott helped them get their weapons and equipment transferred to the van.

"I'll be here if you need me," Mott said.

"Thanks, Charlie," Blancanales said. "We appreciate you stepping up to the plate on short notice."

"For you guys?" Mott shrugged with a warm expression. "Any time. Never a dull moment around you three."

"Yeah," Lyons grunted. "That's for sure."

"Ta-ta for now, boys," Mott said in farewell.

Once loaded up and in motion, Lyons rang up Kurtzman on the inboard mobile communications system. While it wasn't as tricked out as the specialized van Able Team normally preferred for their urban missions, this one did have some decent additions including a satellite link to Stony Man's secure communications array along with a GPS tracker so they could get help from local or state law enforcement if things went hard and they needed support.

"You okay, Ironman?" Kurtzman asked with real concern in his voice.

"I'm no worse for wear," Lyons said. "Thanks for asking."

"He's still as ugly as sin, though," Schwarz quipped.

"You have a position?" Lyons asked while casting a sour eye at his friend.

"I do," Kurtzman said. "We traced some activity on a draw account established for one of Daudi Muwanga's several aliases. We think Muwanga's the mastermind behind the LRA's operations here in the U.S. He came into the country under a student visa. His first few months in the States he had a New Orleans address, but the credit account, funded by parties unknown, was for ten grand. The account was used to pay on a month-to-month lease for an address in St. Tammany. Some kind of lodge house catering to the snowbirds."

Blancanales let out a whistle. "Wow. That's a definite step up for a student."

"Yeah, and you're not just whistling 'Dixie.'"

There were groans among the Able Team trio at Kurtzman's attempt to be witty.

"Any idea what we're up against?" Lyons asked.

"Not really but we're pretty sure it won't be a significant force," Kurtzman replied. "There's little chance Muwanga could've smuggled in any significant numbers. We're guessing the majority of those you've encountered so far are local hire. Probably militia or gun nuts, maybe some radicals thinking they were signing up for a mercenary gig."

"Soldier-of-fortune syndrome," Lyons said.

"Exactly."

"Okay, we'll just have to play it by ear. Give me the address."

BLANCANALES PARKED the van about a hundred yards from where Kurtzman said the lodge house was located. The Able Team warriors made their way through the copse of trees bordering the isolated property, moving slowly to reduce noise and maintain proper direction. It wouldn't do any good to get lost out here, and they sure as hell didn't want to alert the enemy to their presence.

It took them almost twenty minutes to reach the lodge house. They crouched at the wood line, careful to keep themselves spaced at least fifty yards apart. The trio communicated by their VOX system. The lodge house was dark, or at least it appeared that way. Lyons activated a pair of night-vision goggles and scanned the two-story lodge house. A quick but professional study revealed the windows were blackened with slivers of light escaping from the edges.

"Lights are on and somebody's home, guys," Lyons said. "Get ready to move. Gadgets, light 'em up first."

Schwarz opened the breech of the M-203, double-checked the high-yield explosive grenade he'd loaded and then secured the slide with a definitive click. He quickly settled on a second-floor window in the center of the lodge house, aligned the luminescent leaf sight on it and took a deep breath. Schwarz squeezed the trigger. The M-203 bucked with the force of a 12-gauge shotgun, and the grenade hit the window less than a second later. The intense heat shattered the window and exposed the fireball to a sudden rush of air. Schwarz watched with satisfaction as the now-visible curtains spontaneously combusted. Flames licked hungrily at the frame and the flurry of human movement was evident beyond the window.

Lyons keyed his mike. "Move."

They charged the lodge house simultaneously. Blancanales had taken the center, so he made a beeline for the front door while Lyons and Schwarz split off in flanking positions. The screaming continued, as did the obvious pandemonium inside, but the first target presented itself quickly. The LRA terrorist leaped through a first-floor window in a flurry of glass shards and wood pieces, rolling to a stop on his knees. Schwarz got him through the heart with a 3-round burst from the M-16 A-4. The terrorist's body twitched and jerked under the impact.

A second terrorist appeared in the open window frame, apparently unaware of the demise of his comrade. His eyes widened with terror and as he opened his mouth to shout with surprise, Schwarz put a slug through it. The back of the guy's head exploded in a gory gray-red spray of blood and bone fragments.

Blancanales took the front door off its hinges with a front kick just below the handle. He came through the doorway and went prone immediately. The action saved his life. Two terrorists had managed to escape the searing effects of the white phosphorous and taken defensive positions behind a massive sofa. They fired a hail of slugs from semiautomatic pistols that burned the air where Blancanales had been a moment before. The Able Team warrior came to one knee behind a recliner, reached into his satchel and withdrew a flash-bang. He waited until there was a lull in the firing, and then hosed the area with autofire to keep heads down while simultaneously releasing the concussive weapon. It had the desired effect, disorienting the terrorist gunmen just as they were unloading a fresh volley in Blancanales's general direction. Blancanales stepped from cover and dispatched both terrorists with controlled bursts of 9 mm Parabellums.

Lyons reached the side of the lodge house unchallenged. He didn't find any entry point there, so he continued to the back door. He shot up the lock, kicked down the door and entered the lodge house ready for action. He found himself standing in a wide, sparse kitchen. Instead of dodging an expected storm of bullets, Lyons found a ham-size fist rocketing toward his face. He managed to avoid the full force but took a glancing blow on his chin. Lyons spun on his heel, went low and drove the barrel into the aggressor's solar plexus with an upward thrust. Breath exploded audibly from the terrorist. The LRA fighter stepped backward, wheezing for air, but Lyons wasn't about to wait. He fired a rock-solid punch that connected with the terrorist's forehead and slammed him into the wall. His eyes rolled upward as he slid to the floor.

Lyons spun at the sound of movement, and caught sight of a terrorist half running, half sliding down the stairwell. The man was short and muscular, wearing a T-shirt and camouflage fatigue pants. The terrorist spotted Lyons as he reached the first-floor landing and raised the pistol in his fist, but it was too late. Lyons swung the muzzle of the MP-5 SD-6 into action and fired a 3-round burst from the hip. Two rounds caught the terrorist low in the abdomen, and the third ripped through his sternum. The impact drove him into the wall and the pistol he carried flew from his fingers. The terrorist was dead before he hit the ground.

Lyons whirled in time to see Blancanales come through the kitchen doorway.

"We clear down here?"

"I think so," Blancanales replied. "I haven't seen Schwarz yet, though."

Lyons keyed the throat mike. "Schwarz, report status."

Lyons's response came as the *tap-tap-tap* of autofire from his friend's M-16 A-4. Lyons and Blancanales exchanged knowing looks and then moved out of the kitchen in the direction from which Blancanales had just come. It didn't take the pair long to size up the situation. They could hear Schwarz firing just outside a side window and there were the fainter reports of weapons fire coming from somewhere above him. Apparently second-floor residents had pinned down the electronics wizard.

Lyons crossed the living area in three steps and disengaged the window lock. He raised the window and found Schwarz pressed against the wall just to the right of the window. Sure enough, gunners above had him pinned down, and he was exchanging hurried shots. Lyons leaned against the far part of the window frame so Schwarz could see it was him, but he didn't risk exposing his skull and getting his head blown off.

"Need some help?" Lyons quipped.

Schwarz sent one last sustained burst in the enemy's

direction for good measure, and then hauled ass through the window with one-armed assistance from Lyons.

Once inside, Schwarz let out a deep sigh. "That was too close. Thanks, Ironman."

"Let's finish this," Blancanales said.

Lyons and Schwarz nodded in unison and the threesome headed for the steps. When they reached the stairwell, Schwarz offered Lyons a flash-bang grenade. Lyons palmed it as he positioned himself for point, and Blancanales took rear guard. Lyons started up the steps, stopped halfway up, pulled the pin on the flash-bang and visualized a three-count with his fingers. He then tossed the grenade, and the Able Team warriors clapped palms on ears and closed their eyes. As soon as the grenade exploded, the three charged up the stairs.

They hit the top landing and immediately fanned out. Lyons went low, Schwarz took high ground with his back to the wall and Blancanales knelt at the top of the stairs to cover the upper and lower landings. Two terrorists emerged from a doorway at the opposite end of the hallway, probably the same crew that had pinned down Schwarz.

Schwarz opened up with short, controlled bursts of his M-16 A-4. Lyons took a more radical approach by throwing an M-69 HE grenade at the door frame over their heads. The grenade blew a moment later and severed limbs from its intended targets. The terrorists' clothing erupted into flames and melted to their skin. They began flailing and dancing around with pain and terror, finally running into each other before the smothering miasma of high-explosive chemicals seared their lungs. Their corpses hit the floor in short order.

Able Team stood their ground for a few moments, but no additional resistance appeared. The hallway was silent save for the crackles, pops and hisses of the retarding flames burning the pair of corpses. Still, the threesome didn't move for a long time. Lyons finally gave a nod and gestured that he was confident they were all clear.

They scoured the rest of the rooms and found four more in a front, loftlike area that spanned the entire width of the log retreat. Patches of noxious smoke from ashen skin and severe burns in the treated flooring nearly asphyxiated the trio. It would have been damned impossible to remain in the room, save that the majority of the fumes were vented through the opening of the broken window. Lyons and Blancanales quickly frisked the bodies for identification while Schwarz went to search the remaining area. The trio reconnected in the hall a few minutes later.

"What did you find?" Lyons asked Schwarz.

"Colonel Scott," the electronics wizard replied. He jerked his thumb in the direction of the pair at the end of the hallway.

Schwarz's two friends knew what it meant just from the look in Schwarz's eyes, a desperate and harried glint that meant there was a recompense coming to the Lord's Resistance Army. An honorable soldier had died protecting his country. They had no reason to think he'd been complicit to this point, unless he'd outlived his usefulness.

"Something's wrong here," Politician said. "Why keep Scott this long and then kill him?"

Lyons nodded. "That's a good question."

"You'd think the LRA would be thorough enough to at least attempt to use him for a bartering chip," Schwarz said.

"Unless he was complicit, and when they learned

we were on to them they decided to terminate him as a liability," Lyons said. "They certainly didn't have any reservations about killing one of their own."

"We do have to consider that as a possibility," Blancanales said.

"If he was complicit then why torture him?" Schwarz asked.

"He was tortured?"

"Based on the condition of his body, I'd say so."

"Perhaps that's why they returned to the house," Blancanales said. "Maybe they went back for something. Maybe they wanted something from Scott and he wouldn't give it to them so they tortured it out of him."

"Well, there's nothing we can do about it now," Lyons growled. "Let's conduct a search downstairs and see if we can find anything. I left a man down there, too. He should be waking up right about now."

His fellow warriors nodded and they descended to the first floor. They spread out to save time. Schwarz rifled through the drawers and cabinets in the kitchen, searching for any clue as to where the missing Muwanga had gone or what the LRA's plans might be. His search quickly proved fruitless. Blancanales used his combat knife to rip open seat cushions—it was no time for niceties. He found nothing.

"Hey!" Lyons called.

The two quickly located him in a small room off the main living area that they had noticed when coming in. Lyons was blocking the doorway because he could barely squeeze by the table that took up the majority of the room. It didn't take them long to determine that it wasn't a room but actually a large walk-in closet. Blank passports and other documents and literature covered the table, and there was a plastic-coated map tacked to the wall.

"How's sleeping beauty?" Schwarz asked.

"He's secured but not awake yet, unless he's playing possum."

"You said you hit him?" Blancanales said. Lyons nodded. "He's still out, then."

Blancanales went to the map and studied it while Lyons and Schwarz began to rifle through the stack of documents, smaller maps and other paraphernalia on the desk. The map displayed three areas circled in red, each labeled Range Alpha, Bravo and Charlie respectively. There were also grease pencil marks along a road.

"This is a pretty detailed map," Blancanales remarked.

Lyons looked up from his task. "Of what?"

"Camp Shelby. It looks like maybe they've been using the empty ranges to stockpile the weapons and then smuggle them out by a rear-post access road."

"Well, if what we're seeing here is current, they may be planning one more run before they play their exit scenario. There's also an address here for what I'm betting is their smuggling pipeline. It's a waterfront warehouse in New Orleans."

"Sounds like a good working theory," Schwarz said.

A moan from the kitchen got their attention.

Lyons grinned. "Sounds like our boy's waking up."

He pushed his way past Schwarz and Blancanales and hauled ass into the kitchen. They followed him and entered through the doorway in time to see Lyons reach down, grab the terrorist by the shirt collar with one hand and haul him to his feet. He pushed him to a nearby kitchen table, yanked out a chair and shoved him into it with enough force that it struck the wall.

The man was dark-haired with large brown eyes. There was a welt on his forehead where Lyons had punched him. It would take a day or so for the bruise to show, but his knuckle imprints were clearly visible in the dim light. The man's head spun and then he vomited on the floor. Lyons had to jump back to avoid having his boots covered by terrorist puke. Lyons knew the man's body was reacting to the trauma.

"Welcome to the land of the conscious," he said.

The terrorist looked up and squinted at him. His eyes burned with hatred as he looked at Lyons with smug defiance.

"Let me get right to the heart of the matter, you scum-sucking fanatic," Lyons began. "We know you're a member of the Lord's Resistance Army and we know that your master, Daudi Muwanga, has plans to smuggle weapons out of Camp Shelby. We also know that you're a murdering piece of shit who killed an American Army officer for no reason."

"It was not without reason," the man said.

"Oh…good." Lyons glanced at his two partners. "He speaks English. Well, let's get right to business, then."

Lyons reached up and clamped a viselike hold on the terrorist's throat. He began to squeeze, rock-hard fingers digging into the LRA terrorist's neck muscles. Lyons was careful to keep the palm of his hand clear of the man's trachea. He wasn't trying to choke him out, rather to apply an implicit threat with bone-crushing effect to the brachial-cephalic nerves in the man's neck.

"Now listen to me very carefully," Lyons said. "You're going to talk to us and you're going to spill everything you know. And you're going to tell us the truth about your operations here because if you don't I'm going to set you up in some cushy little federal penitentiary awaiting trial, or even ship you to Guantanamo Bay. No, what I'm going to do is wring your neck like a little bird. You understand me?"

The man produced a squeal of pain mixed with outrage but he nodded his willingness to cooperate.

"Good," Lyons said. "Let's start with your chicken-shit leader, Daudi Muwanga. Where is he?"

CHAPTER SIXTEEN

North Sudan

Dusk approached rapidly as Jack Grimaldi put down the chopper carrying his friends on a small helipad at an SAF military compound. According to McCarter, they had actually crossed over the DMZ and were now operating in northern-held territory but at some level the borders were still largely unpatrolled. Given they were utilizing what could be deemed as an "enemy chopper," Grimaldi had to fly below radar until out of South Sudan airspace to avoid being shot down by air patrols. Still, they arrived without incident, and after his passenger debarked Grimaldi set about the task of spreading a radar-scattering camouflage to conceal the chopper from high-level observation.

Their SAF guide from the 144th Counter-Terrorism Unit, Ninth Airborne, introduced himself as Seneqat Hamun. Hamun was tall and good-looking, with short-cropped dark hair and a trimmed mustache. His eyes were almost black, his chin strong, and even through the uniform khakis with blouse rolled at the sleeves, McCarter could see that Hamun kept in shape.

Hamun offered his hand to McCarter. "You must be Brown."

McCarter nodded and returned the handshake. "I'm guessing our people contacted you."

"This is correct," Hamun replied.

Jack Grimaldi joined the group and jerked a thumb in the direction of the chopper. "Is this thing really going to be okay?"

Hamun nodded. "It will be fine, I assure you. We had this area blocked off for months before building here. No one who is unauthorized will come anywhere near the area."

"And if they do," McCarter cut in, "you know what to do."

Grimaldi nodded, wished them luck and returned to the chopper to complete setting up the overhead camouflage.

After introductions all around, Hamun led McCarter, Encizo and Hawkins to a waiting jeep. They piled in, Hamun taking the wheel, and left the makeshift military compound on a secondary access road headed south.

"You're sure we can pass through the DMZ into Bor undetected?" McCarter asked.

"Of course. I've been fully told of the reasons for your being here."

"You have?" Encizo asked with surprise.

Hamun nodded. "It should come as no surprise to you that eliminating the leaders within the Lakwena is very important to all peoples in my country. These terrorists have operated here for too long. My government was not happy with the idea of this treaty but we also understood that once it was in place, the Lakwena would no longer be our problem."

"And why is that?" Hawkins asked.

Hamun shrugged. "We are not equipped to fight a war within our own country on two fronts. Imagine if the citizens in America were battling both the police and your standing military, and the military within your states were a law unto themselves. This would be anarchy."

"Not to mention a real bitch," Hawkins said.

"So the neutralization of the Lakwena you believe will bring stability to this region?"

Hamun scoffed noisily and then replied, "It would take much more than this to bring peace to Sudan. But it would be a good start. The problems in my country are vast. There is starvation and violence, bloodshed such as you've never known before."

"I wouldn't be so sure about that," Encizo interjected.

Hamun had no reply to that, probably because he was intelligent enough to know exactly what it is the men of Phoenix Force did to earn their paychecks. Still, even with the violence they had seen it could not compare to a country that had been at endless civil war for the past four decades, with warlord after warlord vying for ultimate power in a region rich in natural resources and poor on socioeconomic advancement.

"Okay, so we have a bit of politics to worry about," McCarter said. "But what about the pair we're looking for? I take it you haven't found them yet."

"Unfortunately we haven't," Hamun said, frowning and shaking his head. "We have our spies in Bor keeping a careful lookout for them. We did receive reports that a civilian vehicle ran a roadblock early this morning but it then disappeared. We've also been told that a vehicle stolen from Khartoum was encountered by a civil patrol and fled. One of our men was injured. The driver was described as a young white woman but we do not have any more information than that."

"A woman," McCarter said. "Very odd."

Of course, the Phoenix Force trio knew exactly who Hamun was talking about: Kendra Hansom. McCarter had always suspected she could become a wild card, one of those unknown factors that always seemed to crop up in missions like these, but he'd believed she wouldn't get this far south before the SAF or SPLA caught up with her. Now they had a potentially new complication to worry about. If Hansom had gotten it in her mind to attempt to rescue Leighton, there was a better than good chance she'd be very disappointed.

McCarter hadn't been holding out much hope that Leighton was still alive. If he was, he'd surely talked by now. This was the one factor that might have contributed to Bukatem and his people seemingly being just one step ahead of Phoenix Force. Somebody had ratted them out, told them about the planned assault against Bukatem's weapons depot. McCarter was betting that was the same somebody who had leaked information about Phoenix Force's presence in the country. Even if it did force the LRA to speed up their timetable, it removed the element of surprise critical to wrapping this mission up and giving Leighton even a marginal chance of living through it all.

"We think there may be a traitor inside the SPLA," McCarter ventured, looking at Hamun for any reaction. "It might have been this person who leaked information about a CIA agent attempting to gather information on the LRA's activities in Bor and other parts of southern Sudan."

"This comes as no surprise to me," Hamun admitted. "The network of informants is considerably vast in this part of the country, particularly where there are shifting alliances and the balance of power can turn at any moment."

"It sounds as if you have a pretty solid grasp on the situation in your country," Encizo remarked.

Hamun nodded his head in acknowledgment. "I have been a soldier for many years, sir. My father was a soldier before me, and I have many brothers who have served. Some met terrible ends fighting for peace, to cease the reign of bloodshed and terror spread by so many armed groups. We were against allying ourselves with the People's Liberation Army for a very long time, due mostly to our disagreement with their basic religious beliefs. That was until we realized that this war has never been truly about religion. It was then that my brothers convinced me to join the army and to carry on the tradition of fighting men in my family. It is an honor I take seriously. I worked hard to learn many languages, both those of allies and friends. This has helped with the communications we've intercepted over the years, making it easier to detect where our enemies would strike next."

"Well I, for one, commend you for your efforts," Hawkins said.

"It is good that you say this. Thank you."

McCarter nodded. "I don't want to break the mood of this little love fest but about my men. We have a way of locating them if you can help us navigate Bor. I'm afraid we're not that familiar with it."

"It is nothing in comparison to Khartoum but it is a large city, becoming more prosperous. Because of its location on the White Nile, it is a key location. I shall help you in any way that I can. We will find your friends if they are alive or dead. On this you have my word."

"LADY, YOU ARE way out of your league," Calvin James said.

"The same thing could be said about you…mate," Kendra Hansom shot back.

"Oh, our team leader's going to love you."

Gary Manning stepped between the pair and raised a hand. "Okay, friends, right now isn't the time for this. We are basically outgunned and outmanned, and in a very short while there's a good chance a whole lot of very nasty LRA terrorists are going to bust through that door and then we're going to be in a world of hurt."

While they were both hardheaded individuals, James and Hansom knew he was right. The Phoenix Force pair had managed to get into Bor without a problem and even avoided additional patrols. But once inside the city their attention had been drawn to some rather unusual police activity focused on events occurring in the heart of a downtown commercial district, the largest in the city in fact. This led Manning and James to observe a full-out encounter with a half dozen LRA terrorists who were in pursuit of none other than Kendra Hansom.

Hansom had made her final stand in an abandoned wreck of a building among the toppled concrete, brick and rebar. That was after the tires of her stolen vehicle had been shot to shreds and she'd finally had to abandon it after driving it down to the rims. Some areas of Bor had suffered during parts of the civil war and still hadn't seen reparations due to more pressing concerns by state and local officials. It was in this area that Manning and James decided to intervene.

"Let's get to business," Manning said. He looked Hansom directly in the eyes. "Why don't you fill us in what you're doing here and who authorized you to do it? And try the truth because we already know you're most likely a fugitive from the British SIS and been denounced as rogue by now."

Hansom feigned surprise. "I don't know what you're—"

"Ah!" Manning raised a finger. "I told you to shoot straight."

Hansom glared at the pair a moment, then shrugged with a gust of air to blow her hair out of her eyes and sat on the edge of the bed.

"I've been in-country for nearly a year. About three months ago I became romantically involved with one of your CIA case officers assigned to Khartoum. Sort of."

"What do you mean 'sort of'?" James interjected. "Either you are or you aren't."

"It wasn't love or anything that sappy, Yank, if that's what you're suggesting."

"He's not suggesting anything," Manning said. "Back on topic. What happened?"

"Yesterday I was contacted by one of his associates in Khartoum. They said he'd disappeared, reported as MIA, suspected dead. It was obvious they weren't going to do much to try to find him so I decided someone had to look into it."

"Was the concern personal or professional?"

"Both." Hansom reached into the cargo pocket of her pants and retrieved a pack of cigarettes. She lit one and continued. "We never got into each other's business, gentlemen, but I do know that Jodi left strict instructions with his colleagues that if anything happened to him that they should look in the direction of the Lord's Resistance Army."

Neither of the Phoenix warriors had seen that coming.

"So you're saying that he was looking into the LRA," James said.

"I'd imagine." Hansom shrugged. "Like I said, we kept our professional lives out of it. Too risky to hop into bed with somebody and then blab company business. That's the fastest way to get yourself or a colleague killed. Professional bloody courtesy, that's what I think."

"So what brought you here?" Manning asked. "Why would you come to Bor?"

"You're kidding, bloke, right? You Yanks aren't the only ones with eyes and ears in this country. Her Majesty's government likes to keep close tabs on places like Sudan, especially of recent with all the political hotbed of activity down here. This area is still ripe for a hostile takeover by guerrillas, and the LRA is a damn sight closer to being equipped and manned well enough to do that."

"You can't argue with that," James said with a glance to his teammate.

Manning nodded. "Okay, so maybe you have some business here after all. But understand that you don't make any more moves until we say jump. Got it?"

"Who the hell are you that I should follow your orders?"

Manning remained calm. "We're the ones who just saved your ass from a nasty bunch of terrorists. Not to mention that our mission objectives here coincide with yours, and we're much better equipped to deal with this type of situation."

"So it's a macho thing."

"No," James interjected, "it's a reality thing. Our entire careers are built on handling situations exactly like this one. Eventually, our people are going to come for us. Until they do, we're going to keep our heads down because those are our orders."

"But—"

"But nothing," Manning said, putting an edge in his

voice to make his point explicit. He then softened some and leaned toward her, one foot propped on the bed. "Listen, we're not here to rain on your parade. Our goals are the same. You obviously have information that could prove of great value to us. If there's any chance of extracting Jodi out of their hands without getting him and the rest of us killed, then we will do everything in our power to make it happen.

"What we can't have is you going off half-cocked and compromising our situation. All that will likely result in is getting you, us and every one of our other team members killed. We can't have that. And I mean no offense, nor do I wish to threaten you, but before that happens I'll shoot you myself. Are we clear?"

Hansom stared at Manning with the venomous eyes of a cobra but she lowered her shoulders and delivered a curt nod. The Canadian hadn't wanted to take such a hard line but Hansom had proved unpredictable and stubborn. He understood her reasons, figured if he were in her shoes he'd probably feel the exact same way. But feelings weren't going to increase Leighton's chances of getting out alive, nor would they do anything to improve Phoenix Force's chances of locating Bukatem's base of operations and eliminating the LRA threat for good.

Manning nodded at James, who reached into his bag and returned the pistol they'd taken off Hansom once they escaped from the LRA terrorist hit team. She mumbled thanks and returned the pistol to the shoulder holster she'd worn beneath her light jacket.

"What now?" James asked.

Manning scratched the stubble on his chin. "That's a good question. We don't risk leaving here. Too much chance we'll encounter more of our terrorist friends.

And even if we don't, heading back to Juba at the peak of day will probably only buy us trouble from the Sudanese cops. No doubt they're looking for our truck. Speaking of which—"

James waved him away. "It's fine. I parked it about a mile away in a trash disposal site and threw a tarp over it. Not likely anybody's going to find it."

"Okay." Manning yawned. "We probably ought to get some shut-eye. We'll clean the weapons and then I'll take first watch."

"Sleep? You guys actually want to sleep?"

"We're no good to anyone if we're too exhausted to fight."

"You can have the bed," Manning said.

"You know if we're going to bunk together— platonically speaking, of course—it might be nice to know your names."

"I'm Mr. Black," James said, jerking a thumb at Manning and adding, "he's Mr. Green."

"Black and Green. Well, isn't that bloody trite." Hansom stabbed her cigarette out on a bare part of the floor and then lay down, tucking one pillow under her head and tossing the other in Manning's direction. "I'll let you boys fight over that one."

"Gee, thanks," James muttered.

CHAPTER SEVENTEEN

When they were all assembled, McCarter began their briefing. "Okay, team, you know what these bastards look like and you know what they're capable of. We should take them hard and fast, but try to take them alive. If everything goes according to plan, we should be able to get in and out without problems."

"What exactly is our plan?" Hawkins asked.

McCarter looked at Hamun with raised eyebrows, a signal that it was now his show. "We have a few informants in Bor on our payroll. The spies I mentioned before. There is some agreement that your people may have taken shelter in a small hotel in the southern inner city. They were spotted accompanied by a woman, a woman who matches the woman I told you about before."

Hamun paused to gauge a reaction and McCarter finally said, "Hey, I don't know anything about that. She's not with us so if these are our men who were seen with her, I'm sure there's some reasonable explanation."

"We shall see," Hamun said.

McCarter said, "Okay, so once we've seen the layout, we'll figure out the quickest way in and I'll dole out assignments at that point. We'll run with two teams." He looked at Hawkins and Encizo. "You two will stick together and cover the rear of the motel. Hamun, you're with me."

"And what happens if you can't find them?" Hawkins asked. "Once we make an appearance we're sure to draw unwanted attention."

"If it comes down to either you or potential hostiles, then don't bloody well hesitate to put one between their eyes," McCarter replied harshly. "We can't afford to take any chances. Getting our boys out is numero uno on the priorities list. Got it?"

Encizo and Hawkins nodded their understanding in unison and then they vacated the back room of the small shop where one of Hamun's contacts maintained a sanctuary of sorts. Hamun urged them that the fastest way to the inner city area of Bor would be by car. He led them out back of the shop to a jalopy of a Citroën. It was an early model but they were well-built then and it had somehow survived all of this time. Its dodgy condition would only serve to enhance their cover since even having a car in Sudan was a sign of prosperity most couldn't afford.

It only took five minutes to reach the southern inner city. When they arrived in the area with the hotel where they believed Manning and Encizo—along with Kendra Hansom—were hiding, Hamun led them to a small, one-story brick structure with a darkened interior. Mc-Carter went on high alert and he could almost detect the increased energy and sensitivity of his teammates. They were as ready as he was for deception. The Briton still wasn't entirely sure he could trust Hamun. Phoenix Force had been deceived before and it wasn't inconceivable such a thing could happen now.

Despite any reticence on the part of the Phoenix Force warriors, they quickly discovered the little mud-brick hovel was unoccupied.

"That building across the way?" he asked them.

Encizo stepped forward and peered across the way. "You mean, with the watcher in front?"

"Yes. That is where your friends were last seen. The man in front is another one of our spies who was ordered to stay there until we arrived."

Hamun pulled a rope dangling over their heads and bathed the room in the glow of red lights. It wasn't overly bright, but it was more than enough light to see things well and to read by. The room was large, boxy and sparse, with chairs spaced at regular intervals throughout. A long, heavy table took up the center of it. It was covered with everything from maps and coffee-stained documents to soda cans, paper cups, plastic ware and empty containers.

"You've got quite a setup here, Hamun," Hawkins remarked. "How many you got on the payroll?"

Hamun's smile was genuine, but with obvious reservation. "I believe your American CIA would say that is need-to-know, yes?"

Hawkins shrugged, apparently not feeling it was important enough to press the point.

"Okay, what's the gig?" Encizo asked.

Hamun spread a large paper on the table that contained a crude drawing of the motel's layout. The group gathered around as Hamun explained the general interior of the two-story structure. When he'd finished, McCarter orientated them to the building by quadrant lettering, starting with Alpha on the left and moving counterclockwise to the rear designated as Delta.

He looked at the group and said, "We'll stick with the same team designations. Any trouble starts, you sound the alarm."

Encizo nodded.

Hamun said, "There are two stairwells but no ele-

vators. Your men will have to watch them for trouble.
When the Lakwena strike they are known to hit fast and
without mercy. You will have to be prepared for almost
any eventuality. They will also be heavily armed, including explosives and other ordnance. I do hope those
bags contain a sufficient supply of arms and munitions
to repel such an attack."

McCarter nodded. "They do. Okay, let's do it, mates."

The team traded tennis shoes for combat boots,
zipped out of the athletics clothes and then prepped their
weapons. All were carrying MP-5s except Hawkins,
who preferred an M-16 A-4/M-203 combo. It was just
as well since he would have the rear guard with Encizo
anyway, and if anything went down there, the need for
stealth would probably become a moot point.

Hamun got himself ready, disappearing into an adjoining room and returning five minutes later in urban
camouflage fatigues and wearing a knife and holstered
pistol. He studied the other weapons that were now in
Phoenix Force's possession with some interest.

"You are very precise in your operations."

"We're like the Boy Scouts," Hawkins said. "We like
to be prepared."

Hamun only smiled.

Once they were dressed, locked and loaded, the team
moved out with McCarter and Hawkins at point, Hamun
and Encizo on rear. They moved quietly between the
buildings, staying in a single file as Hamun led them
through a half dozen alleyways until they reached a
sidewalk at an alley entrance directly across from the
motel. McCarter quickly scanned the team who all
gave thumbs up, and then he gestured for Hawkins and
Encizo to proceed. The pair moved across the street
quickly and quietly and disappeared into the shadows

of the building. They'd agreed on one minute, no more, to make access.

"You sure your guy will have that door unlocked, bloke?" McCarter asked Hamun.

"We shall do our part as I have promised," Hamun said as he pulled his 9 mm CZ-85 pistol from its holster and checked the action and load. "It is not us you will have to worry about, my American friend. It will be the Lakwena that is cause for concern."

McCarter then turned and led Hamun toward the front entrance. The watcher Hamun had out front checked the immediate area to ensure nobody had observed the pair. For all they knew, someone was watching who wasn't even visible to them. Still, they had done nothing to alert the LRA terrorists they were even in the city, so there would be little reason for them to have anyone shadowing the establishment unless they'd had someone follow James and Manning to this location.

McCarter and Hamun passed the desk clerk, a young man who didn't even look in their direction. Everyone was playing it cool, and McCarter was thankful that at least the clerk hadn't freaked out at seeing a couple of mean-looking dudes in fatigues and carrying weapons scurry through the lobby.

McCarter and Hamun continued to the stairwell and quickly ascended to the second-story landing. McCarter paused and knelt, watching the stairs ahead and above while Hamun covered their rear flank. McCarter adjusted the earpiece and cranked the volume just a bit to make sure he could hear Encizo and Hawkins call in their ready signal. Taking out any bad guys in such a public environment hadn't been McCarter's first choice. He preferred a more direct approach: burn their bloody arses to the ground. Instead of that, they had to apply these more covert tactics, the circumstances being what they were and all. It wasn't McCarter's kind of show, but he was ready and well-trained for it, not only because of his years with Phoenix Force but also because old skills gleaned from the SAS died hard.

"Red Team to Gold Team, we're in position," Encizo announced quietly.

McCarter acknowledged them as he and Hamun cat-footed it down the hallway to the target room. McCarter rapped quietly twice, and then he and Hamun stepped back and waited with their weapons pointed at the door. Nearly a minute elapsed before a woman's voice answered softly from behind it, muffled by the barrier.

"Yes?"

"Miss Hansom?"

"Sorry, I do not know anyone by that name."

McCarter heard what sounded like another whispered exchange and suddenly the door came open to reveal Gary Manning. He stood there grinning like a cat. "Well, it's about damn time. You get lost?"

"We stopped at a McDonald's," McCarter quipped, extending a hand. "Time got away from us. You guys all right?"

Before any of them could make a reply, the voice of Hawkins crackled in McCarter's ear. "Gold Team, we've got company."

McCarter heard the reports of automatic weapons at the same moment that James went to the window that faced onto the back alleyway in time to see eight men emerge from a building two doors down and head up the alley in the direction of the motel's rear entrance.

"We've been waiting for something like this," James said.

Hamun turned to leave, but McCarter grabbed the lapel of his fatigue blouse and restrained him.

"Not yet," McCarter said.

"But your men downstairs—"

"Can take care of themselves, so just wait."

Hamun fell silent and McCarter could tell he was furious. McCarter understood Hamun's enthusiasm. Yeah, he was concerned about the situation but if there was a time to stay calm and collected it was now. Panic wouldn't solve a damn thing, especially not when his colleagues would suffer a lot more heat in the next moment than they would.

"Mr. Black, are you loaded?"

James stepped to a nearby bed, bent and came up with an M-16 A-4. "Don't you know it."

"Let's give our boys a little high-ground advantage."

James nodded and turned back toward the window. McCarter ordered Hamun to stay with Hansom, make sure he didn't let her out of sight or reach and then waved for Manning to accompany him. The pair ran down the hallway and headed for the first floor.

HAWKINS QUICKLY RAISED the over-and-under to his shoulder and rotated the quadrant sight on the side of M-203 into place. He adjusted for just forward of the building exit where the LRA terrorists had emerged, accounting for distance and speed and matching that to the approaching figures. He needed the blast to be debilitating enough that it would neutralize the enemy, but simultaneously he needed it to remain far enough out so there was no chance of injuring innocents.

Hawkins acquired his final strike point for the grenade, then took a deep breath and squeezed the trigger. The 40 mm HE sailed on a true course and landed on target. The resulting explosion at ground zero devastated the terrorists before they could get halfway to the rear doors of the motel. The concussion scattered several of them in varying directions. One man's face visibly melted under the searing gases, and the concussion separated his arms from his body. The other lost a leg and was sent flying through the air to land headfirst. His skull split open and blood poured freely from his head as his body smacked the packed dirt of the alley.

The remaining five were far enough away to avoid the full effects but they were disoriented at the sudden swiftness and ferocity of the attack. They were obviously also unprepared for the tenacity and resolve of their attacker.

"Time for fire-and-maneuver?"Encizo asked.

Hawkins nodded.

"Then let's do it. You go right, I'll take left."

Hawkins didn't even wait for a reply. He sprinted from the cover of the alleyway and laid down the first volley on the disoriented troops, firing in 3-round-burst mode. Encizo waited only a moment, just long enough for Hawkins to get their heads down, and then he erupted from the spot—MP-5 in hand—and began squeezing off short bursts as he sprinted across the alley. One terrorist caught a salvo to the upper torso that ripped flesh from his neck and split open his skull.

The terrorists quickly realized they were still under attack—taking small-munitions fire now—and not just the victims of a bomb. Hawkins reached a thick wrought-iron pole and dropped to one knee. He set the front sight post of the M-16 A-4 on the nearest target and squeezed the trigger. The assault rifle recoiled slightly as all three rounds found their mark. One struck the terrorist in the gut, the second in the chest and the third ripped away the better part of his neck and lower jaw. The impact spun him as he reflexively triggered a few rounds into the air from his machine pistol before dropping to the sidewalk.

Encizo managed to hit a second terrorist with two 9 mm Parabellums from the MP-5. The LRA gunner was actually faced away, trying to retreat from the firestorm Hawkins was now pouring out, but he didn't get far. Both of Encizo's slugs punched through the retreating terrorist's spine at a velocity of over 600 meters per second. The terrorist pitched forward and skidded to a halt face-first.

The pair of Phoenix warriors got a pleasant surprise when they heard the supporting fire coming from above their heads. They turned to see Calvin James pouring down a maelstrom of 5.56 mm destruction on their enemies. James took the last two with his M-16 A-4. A 3-round burst lifted one terrorist off his feet and tossed him through a first-floor window. The second terrorist he ventilated with a pair of short bursts to the abdomen, the 5.56 mm rounds ripping the man's stomach and exposing his intestines. The terrorist screamed before succumbing to shock and then death. He dropped to the sidewalk with a dull thump.

Hawkins sprang to his feet and sprinted back toward the rear entrance of the motel as he tossed a thumbs-up at James. His friends were inside and it was possible they needed his help. Hawkins had no idea what their condition was, but when McCarter called in an engagement on the lobby he figured it had gone hard.

Real hard.

THE BLOW Manning delivered with the butt of the FN FAL smashed the terrorist's nose to jelly and sent him sailing through a window. In this kind of close-quarters engagement, and given the size of the lobby, there wasn't really much chance of firing his weapon without the risk of hitting McCarter or an innocent. So when Manning saw the terrorist charging him with a knife, its blade glinting under the bright lights, the Canadian warrior swung the submachine gun at the terrorist's shins to trip him up and then followed up with a butt stroke to the skull.

McCarter fared a bit better, rolling away from the autofire laid down by the remaining five terrorists, and came to one knee with the MP-5 tracking. The report from the weapon was undetectable over the cacophony of sounds coming from the terrorists' machine pistols, but the ratcheting of the extractor as it spit brass told the tale well enough. McCarter took one of the terrorists with a head shot, blowing off the top of his exposed skull. Blood and brain matter splattered against the cheap wallpaper, and the terrorist's body did an odd spin before dropping to the threadbare carpet.

Hawkins had gone to the left flanking position on entry from the rear hallway and dived to avoid the twin muzzles of submachine guns. He felt the heat on the back of his neck caused by the flame the weapons spit, a grim reminder that only his quick reflexes had saved him. Hawkins hit the ground and, as he rolled, he opened up full-auto with the M-16 A-4. The 5.56 mm rounds arced with his roll, forming a corkscrew pattern that was odd but still produced the desired results. One of the terrorist's took several of Hawkins's rounds in the face and his head exploded under the impact. The second sucked in a sudden, wheezing breath as one of the rounds drilled through his chest and collapsed a lung.

McCarter was probably the least surprised they had walked into a trap, but the sudden force and ferocity of their resistance surprised him. He'd expected a couple of armed men in the room, not a half dozen. McCarter hit the ground hard, banged his elbow and bit back the sharp pain that shot down the forearm and simultaneously up to his shoulder. He managed to turn on his side just as Hawkins blew away one of the terrorists. McCarter was aware of Manning's plight but knew he couldn't do anything about it. In these close quarters, any of them would be lucky to walk away from a firefight.

Bullets chopped the floor in front of McCarter, raising dust, patches of carpet and wood splinters in front of his face. The material being raised by the intense autofire partially blinded McCarter. The Phoenix Force leader decided to forego any niceties, like aiming, and sprayed the area full-auto, keeping his arm fully extended to reduce the risk of hitting one of his team members. Initially he couldn't tell if he'd hit anything but it was enough to keep heads down until he could clear the dust from his eyes and regroup enough that his next shot might actually hit something. The Briton decided to do the riskiest thing, which also just so happened to be the most unorthodox and therefore the least expected. He rolled in the direction of the enemy's position and then stood full height to find the remaining pair of terrorists, one to his right and the other to his left. He recognized one as part of the pair they were looking for, so he shot the other one first, putting a short, clean burst through the gunman's chest.

The delay gave McCarter's quarry enough time to aim his weapon at McCarter, but just as his finger began to tighten on the trigger, something whistled through the air and knocked the gun from the terrorist's grip. McCarter could only blink before his ears were filled with screaming. The man's hand was pinned to the wall on his right, and a black throwing knife with holes in it vibrated where it had struck him. McCarter turned to see Encizo rushing forward. McCarter had always known Encizo was talented with a blade—he'd demonstrated this time and again—but he was particularly glad of the fact at that moment.

The area went suddenly quiet as the echo of the weapons fire died. The fading sounds were followed by nearly thirty full seconds of silence save for the footfalls of Hamun and James rushing to join the battle, Kendra Hansom in tow.

Manning and Hawkins cleared the rest of the room as Encizo retrieved his knife and James began to tend to the terrorist's hand wound.

"Is it bad?" Hamun asked James of the LRA terrorist's wounds.

"I've seen worse," James told him with a grin.

"In fact, he's had worse," Hawkins added with a chuckle.

McCarter threw the young Texan a sour "don't try to help" look, so Hawkins clammed up. It only took James a minute to confirm the injury was minor and the Phoenix Force medic quickly used a field pack to dress the wound.

"What happened, mate?" McCarter asked Encizo.

"I'm not exactly sure," Encizo replied. "A bunch of them came out of nowhere and were headed for the lobby. Between me, Hawk and eagle-eyed Mr. Black there, we were able to take them out. Guess we should have covered both the front and rear—otherwise you wouldn't have walked into that ambush."

"Don't let it rub you, man," Manning said. "You guys were undermanned going into this thing and you still did it just to pull our collective butts out of the potential fire. You got nothing to apologize for in my opinion."

"At least we're all in one piece and together again, mates," McCarter said. He looked at the terrorist and said, "Now, let's see what this wanker has to say."

PHOENIX FORCE managed to clear the shambles of the motel with their prisoner before the arrival of police or SPLA units who weren't savvy to what was happening. Hamun had parted company with the team, his obligation fulfilled to help locate Manning and James.

McCarter could tell it would take some significant effort to glean information from their prisoner. The guy was dark-skinned and small, but muscular and strong, obviously the product of months of mental and physical conditioning. It was also immediately apparent that he was above average in intelligence. His responses to McCarter's questions were brief and pointed, and his English very broken. He seemed unafraid of his captors and unwilling to trade information for leniency; he would have preferred dying over betraying Bukatem and he told them as much.

Which brought the Phoenix Force members to another conclusion: the guy was anything but a fanatic. Unlike many they had encountered in the past, he didn't give off any vibes that would have suggested the LRA was doing this for religious reasons, or even that they were performing terrorist acts for the sake of terror. No, there was more to it than that—much more—and the Stony Man veterans quickly surmised that the activities and operations they had witnessed today were cold, calculated and designed to meet a number of specific objectives.

The team now surrounded their prisoner. A tourniquet encircled the terrorist's right arm.

"I think you'll find him much more cooperative now," James told McCarter.

The Briton nodded with a grin and said to their prisoner, "All right, bloke. Let's start from the top."

CHAPTER EIGHTEEN

Phoenix Force warriors had their information—thanks to the truth cocktail introduced by Calvin James—and now they planned to act on it. While James and McCarter got the details, Encizo, Hawkins and Manning cleaned the weapons, reloaded and stocked up on grenades. Simultaneously, the trio kept watch on the perimeter of the small house that had become their base of operations. They weren't taking any more chances. The LRA terrorists had caught them once with their pants down and damn near a second time.

There wouldn't be a third.

"You're sure you don't want to contact Hal before we go?" Encizo asked McCarter once they had left the house for their hotel. They still needed to pick up the rest of their equipment before leaving town.

"I'll contact him on the back side, mate," McCarter said. "There isn't much to report really. All we have is a name and location."

It wasn't much but it was something. The terrorist had resisted the drugs well but eventually his will was overcome. Obviously they hadn't taught discipline under torture to their people. It was irrelevant how well one trained a man in combat if he was not also taught to resist interrogation and torture.

The location where the LRA prisoner had said they were to stockpile some of the weapons was in the factory district of Bor-gon, which was on the southeast side of the city. He'd not known the exact numbers but indicated resistance would be high. Phoenix Force was counting on that. The more of the terrorists they could bring down in remote locations like Bor-gon, the better off they were, since it would minimize the chances of civilian casualties.

"It will have to be a quick hit, mates," McCarter had told them. "We'll do a fast recon of the area when we arrive and then decide the best way inside from there. We hit them fast, eliminate all targets and then we're gone again."

Now they were headed for the factory district with McCarter and Manning in the pickup, and the rest of their team in the Citroën.

"News is sure to travel fast about our activities here to other factions that might be waiting in the wings."

"That occurred to me," McCarter said. "I'm counting on good fortune here, mate, and little else. We can't spend a lot more time on this before we're going to have to produce results. Hal told me the Man's behind us totally now, and he's advised Stony Man to do whatever's necessary to put these LRA blokes down for good."

They didn't speak for the remainder of the fifteen minutes it took to reach Bor-gon. McCarter checked his watch and realized it was still a few hours until nightfall. He would have preferred to wait but there was no time for planning and strategy. Besides, the chances the terrorists were expecting them were slim unless someone had managed to get word to them about the fight in the inner city, which McCarter sincerely doubted.

As they arrived at the road that led to the factory, McCarter produced what Carmen Delahunt had named Siren from the breast pocket of his fatigues.

Their newest toy—its namesake a reference to the way it "sent" information—was the equivalent of a small handheld device with a liquid crystal display and an ASCII-based keypad. The unit was capable of sending encrypted text or numerical data through a satellite linkup, but security was a problem because of the open-ended communication channels that bounced signals using wireless fidelity. Stony Man's cybernetics team used a programming algorithm to scramble the text. However, the communication channel was only one-way, so they couldn't receive information back through the device except when they plugged it into a wired network.

McCarter unlocked the keypad and then entered the encryption codes that initiated a satellite link. Once the communication path was established along the 4096-bit Blowfish-encrypted tunnel, McCarter entered his user name and pass code, and a minute later he sent the information directly to Stony Man's computers that they were commencing their assault. The transmission didn't take long. McCarter severed the connection. The blue-white light on the pad faded out.

They were now committed.

Juba, South Sudan

KATO KAMOGA STRODE through the small warehouse with a purposeful stride. His mission was to find Lester Bukatem as quickly as possible.

He'd told his friend before they had ever begun the mission that he had a bad feeling about these plans, and now the true horror was coming to fruition. Many of their people were dead. *Dead!* That was nearly half the total force in the entire Jonglei region, a force that was vital to the success of their operations. The remaining units were scattered too far apart to come to their aid here in Juba and reinforce this operation. There were only a dozen here to guard their weapons cache, including Lester and himself, and the remainder of that detachment was operating in Bor-gon.

In some ways, Kamoga couldn't help his feelings of sadness and disgust. He didn't want to begrudge his friend and brother of accomplishing his goals, but not every goal was worth this kind of sacrifice. How Lester had ever hoped to keep things together was beyond Kamoga's comprehension. At first, he'd trusted Bukatem's judgment but now it seemed his colleague was getting sloppy. How could they maintain their vigil? And how much longer could their men hold out against these unknown forces?

Kamoga finally found Bukatem standing near a truck, smoking a cigar and supervising as the last of the weapons were loaded into the back of the old panel truck. In fact, it was so old that the vehicle creaked and rocked under the weight of the men as they loaded the last of their cache. There wasn't much chance they would be stopped by Sudanese authorities but Bukatem wasn't willing to take the chance and Kamoga had happily agreed.

"What is it, Kato?" Bukatem said.

Kamoga realized his color must not have been what it normally was. "I have bad news."

Bukatem stood fully erect and shook his shoulders ever so perceptibly.

"An unknown force attacked our people at the depot that you placed there to assure that anyone who followed the trail of our decoys was eliminated. Your plan failed."

"Have they discovered the supply unit in Bor-gon?"

Kamoga shook his head.

"Then the plan didn't fail," Bukatem replied, letting out a deep sigh. Obviously he seemed unaffected—even relieved—at Kamoga's news.

Kamoga was seething now. "The plan didn't fail? How can you say that? Sixteen of our people are dead."

"What's your point?"

"I've repeatedly warned you that this kind of thing might happen, and now it has. We're up against a more resourceful enemy than either of us had originally designed, and that means we're vulnerable now. You should cancel this mission and wait until the odds are better."

"I will not do that."

"You will cost us dearly if you don't reconsider this," Kamoga insisted.

"I have considered it, and I have listened to your incessant protests, and I have decided we shall continue on mission. Don't you see it, my friend? It is either Taha's people or the American special unit here hoping that we'll give up, that we'll retreat like rats and come out fighting another day when the risks aren't so many and the stakes so high. And now you want to play right into their hands? They'd like nothing better! They want us to give up!"

"Who are 'they,' Lester? Just who is it that you're fighting here?"

"I'm fighting them all," Bukatem replied, beating his chest with his fists for emphasis. "I'm fighting every one of these godless dogs who represent part of the element that places a foul stench on the entirety of the human race. These simpletons have never amounted to anything, and I don't think they ever will. From the moment that their first ancestors were put on this planet,

God's been telling us to wipe them out. And up until this point we have failed in that mission. Well, I'm not going to fail! Do you hear me? I'm not going to fail God, and neither are you!"

Bukatem took the cup of hot tea someone had just handed to him and tossed it away. The foam cup struck the wall. Steam immediately rolled from the hot liquid as it ran down the wall. "Our enemies are like the waste of dogs, Kato. It is natural but offensive all the same. We've allowed that to occur all over our homeland. That's our true crime. That's when I get down on my knees every night and pray for forgiveness, Kato. We will *not* give in and we will *not* surrender, no matter what. Do you understand?"

Kamoga nodded slowly but kept silent. There was very little reason for him to bother fighting his friend at this point. Lester Bukatem had gone crazy while going to extremes. The fight wasn't about God or power now for Kamoga; it was about simple survival. Things were changing in this country and he, for one, was tired and wished to return to Uganda. But he knew if he turned his back with the intent of running that Bukatem would put a knife in it. That left only one option.

Kamoga had to contact General Kiir.

THE FACTORY LOOKED abandoned, which didn't mean that it was—it only meant that the terrorists wanted it to look that way. There was a part of McCarter that considered the fact that Phoenix Force might be walking into an elaborate trap, but he dismissed the idea after careful thought. That would have meant not only that their LRA prisoner had lied under drug-induced interrogation, but that Taha and his people were in on the game, as well. McCarter couldn't buy that—it was too far-fetched.

McCarter waited patiently for the rest of his fellow warriors to return. He'd sent them in pairs—Manning and Hawkins, James and Encizo—to conduct soft probes of the factory and see if they could find a quiet way inside. They had ten minutes and less than two remained. The teams returned right on time and delivered their reports.

Manning and Hawkins had found what sounded like the best way into the factory undetected. There were two wide windows, about eight feet apart, on the north side of the factory, and they were opened just slightly but enough to get inside without having to move them. This news surprised McCarter.

"Looks like Gary and T.J. win the prize," James said.

"I don't like it," McCarter replied. "It seems too easy. If these LRA blokes were so paranoid about keeping their weapons under lock and key, they wouldn't have provided such an easy way in."

"That's only the half of it," Manning said.

"How so?" Encizo asked.

"Well, experience tells me that even if it wasn't a trap, we might be better off just hitting this place in blitz mode. We try to go through quietly and they're waiting for us, it's possible they'd have us right where they want."

Hawkins nodded his agreement, and added, "Not to mention that we're now all stacked up on each other. It'd be like shooting monkeys in a barrel for the terrorists."

McCarter was silent for a moment, then studied each expectant face in turn before saying, "Would have, should have, could have… We could discuss this all bloody day and it wouldn't make a damn bit of difference. Let's take the opportunity and hope for the best. Good luck, mates."

They nodded at McCarter and then moved into position. They planned to approach one at a time, Hawkins on point, while the rest covered. A pair of wire snips from Manning's belt made short work of the tall chain-link fence. When they had a large enough egress, Hawkins went through the fence and sprinted as quietly as possible to the window. He kept his back to the wall below it and waited. There were no shouts, no reports of gunfire—nothing. It was damn dead, and McCarter still couldn't shake his suspicions. He just couldn't believe it would be this easy but so far they hadn't met any resistance. The LRA terrorists were probably in the factory just waiting to nail the coffin shut.

Encizo was next, followed by McCarter and James, with Manning on rear guard. Phoenix Force reached the wall unscathed and apparently undetected. McCarter counted out three on his fingers and then gestured to the window. Hawkins raised the window with the butt of his MP-5 just enough to allow entry, and then got to his feet and dived through the opening without even touching the frame. He landed almost noiselessly.

They continued through the window in the same order as they had approached it. Manning had just finished coming through the window, and they were about to fan out when bright lights suddenly flooded the room. Every member of Phoenix Force froze. McCarter realized they were standing amid a huge armament. It was a vast room with large racks throughout it, and there were tools and other gunsmith equipment on the tables and on benches against the outer walls.

And now there were enemy inside of it. Fortunately, the Phoenix Force warriors had avoided immediate detection because the workstations hid them. It was possible they could still utilize the element of surprise if those who had entered the room just now weren't afforded an opportunity to sound an alarm or shout a warning. McCarter looked at Encizo as the sound of voices echoed in the room. He pointed to his own eyes and then in the direction of the talkers. He drew his finger across his throat in a cutting motion, and followed that with a stop signal by displaying the palm of his hand.

Encizo nodded. The instructions were clear: establish a position but don't take them just yet. Encizo's skills with a variety of knives made him the perfect takedown man when Phoenix Force needed somebody neutralized quickly and quietly. In fact, Encizo was so good at it that he'd even taught Mack Bolan a trick or two during quiet times at the Farm. Of course, that had been a long time ago—but it said something about Rafael Encizo's skill.

The Cuban moved forward on hands and knees soundlessly until he reached a vantage point with which he was comfortable. McCarter could tell that the voices weren't getting any closer, but they weren't going away, either. The entire team watched Encizo quietly, but the apprehension was obvious in everyone's expressions. Encizo began to communicate using hand signals and reported four well-armed terrorists. Encizo then pinched his nose and scowled, and McCarter knew exactly what that meant: they had stepped into the room to smoke.

But why in here, where there were likely all kinds of flammable elements? Okay, so they couldn't go outside because then they would give away the fact that the factory wasn't so abandoned if anyone just happened by in broad daylight. And for some reason, wherever they had been, they couldn't smoke. So they'd come in here where there was probably bullet wax and gunpowder and other propellants and accelerants, and they light up.

So they were idiots. Who cared? Either way, Mc-Carter didn't see any reason to take them out just yet, so he signaled Encizo to hold off and maintain his watch. Five minutes passed, then ten, and the foursome just continued to talk and laugh through a second round of smokes.

Finally the lights winked out, and the sound of a door slamming shut signified they were alone once again. Every member visibly relaxed, and McCarter even heard Hawkins produce a faint sigh.

Encizo crawled quietly back to their position. Keeping his voice low, he said, "That was too close."

"It could have been worse," Manning reminded him.

"Yeah, they could have come in and shot holes in us," James whispered.

"Ditto," Hawkins replied.

"Never mind that," McCarter replied with irritation. "You said there were four, Rafe?"

Encizo nodded.

"What do you want to do here?" Manning asked.

McCarter scratched his chin. "I find it hard to believe these blokes have only left four behind to guard all of these weapons."

"Did anyone at the Farm have any idea they had this much stashed?" James asked.

"Not a frigging clue," McCarter said, shaking his head. "We didn't know how deep it went until we found their base with the fuel depot and armor. That's why Hal wanted us to come at this full-bore."

"I'm thinking we could just set some demolitions right here and neutralize the operation without firing a shot," Manning said.

"That would definitely accomplish our mission objectives," Hawkins said, casting a hopeful glance in McCarter's direction.

The Briton shook his head. "Sorry, mates, but no dice. We have to make sure not a one of the LRA guerrillas here leaves this place alive. If this isn't the only place that Bukatem's operating, or there is something else going on like something Kiir's holding back, we have to make sure nobody reports back to Bukatem."

"But Hamun was convinced Bukatem was here," Hawkins said.

"No guarantee of that, mate," McCarter replied. "We have to assume he isn't until we verify his cold, dead body. I don't think he'd be stupid enough to put all of his eggs in one basket."

"Then if he's not planning on operating here, Bor being the strategic location it is, where the hell else would he go?" Encizo asked. "Unless—"

"Unless you were right about Kumar, who seemed all too anxious to point us in this direction."

"So what about destroying these weapons?" Manning asked. "You want me to get wiring this place up?"

"Do what you have to," McCarter said with a nod. "We'll take care of the terrorists."

With the plan in place, Manning turned to the satchel of tricks he had slung around his shoulder as the rest of Phoenix Force moved single-file toward the door. They reached it without incident.

McCarter looked at each of them in turn and said, "As soon as we're through, fan out. We don't know what we can expect on the other side, and I don't want us clustered together if it goes bad. Understood?"

When they had all affirmed his instructions, he said, "Let's do it."

CHAPTER NINETEEN

The Phoenix Force veterans went through the open doorway and immediately fanned out, ready to meet whatever resistance might await them.

They found it.

The terrorists who had been in the room less than a minute earlier were still visible. They had just about reached the end of the hall that separated the two halves of the factory, and they were going through the entrance when the noise of Phoenix Force's entry caught their attention. The lighting was dim but the terrorists had no trouble identifying the newcomers as enemies.

That was all the terrorists apparently needed to know—or ever would know.

Encizo and Hawkins went low so they were positioned in the narrow hallway to take the offensive. Encizo was the first to trigger an MP-5. The weapon barked in response to the terrorist posturing, and a 3-round burst of 9 mm rounds punched through the abdomen of one of them. The impact spun him into the wall before he dropped to the cheap, cracked linoleum.

Hawkins got another of the terrorists with a single-round head shot. The terrorist's face exploded in a crimson-gray haze as the 9 mm flesh-shredder split his skull wide open. The impact pitched him against the door and he slid to the floor and twitched briefly before lying limp and lifeless.

McCarter and James pressed themselves against the walls opposite each other's position and took out two other terrorists quickly. McCarter's 3-round burst punched through his target's chest, stitching an ugly, bloody pattern across the front of his fatigues. The man's body jerked under the high-velocity firepower of the MP-5 and McCarter's lethal aim. The deadly bullets slammed him against the wall before his body pitched forward to the floor.

James's first shot was a bit low and caught his target in the knee. The terrorist's weapon clattered to the floor, but as he bent to grab hold of the bloody chunks left by the bullet's path, James put a second round in the top of his skull. The bullet crushed the brain, traversed the spine and exited from the lower right portion of the gunner's back. The terrorist's butt struck the wall as he twisted in a queer direction, and then he dropped and let out a sigh of death.

McCarter and James held their positions, weapons trained on the door, while Encizo and Hawkins acted on McCarter's signal to advance. When the pair reached the end of the hallway, Encizo covered the door while Hawkins frisked the bodies. He gave a quick shake of his head in McCarter's direction upon clearing the terrorists, and then their attention was redirected as the door at the other end of the hallway suddenly opened inward. McCarter and James turned simultaneously in the direction of the noise, and McCarter cursed himself for not instructing James to cover their six.

A figure emerged from an alcove. The LRA fighter went for the floor as he reached behind him. McCarter almost shouted a warning but then choked it back. They were trying to keep this quiet. James didn't think about that, his earlier training in SWAT taking over.

"Drop it!" James screamed.

The terrorist produced a machine pistol and triggered a salvo, sweeping the muzzle in an attempt to spray the Phoenix Force warriors and increase hit probability. McCarter and James hit the floor simultaneously and opened up with their MP-5s. Their initial shots missed the terrorist but as he rose and turned for the door, he staggered and let out a shout of pain. He got through the doorway and closed it behind him, the clang of the heavy metal door reverberating down the cavernous hallway.

James cursed loudly.

The sound of a door opening behind them redirected their attention before anyone could react further. They turned to see Encizo still had the door covered and as a new pair of terrorists emerged, Encizo made short work of them. He leveled his subgun and triggered a trio of 3-round bursts at virtually point-blank range. The quite visible expressions of surprise the terrorists displayed at seeing Encizo lying on the ground near the bodies of their comrades were replaced by shock as 9 mm rounds punched through their tender flesh. The first terrorist took Encizo's rounds in the gut. He stumbled forward and came to rest on the body of one of his colleagues. The second terrorist was also gut-shot, but the shocked expression disappeared when first his throat and then his skull were bombarded by the rising corkscrew burst Encizo had delivered. The guy tipped backward and disappeared behind the half-open door.

McCarter and James got to their feet simultaneously and rushed toward Hawkins and Encizo. Hawkins was just rising and said, "So much for stealthy."

"Our secret's out, men," McCarter said. "We'd better—"

The hallway suddenly rang loudly with the reports

of autofire. The walls and door near Phoenix Force exploded, showering them with bits of wood, drywall and sharp metal while clouding the air with choking dust and drywall residue. The warriors got beyond the door and into the room and closed the heavy metal door behind them. They immediately noted that the room had no windows or doors. It was poorly lit, cluttered with cots, and a table in the center of the room was covered with some radio equipment surrounded by cardboard boxes of expended military rations and bottled water.

"Great," James said, upon quickly taking in their surroundings. "We're trapped."

GARY MANNING HAD GAINED much of his expertise in demolitions from his father and later working for several different commercial organizations, but it was his time as an antiterrorist expert with the Royal Canadian Mounted Police, the GSG-9 and finally Phoenix Force that he gained the real experience. Manning would have preferred to be helping his friends, given his unquenchable passion and interest in antiterrorism techniques, but he had a job to do, and do it he would.

Hamun's connections had managed to provide him with more than enough demolitions to do the trick. Manning had also noted there was plenty of accelerant to assist his efforts. Several cases lined the shelves containing bulk quantities of nitro solvent and gun oil. There were also reloading machines mounted to the various workstation desks, and where there was reloading equipment there was bound to be gunpowder. It didn't take Manning long to find bundled packages in cabinets beneath the workstations, along with powder measures, scales, dies and a slew of other reloading equipment.

But the thick olive-green bundles about the size of

flour bags interested the demolitions expert the most. Manning checked the labels and confirmed they had been manufactured in some Arab country. Manning withdrew his knife, poked a small hole in the side of the bundle and watched as gunpowder began to pile on the floor. Manning smelled the end of his knife, and then quickly wet his pinky and ran it quickly through the spilling stream of powder. He touched his finger to his tongue and immediately experienced a burning, metallic taste. Okay, so it definitely wasn't cocaine—some kind of gunpowder. Manning began to ponder how the terrorists might have gotten the stuff into the country undetected, but that moment passed when he suddenly felt another presence behind him.

The alarm bells went off in the Canadian's gut and only by turning just slightly to his right did he avoid having his throat cut wide open by a wire garrote. Manning got his forearm up near his head, a reaction that came from years of training. The piano-wire garrote was a simple device, lethal in the hands of an experienced user, but Manning's particular attacker seemed to be anything but that. Manning was sideways to his attacker now and on his knees, and his well-calculated and well-timed movements had given him the advantage.

Manning reached down, grabbed the back of the attacker's boot and yanked forward while simultaneously rising from his position. The maneuver tipped the attacker off balance and onto the floor. The movement caused a release of tension on the wire intended for the soft flesh of Manning's throat, and the sudden absence of that pressure catapulted the garrote across the room. Manning was so fixated on neutralizing his opponent that he never heard it hit the ground. He was on his opponent in seconds but not before his enemy had time to deliver a kick to the face that nearly knocked him unconscious.

Manning's ears rang with the blow.

The man was on his feet as quickly as he was, and there was no mistaking the glint of the outside streetlights on the knife blade. The blade was big and sharp, and as mean as the man's expression. He charged Manning with a hiss and the ferocity of a wounded animal. The Canadian sidestepped the attack and delivered a sharp karate chop to his wrist while simultaneously hitting the side of his head with a palm strike. The sound of wrist bones cracking was audible in the high-ceilinged room and the blow to his head redirected his strong forward movement. The terrorist screamed in pain as he dropped the knife and backpedaled to crash into a stack of empty crates.

Manning cursed at the noise, but only a moment elapsed before it didn't matter. The hallway was suddenly filled with a cacophony of automatic gunfire. It looked as if his comrades had lost their edge. Manning stepped forward to check the pulse of the terrorist but recoiled quickly when he realized he was still conscious. His tenacity and strength surprised the Phoenix Force warrior. He'd seen that maneuver take down men much bigger and stronger than this small, lone man who now reached for a pistol in shoulder leather.

Manning whipped his SIG-Sauer P-239 pistol from its holster, snap-aimed at the terrorist as he finally cleared his own pistol from leather and squeezed the trigger twice. The first .357 Magnum slug hit the terrorist in the right chest, punching through a lung. Blood erupted from his mouth in a foaming spray even as the second round struck him in the chin, traveling onward to rip away the lower part of his jaw. The terrorist's pistol clattered from his splayed fingers. He began to twitch and shudder, and blood started pumping from the open, gaping wound left by the shot. Manning stepped forward and put a mercy round through his head.

All movement ceased.

Manning stood over him a moment as he caught his breath. These LRA terrorists were hard-core, at least more determined than he and his friends had originally been led to believe. Not only were they nondiscriminating but they seemed almost fanatical about not being taken alive at whatever costs. And that kind of loyalty and dedication only made worse the fact that they were now in possession of cutting-edge technical weaponry.

The shooting in the hallway had stopped, and Manning resisted the urge to investigate. His friends could take care of themselves. The first order of business would be getting this place rigged to go sky-high, and he wasn't going to accomplish that standing around. Manning holstered his pistol, after realizing he was still pointing it at the obviously dead terrorist, and turned to the work at hand.

It was time to finish what he'd begun.

"OKAY," McCARTER SAID. "So we have a situation here. What does everyone think we should do?"

"Would it be too early to consider prayer?" Encizo muttered.

"I can't believe we allowed ourselves to get pinned down," McCarter replied. "I bloody well should have thought about putting a guard on our backsides."

"Don't beat yourself up, David," James told him. "It could have happened to any of us."

"Yeah, but it didn't happen to *any* of us—it happened

to me," McCarter snapped. "I almost got us all killed. It was stupid and unprofessional."

"Are we still alive?" Encizo asked.

McCarter looked in the Cuban's eyes and then after a moment he nodded slowly.

"All right, then, so you've learned something and lived to discuss it later. Let's not relive it."

"Agreed."

Encizo grinned and nodded.

"If we're all done with the therapy session," Hawkins said, "I'd like to discuss how we're going to get out of here."

"Grenades," McCarter replied.

"My thought, as well," James added. "They're surely headed this way and we don't stand a chance against those weapons."

"What I can't figure out is how those weapons got here," Encizo said. "All of our intelligence pointed to those weapons being here in Bor."

"Not all of them," McCarter said. "And we were in too much of a frigging hurry to get here that we didn't ask Kumar about there being any more of these weapons elsewhere."

"But if they had this cache, why risk bringing any more into the country through their U.S. pipeline?" Hawkins asked.

"Let's figure that out later," McCarter said. "I'm sure we'll find the answers when we get to Juba. Right now let's just work on getting out of here."

The men nodded in unison, checked the actions on their weapons and then each palmed a grenade. McCarter counted to three before opening the door. There was an immediate response, with rounds slapping the door frame and ricocheting off the metal door.

James and Hawkins tossed their grenades first. One was an M-67 fragmentation and the other an AN-M8 HC smoker. Thick white clouds of smoke immediately doused the hallway, drifting slowly and lazily upward toward the vast open ceiling. The factory was actually divided by thin drywall covered with cheap wood laminate, but the area above was still completely open. Still, it obscured the hallway well enough to keep the terrorists from clearly seeing their enemies.

The frag exploded a moment later, and the Phoenix Force warriors could hear at least one scream. It appeared they were having an effect. McCarter and Hawkins tossed two more M-67s into the hallway, and the thickening smoke hid much of the flashes but did nothing to contain the ground-shaking blasts or the smell of expended explosive and ammunition. The sounds of the autofire from the terrorists dissipated enough that McCarter and his team felt it safe to engage. The warriors stormed the hallway, keeping low as they moved, their weapons directed straight ahead.

Encizo felt a series of rounds buzz past his head but he kept moving. It was possible they had taken out most with the grenades, or at least their users, and that would be enough to seize the advantage. The Phoenix Force warriors were quite accustomed to fighting against terrorists with superior numbers.

Hawkins estimated he was about a third of the way down the hallway when he sensed he'd advanced too far ahead of his friends. It was still damn smoky in the hall, and they were walking as blindly as the terrorists were. For all he knew, he could walk right into one of them, and a moment after the thought crossed his mind he did. The terrorist was as surprised as Hawkins, but not nearly as quick to react. The ex-Delta Force soldier relied on his reflexes, and he swung the stock of his MP-5 in an underhand maneuver. The metal frame struck the terrorist somewhere on the face—Hawkins couldn't really tell—and he grunted with the impact. Hawkins then dropped to his knees, fired another butt stroke to his enemy's groin area, and watched with satisfaction as the terrorist collapsed.

Hawkins was now in a position below the smoke where he could clearly see the enemy numbers. There were still quite a few, also on the move, although they were retreating. Hawkins also counted several dead or wounded, the victims of the heavy grenade action. He shouted for his teammates to go low and as they obeyed, Hawkins opened up with his MP-5. McCarter, Encizo and James followed suit a moment later, and they sprayed the area with lead. The terrorists began to drop like flies, some silently and others with outcries of pain that were clearly audible even above the synchronous ratcheting of four rolling bolt systems.

Two of the terrorists managed to escape the onslaught by ducking into the room where Phoenix Force had made their initial entry. McCarter immediately panicked with the knowledge that Manning was still in the room and probably fixed on blowing the bloody place to kingdom come. He moved forward, signaling for Encizo to follow while instructing Hawkins and James to cover them. The pair reached the door unscathed, but before they could get inside a trio of terrorists appeared at the end of the hallway with automatic rifles that were not familiar-looking.

"Oh, bloody hell," McCarter mumbled as they hit the ground.

The sound coming from the weapons was thunderous, almost mechanical, and the air above their heads was suddenly alive with hot lead. A thick cloud of black smoke curled around the threesome firing on Phoenix Force's position.

McCarter and Encizo raised their SMGs and began firing simultaneously, but McCarter's weapon jammed on the first 3-round burst. The Briton cursed. Rather than waste time clearing the jam, he pulled a 9 mm Browning Hi-Power from his hip holster and began capping off rounds at a rapid but controlled rate. The terrorists quickly realized the error of their ways, having obviously expended all of their ammunition in a few hurried seconds.

Hawkins got the first one with a sustained burst that stitched the terrorist from crotch to head like a sewing machine needle going through a thin piece of cloth. The terrorist dropped his weapon and danced backward under the assault. His back finally reached the wall, and he jerked a few more times as Hawkins added another short burst for good measure. The terrorist was little more than a chunk of bloody, mangled flesh by the time he hit the floor.

Encizo and McCarter got the second terrorist simultaneously. Encizo's 3-round burst cut a swath of destruction across the LRA gunner's lower torso, shattering his pelvis as the pressure from the rounds cracked both hips. Unable to support his weight any longer, the terrorist started to fall. As he hit his knees, McCarter took him with a shot to the skull. McCarter had loaded his Browning with 135-grain jacketed hollowpoints, and the bullet fragmented on impact, splitting open the terrorist's skull and turning the gray matter beneath it to mush.

James dropped the last terrorist with a double tap to the chest that left gaping exit wounds and a third round that severed a carotid artery. Blood began spurting in every direction as the terrorist staggered against a wall and collapsed onto the floor. The echo of the firefight died and the corridor became deathly still for only a moment.

And then the reports of weapons fire resumed behind the door to the reloading room.

GARY MANNING didn't wait for the pair of terrorists to announce themselves.

As soon as they came through the door, the explosives expert rolled away from where he was placing the last igniter into the block of C-4 plastique. The air around where he'd been a moment before was suddenly filled with a hail of bullets. Manning completed his roll and settled in a kneeling position, MP-5 held at the ready with the selector on 3-round-burst mode.

Manning triggered the first trio of rounds, shooting the weapon from the closest terrorist's grip with the first two rounds and catching him in the ribs with the third. Manning immediately followed up with a second volley, but he couldn't see its effect because the sudden sound of breaking bottles and eruption of heat and flame washed over his head and forced him flat to the floor. The remaining terrorists had obviously fired stray rounds into one of the cases of nitro solvent lining the shelves. Sparks and heat had done the rest. Manning lifted his head at the sound of screaming, and immediately noticed that the remaining terrorist was engulfed in flames. The human torch wailed and cried out, dropping his weapon and begging for mercy. Manning started to raise his weapon to deliver a mercy kill when his comrades came through the door and swept the area with their weapons.

Manning lowered his weapon when he noticed Mc-Carter having to sidestep to avoid the flaming figure, who was staggering backward. McCarter watched the terrorist awash in flames stagger pass with a surprised expression, and it was finally Encizo that raised his MP-5 to his cheek and delivered a single shot to the man's skull. The terrorist dropped to the floor with a dull thud.

Manning rushed forward and began to push his friends away from the growing flames. "Get out of here now!"

When they were in the hallway, Hawkins said, "We need to search this place for survivors."

"You guys get out now," Manning replied. "I'll do a quick sweep."

"It would be faster if we all do it," Encizo suggested.

"No time, blokes," McCarter said, shaking his head. "Then we've got all five of us dead if this place goes instead of one."

"Listen, David, I know this stuff better than anyone, which means I'm the most logical choice for the job," Manning insisted. He handed him a simple-looking black box and said, "Here's the detonator. You four get out while the getting is good, and if I'm not out in five minutes then you blow this place to hell and back. Got it?"

The others looked at McCarter, each one with his own expression of protest, but the Briton's expression told Manning he was right. He realized if any of them stood a chance of getting out alive, what they couldn't do was stand around arguing about it. And Manning was the most qualified given his expertise in demolitions. He knew better than any of them how much time he had, and he also knew how the stuff would blow and where the safest spots would be when it did.

"All right, you heard the bloke!" McCarter finally snapped. "Move your bloody arses!"

They all headed in the direction of where they knew they would find the front exit while Manning went off to search for survivors.

It didn't take him long.

CHAPTER TWENTY

Jonglei Region, South Sudan

"Mr. Brown, it is good to finally meet you personally," General Rahmad Kiir began.

"Likewise, mate," McCarter said, taking the hand Kiir offered.

"We weren't sure what had happened to you," Calvin James said to Samir Taha, who stood next to his leader.

Taha smiled although there wasn't really much warmth in it. "Nor was I sure if you had survived."

Encizo couldn't tell if Taha was being sincere or his reservations were due in part to Kiir's presence. The general had been waiting for them at the encampment outside of Juba, accompanied by a significantly large force along with Samir Taha's unit, which had obviously returned from its mysterious mission. Mc-Carter, James, Encizo and Kendra Hansom had met the SPLA leader in the headquarters tent while Manning, Hawkins and Hamun helped Grimaldi with off-loading exhausted supplies, stocking fresh ones and camouflaging the chopper.

"I've spoken at some length with your superiors, Mr. Brown, and I can assure you that you have no reason to be worried," Kiir continued with a forced smile. "We do not tolerate the presence of traitors in our ranks. If such an activity has taken place, we will learn about it soon enough and take the necessary action."

"Tell that to those among your ranks who have fallen under Bukatem's regime," Hansom countered. "Or to the American CIA agent being held prisoner who has been tortured and may possibly even be dead by now."

McCarter tossed Hansom a sour look, although not too harshly since he could understand exactly how she felt. It wasn't as if Kiir hadn't dealt a bit treacherously with them up to this point. He'd been the one feeding intelligence directly to Leighton, maybe even manipulated the CIA agent into investigating Bukatem's activities so as not to risk exposing his own ass. Given what Leighton had been investigating at the time of his disappearance, it certainly seemed like a plausible explanation.

Kiir had obviously realized the conversation was taking a turn for the worse and decided to change the subject in the interest of keeping the peace. "Please, let us not walk so stiff-legged around each other. Now obviously, Taha, we have reason to be concerned about security within our own unit. There is no doubt that someone is reporting our movements to Lester Bukatem. Isn't that right, Mr. Brown?"

"Whatever you say," McCarter replied.

"But if you don't mind, we'd like to take a look at some warehouses up on the north side of Juba," Encizo said, keeping his tone even so as not to come off threatening to Kiir. "Could that be arranged?"

"Quite easily," Kiir said, finally deciding to step back a few inches from the intimidating presence of the fox-faced Briton looming over him.

Kiir put his hands behind his back, turned and walked to the open flap of the tent. "I can arrange just about anything that you would need or desire. But I have already been notified of the events in Bor-gon and that it was your men behind those activities." He spun on his heel and fixed the men of Phoenix Force with a hardened gaze. "I trusted you to be discreet and as you saw fit to betray that trust, I'm not certain I can continue to rely on you."

McCarter opened his mouth, probably to deliver a tongue-lashing, but it was Taha that actually came to their defense. "General, I can assure you that these men aren't just some hired guns. They come recommended by our supporters in America and by top members of the government."

"So they purport to be antiterrorists?"

"We've been around the block a time or two, guv," McCarter announced.

"We shall see."

"Um, General Kiir, about those warehouses—" Encizo began.

Kiir snapped his heels together. "Yes, of course. If you'll come with me, we'll be on our way."

"Actually, we've got our own ride outside," McCarter said. "We'd prefer to use air support from here out."

"That is your choice," Kiir said, and he headed for the door. "Although I would counsel against it, Mr. Brown. There are factions in our country that are still not under our complete control, and they will shoot down any aircraft."

"We'll take our chances," McCarter said.

James followed behind him, then Encizo, with McCarter bringing up the rear. As they reached the door, Taha put a hand on McCarter's shoulder. McCarter turned and found Taha had leaned forward close enough to whisper, "General Kiir is a powerful man and he can be stubborn. It would be unwise to give him trouble. I understand you're here to do a job, to help us, but things have been unstable and I must ask you to understand that I am forced to obey the general's orders."

"Just keep him out of our way, mate," McCarter said. And as he turned to leave he added, "I'd hate for him to get in the way while we're doing *his* job."

"I will do what I can, but I must speak with you on another matter."

"What? Spit it out, bloke. You're acting as nervous as a cat in a room full of rocking chairs."

"I have received a message from a man known as Kamoga. Do you know this name?"

"Doesn't ring any bells," McCarter said with an impatient sigh. "What's your point?"

"Kamoga is second-in-command to Bukatem." Taha looked around and dropped his voice even more. "He has contacted me and wants to talk in terms of surrender."

"Surrender what?"

"He says that Bukatem has become a madman."

McCarter produced a sardonic chuckle. "That's not really news, friend. The wanker's been a lunatic for some time now."

"He has gone over the edge. He is willing to sacrifice his own people to grab power. Kamoga says this is no longer about God but about honor, and that he will not serve under a bloodthirsty man such as this."

"He lost the privilege to make that decision long ago," McCarter said, turning to leave. "Sorry."

"Wait! Listen to me. He is willing to give us the location of the warehouse and to seize all of the weapons that Bukatem has stockpiled. In return, he wants safe passage out of Sudan and back to Uganda."

"How do you know any of this is real, huh? How do you know they aren't just setting a trap?"

"Because he told me who the traitor was among our unit."

"Who is it?"

Taha shook his head. "I cannot tell you. Not yet."

"Then forget it. I have no reason to help you."

"Please, Mr. Brown, you must trust me. If I tell you now it will undermine my plans to catch the traitor and cause further bloodshed. I want this to end, just like you." Taha stood straight and tall, puffing out his chest, and expressed dignity. "I am asking you to trust me as you have asked me to trust you. It is a matter of honor among us."

McCarter scratched his jaw and studied his ally. Finally he said, "Okay, Taha, I'll give you the benefit of the doubt. What's your plan?"

Juba, South Sudan

AT TAHA'S URGING, McCarter had decided to follow General Kiir's advice and travel by ground via Kiir's command vehicles, a pair of Land Rovers, rather than air. He didn't like not having air support but he also knew that cooperating with Kiir was crucial to the success of Samir Taha's plan. He couldn't say why for certain, but something in his gut told him he could trust Taha and only Taha. Loyalties were often divided in such chaotic situations, with alliances shifting at any given moment because some of the combatants only wanted to be on the winning team. But in the interest of good tactics, McCarter had also secretly arranged to have Grimaldi and Hamun wait with the chopper in a location where they could respond at a moment's notice.

Kiir's first stop was a makeshift HQ set up in a commercial building in downtown Juba. Intelligence gleaned by some of Taha's independent operators pinpointed the location of Bukatem's storage warehouse on the outskirts of Juba. It was actually a small industrial complex that had allegedly been abandoned two years before during the peak of fighting in the area, and much of it had been destroyed. Bukatem had apparently decided to take advantage of this fact, and Kiir had devised a plan for assaulting the warehouse.

While McCarter, Encizo and James went inside, Manning and Hawkins waited with the vehicles. Citizens paid scant notice as they went about their business, and the pair tried to look as inconspicuous as possible while they waited. Finally they spotted their teammates emerge from the building accompanied by Kiir. McCarter and Kiir appeared to be locked in conversation. As they reached the edge of the gravel walkway, the area came alive with the sounds of gunfire. And it didn't take long to conclude that Phoenix Force was the intended target.

Kiir went one way while McCarter, Encizo and James went the other. Encizo was closest to cover, a large stone statue attached to a pillar, but McCarter and James weren't quite as close.

Manning and Hawkins went EVA as soon as the shooting started, pistols drawn, while remaining behind the doors of the Land Rover for what flimsy cover they would provide. Pandemonium had erupted on the busy street. It was the end of a work shift, so most of the denizens of Juba's downtown area were on their way home. Women and children began to scream, running in every direction, some of them right into the street. The panicked mob made it more difficult to pin down the location of their attackers. Manning and Hawkins studied their surroundings, looking for the source of the shooting. Hawkins soon spotted the winking of muzzle-flashes from a darkened window in an abandoned building across the street, and alerted the rest of his teammates to the origin.

Manning, Hawkins and Encizo began laying down a heavy dose of covering fire to give James and McCarter time to grab cover of their own. Manning spotted Kiir moving quite quickly to nearby cover.

The majority of innocents were out of the way. Manning pointed at one guy who was sitting inside his vehicle and staring stonily at the Canadian. He waved the guy out of the way with his pistol, and the dude reacted by tromping on the accelerator, not even bothering to make sure the road ahead of him was clear. Fortunately, he didn't run anyone down in his haste to get clear of the situation.

Manning caught a glint of light on metal at the window, sighted carefully down the slide of his P-239 and squeezed the trigger. While nowhere near the marksman David McCarter was, Manning was more than proficient with a pistol, and this round was apparently on target. The window cracked, glass shattered, and there was a shout and spray of blood from the darkened interior.

Only a moment passed before the front door of the abandoned building opened wide and four terrorists emerged. They traversed the front of the building, moving away from Phoenix Force, and then ducked into an alleyway that separated the abandoned building from another that housed a string of shops. Manning and Hawkins immediately gave chase. Manning could hear the shouts of his companions, but he tuned them out. He'd witnessed firsthand the ability of these terrorists to slaughter innocent people on a whim, and he couldn't risk letting them out of sight. If he did, someone else would surely die.

If he had his way, the only ones to die from here out would be terrorists.

"Go for the car, mates!" McCarter ordered Encizo and James.

The Briton jumped behind the wheel with Encizo taking shotgun and James in the rear.

James was about to close the door to the Land Rover when Kiir suddenly leaped inside and pushed his way past them. James barely had a chance to get the door closed and take his seat when McCarter whipped the wheel to the left and jammed on the accelerator while downshifting to second gear. McCarter was quite talented behind the wheel of just about anything. He crossed the lane into the path of oncoming traffic. Everyone grabbed hold of something simultaneously, but another quick maneuver had them up on the gravel parkways common to the streets of smaller Sudanese cities.

McCarter scraped the side of the building with the Land Rover but quickly turned the corner and accelerated up the alley.

"Getting a little rusty?" Encizo asked as echoes of grinding and scraping the wall died inside of the Land Rover.

"I thought I'd remodel," McCarter replied, flashing the Cuban a wicked grin.

"This is exactly what I asked you *not* to do!" Kiir beat McCarter's seat with his fists.

Encizo shot him a hard look and asked, "What do

you want here? They attacked us. And I noticed your people were nowhere to be found."

"That's not the point. You should still be letting us handle this! Your people guaranteed mine that—"

"Who's 'us,' General?" James asked him with an incredulous expression. "If you've got some way to lend us some support or some people to spare, I'd suggest you get them on the horn. You have a way to do that?"

"As a matter of fact, I do!" Kiir announced, displaying his radio triumphantly. He flipped a switch and began talking rapidly in his own language.

The chase continued up the alleyway, and it only took McCarter a few seconds to catch up with Manning and Hawkins, who were still in dogged foot pursuit. The terrorists had a significant lead on them, but McCarter planned to close that gap in short order. He slowed the vehicle long enough for James to open the door and coax Manning and Hawkins into the vehicle, and as soon as he'd given the all-clear signal, McCarter sped up just as the terrorists turned the corner on the next major street.

McCarter reached the street a moment later, downshifted, then disengaged the clutch as he yanked on the emergency brake and jerked the wheel. The Land Rover went into a power slide and stopped in the dead center of the street, engine still running. McCarter dropped the emergency brake, popped the gearshift into second, and gunned the engine as he smoothly depressed the accelerator. The powerful SUV powered up the street. There were few pedestrians here but the terrorists were nowhere to be found.

"Damn it!" Manning spit. "We lost them! I knew this would happen!"

"Maybe not, friend," James replied. He pointed at a

street vendor who, at that moment, was shouting and waving his arms.

There was the unmistakable sound of pistol fire, and then the man tumbled forward and clutched his stomach. McCarter swore under his breath and jammed on the brakes to avoid rear-ending a small two-seater that had suddenly stopped to rubberneck at the scene on the sidewalk. Encizo bailed, and the three Phoenix Force warriors in back followed suit a moment later. Kiir started to jump out, but McCarter grabbed the sleeve of his fatigues and restrained him.

"Best to let us handle this one, mate." He favored Kiir with a warning smile and added, "Trust me."

Hawkins was the youngest and fastest, so he was soon leading the charge up the street and parallel to the sidewalk, his comrades on his heels. The four warriors reached an intersection where some of the crowd cleared and they could see the terrorists splitting up, two taking the side street while the other two continued up the lane. Hawkins gestured toward the pair that had diverted, alerting his friends that someone needed to stay on them, and he continued his pursuit of the two on the straightaway path. He risked a quick glance to see that James was still with him, and then he poured on the speed. Of their group, James was probably second fastest, his lanky form able to keep stride with Hawkins.

Hawkins saw an opportunity approaching and decided to take advantage of it. He was now pacing his quarry at a breakneck pace, and he was sure they were getting tired. After all, they had been running all of this time, and at least Hawkins and Manning had been given a slight break. Although riding with McCarter at the wheel could have been called by a few other terms.

There was a garbage can made from wire and Hawkins

knew it would be his one chance to put an end to this chase. Hawkins pumped the last bit of speed he had from his burning legs, and soon gained a lead. As he ran past the garbage can, he lashed out with a jumping side kick. The metal can was heavy, but its cylindrical shape allowed it to roll, which it did very nicely under the impact of Hawkins's kick: right into the path of the terrorists. The two men tripped over the wire that entangled their feet and landed on their faces, splayed on the gravel and just ripe for the taking.

Hawkins doubled back and grabbed the nearest terrorist by the shirt lapels. He started to haul the man to his feet, but the flash of light on metal caught his attention. The second terrorist had recovered quickly from the fall and produced a knife. Hawkins watched the blade start to fall, knowing that to defend himself meant to release his quarry. He couldn't let that happen, and so he pivoted with his body weight and used the terrorist he was holding as a shield. The knife wielder couldn't stop his motion and stabbed his own partner. The terrorist screamed with the agony of having had a five-inch steel blade buried in his back.

The terrorist didn't have time to recover from the shock of stabbing his partner, because suddenly his jaw was dislocated by a well-placed punch from Calvin James. The terrorist's hand dropped from the knife, the blade quivering as his head snapped sideways. James followed with a kick to the knee that shattered bone, dislocated the patella and dropped the terrorist to the pavement.

Hawkins spared only a moment to look into the eyes of the terrorist he'd been holding by the lapels, the shock and fear evident in the deep brown eyes, and then they started to glaze over. The knife had obviously struck something vital because the next moment the terrorist slumped in his grip. Hawkins let him fall to the ground in a heap. He then turned and fixed the remaining terrorist with a hard stare. The terrorist returned his look with resolute hatred, but kept his silence.

"We've got some questions for you, partner," Hawkins told him.

GARY MANNING wheezed with the exertion of their little excursion, and Encizo saw him turn a backward glance, probably to see how he was holding up. The Cuban felt as if he was losing steam quickly. Manning suddenly slowed enough to reach in and withdraw his SIG-Sauer. Encizo had hoped to take the terrorists alive, but it seemed clear they weren't going to halt on their own accord, and it was even more obvious that Manning didn't see any chance of catching their younger, faster quarry. The Canadian started to aim on the run but hesitated, and Encizo figured the realization had struck his friend that there were just too many bystanders to risk a wild shot delivered on the fly. If it had been just them and the terrorists, the story would be different, but this many people heightened the risks. They had enough blood on their hands, and Encizo was happy with Manning's judicious actions. They didn't need to add any more innocents to the count.

The chase continued up an abandoned street and the terrorists slowed.

"Down!" Encizo screamed.

Manning obeyed just as a hailstorm of rounds filled the air above their heads. Milliseconds later, the windows of three shops imploded and showered glass on the Phoenix Force duo. Manning's elbows were sliced by the razor-like shards, and Encizo's pants were torn at the knees as he ducked just in time to avoid having his head blown open by the deadly firestorm. Two newcomers were leaning out the back of the plain gray truck, gripping the handholds on either side of the frame as they triggered assault rifles.

Encizo had noted the truck passing a few seconds earlier, and then noticed that it slowed suddenly when there was no traffic in front of it. The markings didn't indicate it was a delivery vehicle, and for the vehicle to suddenly halt like that had been a bit too strange to ignore. It was when the rear door had rolled up that Encizo shouted the warning. It was the Cuban's quick identification of the truck as a potential threat that had saved his and Gary Manning's lives.

The truck slowed a bit more, giving the terrorists an opportunity to reload. A third figure appeared at the back and called to the two terrorists who had been running from Manning and Encizo. The first one managed to make it up into the back of the truck with the assistance of his friends, but when the second tried to hop in, Encizo seized the advantage by clearing his Colt M1911 A1 from shoulder leather, snap-aiming at the terrorists and triggering a round in one motion. The sleek pistol bucked in his grasp and a 230-grain .45-caliber ACP struck a spot square between the terrorist's shoulder blades. The man's body arched as he released his grip on his comrade's hand and fell onto the pavement.

Encizo sought the cover of a parked car as the terrorists opened up with another volley from their assault rifles. He could hear Manning cursing and turned to see the Canadian's back pressed against the thick concrete base of a streetlight. Traffic had now ground to a halt, and people on the sidewalks were quickly heading for the nearest shelter as a flurry of metal struck the walls and ripped up concrete chips from the sidewalks all around them. One civilian was unlucky, several of the rounds perforating his belly, chest and skull simultaneously and tossing him through a front display window.

Encizo watched the destruction helplessly, crossing himself and citing a brief prayer for the innocent victim and any family he might have. He then turned in Manning's direction and shouted for the Canadian's attention.

When he had it, Encizo said, "We've got to disengage. There are just too many people in the way!"

Manning nodded, but the sudden roar of engines down the street demanded attention before he could conjure a reply. Two SPLA jeeps closed the distance with the terrorists' truck, which couldn't make a quick escape because no driver was present. Encizo began to scream at them, leaving his cover and running in their direction, but they didn't see him. Their focus was entirely directed at the men in the back of the truck holding the weapons. And by that fact, the SPLA had now become the focus of the LRA gunners. Encizo looked back and watched with horror as the terrorists reloaded and leveled the weapons at the approaching jeeps. He and Manning obviously realized the terrorists' intent simultaneously because they both risked breaking cover to move into the street and fire their pistols repeatedly at their enemies. One of the terrorists lost a piece of his ear when a round grazed his head, but not before he and his cohort delivered a cloud of firepower that rivaled a swarm of hornets.

The windshields of the two jeeps literally disintegrated under the terrorist onslaught. One of the vehicles swerved immediately, catching the back panel of the other before crashing into a building wall. The second jeep vehicle spun out of control, and with two corpses as passengers, it continued uncontrollably on that course until pitching onto its side and grinding to a halt. A moment later the vehicle exploded.

Encizo dropped the empty magazine of his pistol, slammed home a fresh one and released the slide. He heard the screeching of rubber on pavement and turned to meet whatever threat awaited, but he couldn't describe the relief at seeing the Land Rover. McCarter emerged from the driver's side with an MP-5K machine pistol in each fist. The 9 mm H&K machine pistols were reliable, deadly and particularly effective in the hands of David McCarter.

The Briton let out a blood-curdling scream of ferocity, leveled the weapons and triggered them simultaneously. The truck had started moving again in herky-jerky motions, a driver now behind the wheel, but not before McCarter targeted them with a heavy dose of destructive lead. He swept the muzzles of the machine pistols side to side, raising and lowering the muzzles with unerring accuracy as he pounded the back of the truck. The one terrorist who had made it into the truck alive died in the onslaught and another, toting an assault rifle, tumbled from the back of the truck.

Another terrorist was pitched onto his back when his arm suddenly detached from the rest of his body. The one remaining terrorist who had managed to escape McCarter's deadly assault reached up and started to pull the truck door downward, but he took a hail of slugs in his thigh. He pitched forward, holding on to the strap of the door even as both legs dangled from what was left of the bone, sinew and muscle that had once held them intact. The vehicle lurched from the scene and he could no longer maintain his hold on the strap. The door of the truck reached the floor before the terrorist who had closed it reached the rutted road.

Phoenix Force watched helplessly as the truck disappeared down the street.

CHAPTER TWENTY-ONE

"Mr. Brown, I protest this madness!"

McCarter looked at Kiir as smoke drifted from the muzzles of the machine pistols now pointed skyward, and replied, "I'm sure you do, General."

Manning and Encizo approached. They had retrieved the assault rifle one of the terrorists had dropped. It was a Soviet-era SKS modified for automatic fire. Encizo noticed McCarter studying the weapon and handed it to him. McCarter took it, looked it over a brief moment and then passed it back to Encizo.

"There's still a chance to catch them," Manning told McCarter.

"Sorry, mate," McCarter replied, shaking his head, "but not until we know the status of the others."

"They're still MIA?" Encizo asked with concern.

"They'll turn up soon enough," McCarter said with a frown, signaling that he wasn't really sure if he believed it or not.

As if on cue, a loud whistle resounded. All eyes turned in the direction from which McCarter had come, and they could see Calvin James waving at them from the intersection. McCarter issued instructions for everyone to get into the Land Rover. The Briton whipped the vehicle into a J-turn and sped to their waiting comrades. Wedged between the two warriors was one of the terrorists who had fired on them. James detached the man from their support, and roughly shoved him toward Taha. The weary pair then climbed into the Land Rover.

"Would he talk to you?" Manning asked.

James shook his head. "He's the strong, silent type."

Hawkins immediately noticed Kiir's eyes dart to the terrorist's injured knee, which was clearly deformed. He had put one of the terrorist's arms around his thick neck and had his other around the man's waist. There was a small, dark spot on the inside of the terrorist's ankle, an indication that he probably had an open fracture. Taha looked at James, who was essentially ignoring the terrorist, and then he looked pleadingly in Hawkins's direction.

"This man needs medical attention," Kiir protested.

"Then you'd better get him some," Hawkins replied.

"And you might want to see about your men, too," Encizo said, jerking his thumb in the direction of the wrecked jeeps. "We'll send your driver with the other vehicle."

McCarter leaned over the steering wheel to look past Encizo. He studied Kiir for a long moment and said, "We're going to the warehouse complex. I would suggest if you plan to show up with your men that you let us know."

Kiir's face darkened to a flush hue. "If you choose to go against Lester Bukatem's army alone, the next time I see you it will be to identify your bodies."

"We'll see," James snapped.

Then the door closed and McCarter set off for the warehouse district.

LESTER BUKATEM and Kato Kamoga watched as the truck tore into the broken, unkempt parking lot and ground to a noisy halt. They stood at the door to the warehouse and waited for the driver to climb down from the cab. The expression on the man's face made it abundantly clear what had happened. The attack on the Americans had failed and just as Kamoga had expected might happen. Rushing to avenge their brothers and sisters in Juba had simply cost them more aggravation and embarrassment and more unnecessary deaths.

Kamoga's voice dripped in defeat. He turned to Bukatem and said quietly, "They failed, Lester."

The driver appeared with a survivor. He had the stump of the man's arm tied off with a tourniquet just below the shoulder area. The wounded man's skin was pale and he looked as if he might pass out at any moment. Bukatem looked down and noticed that the guy was carrying what was left of his arm in his other hand. Pretty unlikely that they would be able to save it but there was always a possibility.

"He's going into shock," Bukatem told the driver. "Get him inside before he bleeds to death."

The driver nodded and assisted the man into the warehouse. Bukatem turned and gave his disheartened friend a warm smile. Then he fixed him with a practiced gaze. "It would seem that Taha and these Americans are more resourceful than I had originally thought. We must move up the operation and remove these weapons before they have time to locate us."

"Is that wise? If we move now, it might alert them to our plans."

"It's clear to me now that they know of our intent," Bukatem replied. "It is also obvious that the individual we placed in their midst has been discovered. We have received no reports of their recent activities, nor have we heard from anyone at the base in Bor-gon."

"Feeds over the international news wires seem to point to some type of skirmish that occurred in the city late last night. It occurred between our men and what were described as foreigners dressed as commandos. We've also lost shortwave contact with those who were assigned to guard our weapons cache there."

"Have you sent a team to investigate?"

"Yes, sir, but it will take some time for them to get there. Police patrols have been reinforced with SPLA units and a number of them have been seen working with support personnel from the Sudanese Armed Forces."

Bukatem slammed his fist into his palm. "Blast these cursed, filthy dogs! I cannot fight this war on two fronts, no matter how many weapons I have!"

"I agree," Kamoga replied. "This is why I don't think it's wise we leave this location."

"If we don't, we risk losing everything. We've already had much of our petrol and vehicles either confiscated or destroyed, and now it would appear that they might have reached our facility in Bor-gon if the press is to be trusted."

"You think it's only a matter of time before they strike here."

"Yes." Bukatem rubbed his eyes and then said, "Order our men to get the loading completed as soon as possible. We leave in two hours."

"We cannot be completed by then."

"Then we take what we have and destroy the rest. We must get under way to Bor soon."

"And what of the American agent?"

"He's of no further use to us," Bukatem said as he whirled and headed inside. "Kill him."

"THERE'S THE TRUCK," Encizo said, pointing toward the vehicle visible through the side window.

McCarter braked smoothly and then traversed the fence at a slower pace until they reached an opening that led onto a crumbled lot damaged by shell fire. He stopped there and Phoenix Force studied the place. It was damn quiet and McCarter wasn't sure what they could expect. If there were any more weapons like the ones that had been used against them on the street, there was a pretty good chance their Land Rover could become Swiss cheese before they'd gotten five feet inside the fence line.

"For once, mates, there's a possibility we're expected," McCarter said.

"Yeah," Encizo said. "And even if the LRA wasn't expecting us, there's a number of buildings in this complex. We have no idea which ones they're using."

"We also don't know if Leighton's inside," Calvin James remarked. "Otherwise we could just wire the whole place and blow it sky-high."

"I didn't see any evidence he was at Bor-gon," Manning remarked.

"Ditto at their fuel depot we hit," Hawkins said.

"Which means the LRA is probably holding him here," James said.

"Possible," Manning admitted. "At least, we have to assume they are."

"Either way, we don't have time to debate the bloody thing," McCarter said. "I suppose this is the kind of time that Lyons would just tell us to nut up and do it."

"Probably," James said.

The ex-SWAT team member reached into the back of the Land Rover and began to distribute weapons. They had reloaded their pistols on the ride over and their

heavier weapons were already primed for action. Mc-
Carter and Encizo took MP-5s and also slung MP-5Ks
for any close-quarters work that might arise. James
opted for an M-16 A-3/M-203 combo, and Manning
toted the granddaddy of all automatic rifles, a Bel-
gium-made FN FAL. Hawkins primed and readied a
Sturmgewehr Model 551. Manufactured by the SIG
Concern of Switzerland, the SIG 551 was an early development effort commissioned by the Swiss Army.
Like its military version, the Stgw 90 assault carbine,
it chambered standard 5.56x45 mm NATO ammunition,
and was particularly effective when loaded with SS109
hardball rounds, which just happened to be Hawkins's
preference for the rifle. It was tough and durable, with
30-round detachable box magazines that could be
clipped together for easy change-outs. Because of the
craft worthiness of the design and its light weight, it
was a perfect antiterrorist rifle, capable of delivering
up to ninety rounds of death at a rate of 700 rounds per
minute and a muzzle velocity of 3000 fps.

Hawkins traded positions with McCarter, taking the
wheel. He would make the initial entry and position the
vehicle so as to make most effective use of the machine
gun in back, a loaner from Taha's platoon. The Phoenix
Force warriors donned their digital VOX headsets and
checked each other's gear to ensure that it was ready.

McCarter called for their attention. "We'll have less
than a minute to make entry, mates," he told his team.
"Hawk, you'll have the best cover when we split off. The
windows in that warehouse are eye level, which means
they'll have the initial advantage. See if you can get that
machine gun on top of the roof of that truck. It will give
you a better chance of giving us some useful cover fire.
Like I said, we'll have less than a minute. Any longer

than that and we'll be sitting ducks to however many of the terrorists are inside."

"And don't forget that they may also have grenade launchers," Manning said.

"Thanks for reminding us," James quipped.

"What are you blokes worried about?" McCarter asked them. "None of us are good-looking enough to live forever."

Just as McCarter feared, the shooting began as soon as they were inside the fence line surrounding the parking lot. It was going to get nasty. Even inside the relative dampening effects of their modern Land Rover, there was no mistaking the sound of rounds ricocheting off the pavement. A few managed to chip the rear side window and one even penetrated the windshield and narrowly missed Hawkins's head.

"Steady as she goes, Hawk," McCarter said.

Hawkins didn't reply, obviously choosing to keep his mind on what he was doing. Through some miracle, he got them to an area behind the parked truck, where the men of Phoenix Force bailed. They pressed their backs to the relative safety of the truck as James peered around the corner and studied the door.

He looked back at his teammates with a grin, pulled back on the shell of the M-203 to validate that the weapon was in battery, then peered around the corner and, with a quick adjustment of his muzzle, squeezed the trigger. The *plunk* of the weapon was followed a moment later by a massive explosion as the 40 mm HE grenade struck the door and immediately blew a massive hole in it.

James loaded a second HE grenade on a path just slightly parallel to the first, and then Manning passed him two AN-M8 H3 smokers, which he rolled toward the door. They immediately popped and hissed, the thick smoke issuing from them and quickly clouding the area. Fortunately for Phoenix Force, there was no wind. The shooting wasn't the steady buzz it had been when they first arrived. The terrorists were firing from the windows of the warehouse, just as McCarter predicted.

"They're firing for effect only," Encizo said.

"Don't get comfy," McCarter warned him. "Let's move!"

The Phoenix Force warriors filed out, heading toward the door at a low run while watching for any opposition. McCarter couldn't shake his uneasiness. The terrorists had been given the opportunity to strike out with the new weapons, but they had instead chosen to attack with standard fare. The only way that made sense was if they weren't planning to put up much of a fight, which didn't make much sense, either. But it didn't matter, because if he had his way this would be the final confrontation with the Lord's Resistance Army.

James went through the jagged, smoking hole that was the only remaining testament to what had once been a set of large double doors. Encizo followed behind him, and then McCarter, with Manning on rear guard. They spread out as soon as they were inside, and the enemy didn't hesitate to engage them immediately. The perimeter of the warehouse was lined by a catwalk, but the center area was clear. They'd walked into a bad situation. Aside from a few wooden shipping crates and couple of trucks, they didn't have much in the way of cover.

McCarter felt two rounds sizzle past his ear, and he turned in the general direction of the fire and sighted for a target. He didn't get the opportunity to act on it, though. The air outside was suddenly filled with the familiar chatter of the machine gun, and McCarter's would-be assassin was Hawkins's first target of the encounter. The window next to the terrorist exploded inward, and the man's body began to twitch. He staggered forward, his machine pistol falling from his hands, and then teetered precariously a moment at the railing of the catwalk before going over the side. McCarter didn't wait to see his body hit the ground.

The machine gun continued to hammer the terrorist positions.

Encizo and Manning split away from each other, firing their weapons on the run. Encizo managed to grab a lucky shot, catching one of the other terrorists lining the catwalk in the ribs. The man twisted, surprised that he'd been hit, and Encizo put two more rounds in his back, slamming him face-first into the wall.

Manning rolled away from a terrorist, coming to his feet and charging toward a crate for cover in a zigzag pattern. He made it to the crate unscathed, and then aligned the sights of his battle rifle on the terrorist who was trying to reposition for a better shot. Manning triggered one round, two, and then paused. The Canadian was a crack marksman with a rifle and both rounds landed on target. The 7.62 mm round shattered the stock of the gunner's Czech-made SMG, and the second took off the top of his skull. The SMG fell from the catwalk and the terrorist followed a moment later.

Calvin James eventually reached cover, but not without sacrifice. A bullet tore a furrow in his thigh and nearly dropped the warrior. James got his back against another crate. He quickly inspected the wound and saw that it was bleeding profusely. He hadn't really felt it, probably more because of the adrenaline pumping through his veins than anything else, but it wasn't more than a bite and certainly nothing debilitating.

You don't get off that easy, he thought.

James loaded a 40 mm version of the TH3 grenade filled with thermate chemical. Based on the ever-popular white phosphorous, the thermate burned hotter and longer than a conventional white phosphorous filler, in addition to containing a special chemical that doubled as both an antipersonnel weapon and an incendiary. James jacked the slide on the launcher into place, located the pair who had fired on him and with the pull of the trigger proved that human hair and flesh didn't have a terribly high ignition point. The thermate grenade hit the wall above the terrorists and exploded, raining white-hot molten iron onto them. They screamed, their clothing ignited as the iron burned into the skin at a temperature exceeding 4,000 degrees Fahrenheit.

McCarter saw James's plight and immediately noted the blood running from his thigh. He slapped the VOX device, and over the din of the autofire he demanded the man's status. James looked in his direction and tossed a thumbs-up.

McCarter wasn't sure he believed it but he had bigger troubles of his own at the moment as he noticed two terrorists coming down the stairs of the catwalk and trying to flank his position. McCarter raised the MP-5 to his shoulder, sighted on the terrorists and squeezed the trigger. The weapon was set to 3-round bursts and the Briton's marksmanship was as superb as always. The first trio of rounds slammed into the chest of one of the terrorists and sent him sprawling into a stack of empty cardboard boxes, much to the surprise of his comrade. The remaining LRA terrorist tried to draw a bead on McCarter but he had him dead to rights. Mc-Carter's second 3-round burst punched through the LRA gunner's skull, leaving his corpse effectively headless as it teetered forward and smacked the concrete floor.

Encizo noticed immediately that a number of the terrorists were beginning to pull back from their positions, although they still had the upper hand and the advantage of overhead cover.

He keyed his radio. "Targets are retreating."

"Watch for a sucker play," McCarter replied.

James, who had been pinned down, wasn't even taking fire. Only Manning seemed occupied and even he appeared to be the aggressor rather than the defender. McCarter watched as the Canadian took two terrorists who were running in opposite directions, both of them with head shots. The guy was a phenomenal rifleman and one to be rivaled.

"There may be an explanation for that, boys." Hawkins's voice broke through. "I've got bogies making like bats out of hell. They're on large trucks."

It dawned on McCarter why the terrorists hadn't been using more weapons against them. They needed to get them out of the area. With their jungle depot destroyed and their warehouse in Bor-gon destroyed, they didn't have any choice but to protect what remained of the investment. They were trying to escape with maybe a few hundred small arms and munitions, and there wasn't much chance they could get any more out of the States before Able Team cut off the supply line.

"Stop them!" McCarter said as he lurched from his position and signaled for the rest to follow.

They emerged outside in time to see Hawkins trying to stop the small fleet of trucks heading for the opening in the fence line but he was taking some additional fire from inside. McCarter ordered his teammates to spread out and provide some covering fire but he knew even as they did that they stood little chance of stopping the enemy trucks. Once more, the LRA had eluded them and with the weapons still in their possession.

And McCarter didn't have the first bloody idea where they were headed!

IT DIDN'T TAKE LONG for Phoenix Force to locate Leighton inside the warehouse.

They were relieved to find him alive, even after having to mop up a few stragglers. As James rendered first aid, McCarter called for the chopper. Grimaldi and Hamun arrived within ten minutes, Kendra Hansom in tow. When she saw Leighton she threw her arms around the CIA agent. The Phoenix Force warriors tried to give them a little room but it wasn't really the most practical situation for a reunion.

After a minute, James went back to tending to the severe electrical burns where they had tortured him. Smelling salts and a rubdown with alcohol sponges on the areas where his skin was intact did much to revive him.

"You feel up to a few questions, mate?" McCarter finally asked.

Leighton nodded slowly, his breathing a little erratic. McCarter looked at James, who nodded but held up his hand to indicate McCarter keep it as brief as possible. It was clear the guy had been through hell and back; his body would be susceptible to go back into neurogenic shock if it were exposed to long bouts of questioning.

"The weapons they took out of here. Do you know where they were headed?"

Leighton replied through cracked lips, "They've got

a big op in Bor. They plan to overrun the civil government in place there, take control of the city by force."

"Okay, that's good," McCarter prompted. "What about Lester Bukatem? Was he with them here?"

"Y-yeah, he was here. Bastard was the one who tortured me. I finally broke but I couldn't tell him anything." Leighton coughed and produced a laugh more like a sputter. "Dumb son of a bitch kept bragging about all of his plans. Feeding me information. I knew then he'd kill me."

"Why didn't he?" Manning interjected.

"He...he told his man to do it," Leighton said. "His second-in-command. But when he came in here he just ordered the guards to get out and then he fired two shots. But he didn't kill me. H-he said to give a message to someone called Taha."

"What?" McCarter pressed. "What message?"

"The message...the message is that General Kiir..." Leighton's eyes started to glaze and his words became unintelligible.

James said, "Sorry, boss, but it's going to have to wait. That's all he can take."

McCarter muttered a curse under his breath but the sound of Kumar's voice from behind the group echoed through the vast room as he walked up and stopped next to the Phoenix Force leader. "I am certain I know what the message was."

"And what's that?" Encizo asked over the sound of footfalls as the SPLA unit fanned out to search the rest of the warehouse and secure the perimeter.

Kumar looked at the Cuban. "That it's General Kiir who is the traitor of our people."

"What?" Hawkins said. "How the hell is that possible?"

"It is simple. Lester Bukatem has only ever been interested in one thing, my friends. Power. He does not care for God, neither does he care about the Sudanese or even his own countrymen in Uganda. The only thing he cares about is ruling over all and making a name for his revolution in Africa. General Kiir is very much like him. While their purposes are very different, they are united in their goals. They care about nothing but themselves. Bukatem was able to get the weapons into the country because General Kiir let him."

"I can hardly believe it," Manning said. "But it really does make sense if you can put it together."

"But wasn't it General Kiir who requested us to come here?" Enzico said. "Why would he actually want us here if he's been in on this thing the whole time?"

"Because of my brother's insistence," Kumar said. "It would have been suspicious if General Kiir had refused to call for outside help after American arms were discovered here. But we also knew that the general would arrange for your destruction as soon as you came into the country. It was I who arranged to smuggle you over the border from Uganda, and my brother's idea to tell only General Kiir of the rendezvous point."

"But we thought—"

"I *know* what you thought, American," Kumar said to Enzico. He looked at McCarter and added, "What all of you thought. But we had to let you believe it was someone else so that the general didn't suspect that we knew it was he that had sold us out to Bukatem."

"And what about General Kiir?" McCarter asked. "Where is he now?"

"He is being held in our encampment outside of Juba. When we have finished here he will be tried and executed."

"And what about the weapons? Did Kiir know they were headed to Bor?"

"He did," Kumar said. "But so did Samir, and he is already on the road to Bor. He said to tell you he would meet you there."

McCarter nodded. "Then it's off to Bor we go."

CHAPTER TWENTY-TWO

Bor, South Sudan

Samir Taha met Phoenix Force at an SPLA checkpoint on the edge of the Sudan city in a clearing where they'd established a small makeshift landing pad for the chopper.

The Phoenix Force warriors were restocked and ready for whatever trouble might await them. They were only going to get one last shot at this and if they didn't stop Bukatem this time, the odds of ever capturing or killing him would be astronomically long. He could disappear into the terrain, hide and run for as long as it suited him, and there wouldn't be much they could do about it.

Taha led the team in a convoy of jeeps to a small bunker they'd built and maintained throughout the civil war. The SPLA had acquired additional arms and modern equipment while working as part of the JIT program with the Sudanese Armed Forces. It seemed Taha wasn't overly friendly with Hamun, but the men didn't bristle around each other, either. There had been a lot of give and take on both sides required, and the two men appeared to be getting along for the sake of professional courtesy if for no other reason.

When they were assembled, McCarter said, "That was good thinking about Kiir."

Taha grinned. "Now you can understand why I couldn't tell you."

"Yeah, I understand. What's the current situation?"

"We have men inside the city. There are specific targets we think are of tactical significance to Bukatem. They include the city center, where several high-ranking government officers work. There are also residences in there for dignitaries and visitors, along with a larger number of support staff."

"So we could end up with a hostage situation," Encizo remarked.

"I think taking hostages is the least concern for Bukatem," Manning said. "It seems more probable that if he's interested in hitting the seat of power, he'll go in and simply eliminate anyone standing in his way. I don't think he'd attempt to use that as a place to hole up."

"You could be right," McCarter said. He looked at Hamun. "You've dealt with Bukatem before and you have a number of intelligence assets inside of Bor. What's your assessment?"

"Your friend is correct. Lester Bukatem will be interested in crippling only those powers he feels might offer resistance. He will not concern himself with bystanders unless they threaten his plans. But it would not be like him to spare them, either, if he sees it's not to his advantage to do so. His men are trained to kill anyone that might cause trouble. He has no use for hostages."

"Well, one thing we can't do here is assume the LRA will be discriminate about who they do or don't drop the hammer on," McCarter said. "So we have innocents to worry about either way. What about other factions that could get involved in an engagement?"

"My men have orders to follow your lead," Taha said. "And the agents we have inside the city will get involved only if they are forced to defend themselves," Hamun added. "They will not execute any offensive without orders from me."

"Okay, so we can probably bet on a pretty clear battlefield as long as we stay in the open," McCarter said.

"That assumes we can get our collective ass in place before Bukatem reaches the city center," Encizo pointed out.

"Wouldn't it be better to head him off as far from the center as possible?" James asked.

"It would if we knew which bloody route he plans to take," McCarter said.

"Maybe the Farm can help us with that," Hawkins said. "Maybe get us a satellite path on the route. Surely he'll be traveling in a convoy."

"There's a good chance he'll change out vehicles going in," Manning replied. "Especially if he thinks we can identify him."

"He will be more cautious," Taha said. "Of this I am certain."

"Because…" McCarter said.

"He will know by now that we've identified General Kiir, or he will at least suspect this. That will give him reason to think his entire operation has been compromised. Bukatem is a very wise tactician and an experienced fighter. He will have other plans that he can use if he thinks his primary objectives are compromised."

"A contingency plan," Hamun said, scratching his chin. "I agree. This is very probable."

Taha nodded an acknowledgment at Hamun, who returned the gesture.

"So if I were Bukatem," McCarter said, "how would I most likely do this?"

The group fell silent, each man staring at the large

map of the city spread out in front of them. The quality wasn't as good as they were used to dealing with, not to mention they had to rely on their Sudanese counterparts to translate the legends and other writing.

Taha pointed to an area circled in blue grease pencil and shaded with a brown overlay. "This is a large area that has been condemned due to the instability of structures there. Much of them were destroyed during some of the fighting, shelled or completely destroyed. Many of my men lost their lives here and it has since been declared uninhabitable."

"I remember this," Hamun confirmed. "There are even some undetonated explosives in this area. An engineer detachment went in to clean it out but there are still areas that could pose a hazard."

"Seems like a good place for them to hole up, then," Encizo said.

"And that's not too far from Bor-gon," Manning added. "At least we're somewhat familiar with the area."

"It also looks like it has a direct route into the city along this artery here," James said, tracing his finger along a red line that marked a road artery into the downtown section of Bor.

"What's the condition of this road, mate?" McCarter asked Taha.

Taha scratched his neck and sighed. "I cannot tell you for sure."

"I can," Kumar interjected. "It is mostly in good shape although there are parts of it that are not covered with cement."

"But most of it's paved?"

"Yes."

McCarter scanned the faces of all assembled. "I'd say that sounds like our best bet. Maybe we can utilize the Farm's satellite to scan the abandoned area for heat signatures. Anything more than a few animals or even children who might be playing in the area would probably reveal that's where Bukatem's staging for his little plan."

"And if we use Taha's unit to block the road into the city, we can set up a forward offensive and let them pick up any stragglers," Manning added.

"Sounds good. I'll touch base with the Farm. The rest of you get set. We'll probably have to leave on short notice."

"So what do you think?" Brognola asked McCarter.

"I think we need to stop these buggers and quick-like," McCarter said into the sat phone as a jeep bounced along a back road from the bivouac area.

"Agreed. Bear's getting the satellite into position now and we should have IFR signature data to you in a short while." Brognola paused and then said, "I'm sorry to hear about General Kiir's deception. Looks like I almost committed you boys to your final resting place."

"Not your fault, guv," McCarter replied. "This is what we signed on for and it's not the first time it's happened. Sure it won't be the last. Kiir deceived a whole lot of people including his own. I wouldn't want to stand in that bloke's shoes for all the beauties in London."

"Hear, hear. I want you to get a good feel for the present situation before you engage. A few days ago, the local Sudanese officials in Bor and Juba had to ramp up security across the entire region due to the violent outbreaks instigated by Bukatem. The security is tight going in or out. The local police units control most of the roads so your plan of having the SPLA monitor roads going into Bukatem's possible staging location is a good one."

"It seemed our most sensible option. Somehow the LRA's managed to evade us at every juncture. We're hoping to make this hit count while there's little to no chance of endangering bystanders. According to the dirt we got from our military's contacts and assuming Bukatem is there, our main worry will be some unexploded ordnance."

"What concerns me is that they plan to go into a populated city and massacre everyone," Brognola said. "I don't think they're going to be sparing of either side. Remember, they hate the Sudanese so any blood spilled there will be no loss. The key objective, though, sounds as if it will be to eliminate the highest-ranking municipal leaders, as well as anyone who could testify the LRA initiated the bloodshed."

"Bukatem could probably get some of the bloody press corps to spin the story in his favor if they manage to get that far."

"Possibly, but we're not too concerned about that. Our profile and intelligence indicates that Lester Bukatem is also very distrustful of the press. We're depending on you to head this thing off before it turns into a disaster."

"We'll come through," McCarter replied.

"What's that?" Brognola's voice said faintly, indicating he'd moved away from the phone. "Okay. Stand by, I'm putting Bear on."

"David," Kurtzman said a moment later. "We have the satellite in position and it looks like you called it right. There are a score of IFR signatures smack dab in the middle of the triangulation relative to the coordinates you provided. We also count about a half dozen nonorganic signatures from what looks like heat off vehicle engines."

"Any armor?"

"Too difficult to tell, but I don't think so. Is that a concern?"

"Only inasmuch as we found that American-made APC at the fuel depot we hit before."

"Ah yes, forgot about that. Well, the shapes we're seeing indicate probably SUVs or trucks. Nothing that fits the profile of armor, at least from anything in our database."

"Roger that," McCarter said. "We're almost to the checkpoint so I'm going quiet."

"Good luck, my friend."

"Out here," McCarter said.

McCarter disconnected the call and then started to check the action on his FN FAL. He stopped himself, chalking it up to habit. He wasn't entirely comfortable going against the terrorists on such scant information, but he was equally convinced surprise would be their ally. From all of the intelligence they'd been able to gather, they would be equally matched in the arena of firearms. Each one of the terrorists could only carry one or two weapons at most, and if they could hit them while they were grouped together then they stood a good chance of ending this once and for all.

Hawkins had his M-16 A-3/M-203 and the rest of the Phoenix Force warriors had elected to utilize MP-5s, although these particular models had extended magazines that gave them forty-two rounds versus the standard thirty. Manning had also brought along an older, Finnish-made grenade launcher. All of the Phoenix Force warriors also carried their preferred side arms in shoulder leather, and Taha had equipped them with Russian-made RGN grenades.

Their Sudanese driver tapped on McCarter's shoulder and held up five dusty fingers. McCarter nodded and then signaled to the others with a twirling finger that they should be ready to go EVA. The road that approached the hot zone was filled with ruts, gravel and sand. Even a high-quality vehicle like the Land Rover could become easily stuck in the precarious ditches along the side of the narrow road. But their driver seemed to know his way along this route pretty well and he handled the vehicle like an old pro.

The five minutes elapsed quickly and as the vehicle topped a rise in the road, McCarter could see the LRA terrorists were grouped together and preparing to depart in a mix of assorted vehicles from sedans to large trucks. Damn it! He could only hope they weren't too late. If the LRA managed to get their convoy in motion it would prove a much more difficult and terrible task to shut them down. Not to mention that it would probably start the SPLA backup units on the road moving in this direction and they couldn't afford to leave open any gaps.

McCarter had no illusion that if Taha thought Phoenix Force was in trouble he'd move his people in. "Stop here!" the Briton told the driver.

Phoenix Force bailed out before the Land Rover had come to a complete stop.

James and Manning immediately headed for a row of toppled building materials nearby and McCarter rushed for the cover of a shell crater. Encizo and Hawkins took up positions behind a large abandoned vehicle near the roadway and swept the area ahead of them for targets. They didn't appear immediately but it had obviously taken the LRA guerrillas time to figure out that their enemy had arrived.

McCarter skidded to a halt in the crater as the first band of terrorists opened fire. He heard a brief popping sound and he knew that they had only a few seconds before they became dinner for African carrion. He keyed his transmitter and ordered the rest of his team to keep their heads down but fire for effect. They'd practiced this kind of thing many times before—they'd know what he meant. McCarter landed with belly against the upslope of the crater, acquired his first target and squeezed the trigger of the FN FAL. A volley of 7.62 mm slugs rocketed toward the enemy position, but McCarter wasn't looking to hit human targets. His shots were rewarded with a belch of steam as he put a half dozen rounds into the grille of an antiquated truck.

The LRA terrorists were still trying to find cover as McCarter redirected his fire to a point just above the truck. The windshield exploded and McCarter saw blood spray from the gap, signaling that he'd hit the driver dead-on. With the vehicle and driver out of commission, those weapons wouldn't be going any place fast.

There was an eerie silence in the next moment, and then the ground beneath him suddenly shook with tremendous violence.

McCarter felt the sensation of his back burning. His feet left the ground and he felt the rush of hot wind against his face as he sailed through the air. Another moment passed. His face hit the ground and the air rushed from his lungs. McCarter remembered looking down and seeing that he still had hold of his FN FAL but it had a patina of blood on it.

"TEAM LEADER'S DOWN!" Hawkins looked at Encizo.

"I see it," Encizo replied calmly. "Hold your position and open fire on that grenade launcher."

The Phoenix Force soldiers aimed the whole of their arsenal in the direction of terrorists who were now seemingly focused on celebrating their first major victory and triggered a full-auto salvo simultaneously. The air around them grew deafening as a swarm of 9 mm and 5.56 mm rounds hammered the LRA terrorists, taking out equipment and manpower in turn. Screams resounded through the air as Phoenix Force unleashed a furious storm of hot lead.

"We could use a machine gun," Hawkins said triumphantly as he slammed home a fresh magazine.

"Your wish is my command," Encizo said. "See if you can put that M-203 to use while I get us some support."

"Phoenix Two to Eagle, you copy?"

"You're coming in five by five, Phoenix Two," replied Jack Grimaldi's voice.

"Phoenix One may have been hit. We've got bogies at our two o'clock. We could use some help."

"On my way," Grimaldi said, even as the roar of the chopper engines buzzed over their heads.

Flashes pulsed from the .50-caliber door gun manned by Hamun on one side of the SAF gunship as Grimaldi circled the enemy position like an eagle circling a lake with its eye on a big, juicy fish. Hamun made short work of the terrorists who had taken up position behind the jagged walls of another building. Dust and stone crumbled under the brutal assault and as Grimaldi completed his first pass, Hawkins followed with a 40 mm high-explosive grenade from the M-203. The grenade launcher that had bombed the area around McCarter went up in a red-orange ball of flame, followed a moment later by secondary blasts that went as high as a hundred feet.

Hawkins had obviously hit their ordnance cache, as well.

"On my mark, boys," Encizo told them.

The Phoenix Force warriors aligned their weapons on the enemy's position once more and braced themselves for another volley. The Cuban ensured he had the target sighted correctly, and then he gave the order. Once more they fired one hundred rounds at a new position. There was a short delay between when their rounds hit, and Encizo ordered Hawkins and James to reach McCarter quickly and deliver a status report.

"Phoenix One's okay, boys, conscious and breathing."

"Tough old bastard," Hawkins muttered to Encizo with a grin.

Manning replied, "Get him evac'ed to the rear. We'll advance on the LRA and mop up."

"Acknowledged," James replied.

Manning met up with Encizo and James, and after a quick reload the trio leapfrogged down the road in a fire-and-maneuver pattern. Some of the terrorists held their positions and kept fighting while others retreated. Some men were screaming and others tried to quiet them so as not to give away their positions. The Phoenix Force warriors kept to the edges of the road, using the irregular framework of the crumbled buildings to provide cover. They were all cognizant of the positions of their teammates. Every so often a terrorist would emerge from concealment and fire at the group and then duck behind cover again, but most of it amounted to little more than harassing fire. They were trying to intimidate men who'd become experts at the craft and they were losing.

Grimaldi buzzed the area once more, this time sweeping in a tighter arc. Hamun appeared to be having the time of his life as he swept every position he could find with a fusillade of .50-caliber rounds. In some cases, the massive slugs decapitated the heads of some of the LRA terrorists while others separated arms or legs from their torsos.

"Keep your eyes open," Encizo said into his mike. "We don't know how many or where."

They both acknowledged the message and then continued on their mission. They were here in one capacity and one capacity only: to search and destroy. Encizo thought of it now, envisioning how easy it would have been to simply let Hamun rip on a full-auto burn until he leveled the place. But these weren't just a bunch of dilapidated buildings clustered together; every corner was a potential terrorist hiding place.

"Trouble at high noon," Hawkins's voice called.

Encizo looked up and watched the terrorists coming straight for them. They were armed to the teeth with assault rifles leveled and their gait said they were determined to unleash hell on their enemies. There were only a dozen or so and Encizo surmised they were looking at the remainder of the LRA force.

"Down!" he screamed.

They dropped to the ground even as the report of assault rifles echoed through the hot air. The space above their heads was filled with a firestorm of lead, and Encizo could actually feel the heat and pressure changes in air density as the area immediately above them was suddenly filled with deadly missiles. He heard the crumbling of walls and experienced a moment of dread. He felt something warm and wet smack his hand and he looked in the direction in time to see the lifeless eyes of a head staring back at him—it was no longer attached to its owner's body.

Encizo's heartbeat skipped and something seemed to catch in his throat as he realized he was staring into the face of none other than Lester Bukatem. He recognized the man from the photos and it almost seemed, just for a moment really, that Bukatem had a ghastly smile frozen to his features. Encizo dismissed the thought, realizing that what had really happened was that heat from some unknown source had melted part of his skin and drawn up his cheeks, pulling the lips into a natural, upward curve.

Still, Encizo realized that picture would probably haunt him for a long time.

"Let's finish this," Encizo told his teammates.

The trio brandished their weapons and then took aim. The terrorists—who had stopped to reload—realized that their enemies were about to unleash a firestorm of their own. At that point, there was little more they could do and the Phoenix Force warriors knew it as well as their opponents did. In fact, they knew it better. They opened up simultaneously and twelve terrorists fell under a hail of bullets. Some had limbs torn from their bodies, others literally lost their heads, and still others were simply cut in two.

Hawkins leveled his M-203, called for fire in the hole and then triggered the grenade launcher. All of the Phoenix warriors went prone and a heartbeat later the high-explosive ordnance blew. Blood, bone and brain matter sprayed in every direction and a few terrorists went airborne as the shockwave propelled them back.

The sounds of battle died away, leaving only the blood-ied and burned corpses of the LRA remnants.

And deathly silence followed.

CHAPTER TWENTY-THREE

New Orleans, Louisiana

Able Team rolled through a seedier part of one of the many wharf areas in New Orleans.

The trio had a target and they were gunning for bear. Lyons had already notified Saroyan and Shubin that there were possible terrorists operating at one of the several ranges currently abandoned, and that given the size of the post and Able Team's current assignment it would be some time before they could return to assist them. Saroyan had assured Able Team he would activate the Department of the Army Civilian Police and MPs.

"If those bastards are here, we'll find them," Saroyan had told Lyons.

"Understood, General. But if you do locate them we'd prefer you wait for us to arrive before attempting to engage them. We're much better equipped to handle this kind of thing and we do have some information that could save the lives of the civilian police. In other words, don't rush into the situation unless absolutely necessary. Just locate and observe."

"I give you my personal assurances we won't engage unless we're provoked and forced to defend ourselves or they try to leave the base."

With Saroyan's promise, Able Team could focus on the task ahead.

Lyons had been tempted to rush straight back to Camp Shelby and stop Muwanga's operations there, but the Able Team warriors ultimately agreed that if they focused on neutralizing the exit pipeline, it would buy them more time and remove any place for Muwanga and his people to run. Essentially, the LRA smugglers would be like trapped rats and Able Team would be the exterminator.

"It's win-win for our side," Schwarz pointed out.

Blancanales pulled the van up to a side street off the main road that led down the waterfront and killed the engine and lights. He gestured through the windshield at a small, darkened building on the waterfront. A single light burned inside, its glow visible around the edges of the otherwise blackened windows.

"That's the place," Blancanales said.

"Looks tight," Schwarz remarked, leaning forward from the backseat and peering through the windshield at the gloomy environs.

"Anybody got a guess how many might be waiting for us?"

"Hard to tell," Schwarz said.

"We took out quite a number of them in St. Tammany."

"If the guy we took prisoner back there told the truth, we're probably faced with a fairly good-size group. He indicated there weren't too many at Camp Shelby."

"That'd only make sense," Lyons mumbled. "Too many on base would draw some unwanted attention. The smaller they keep the operation there the easier it would be to get on and off the base."

"I wonder how they've managed to keep it going this long without getting caught."

"My guess would be wannabes and mercs," Blancanales said. "If you think about it, the country is ripe with these kinds of whack jobs. Unemployment's high and people are down on their luck. That sort of socio-economic environment is bound to produce more guns-for-hire, not to mention ex-military or disgruntled vets."

"And a whole boatload of felons willing to shoot a few bystanders for a quick buck," Lyons added.

"True," Schwarz said. "I mean, it's not like the LRA would be doing background checks on every recruit that answered a magazine or newspaper ad."

"Well, we're not getting any younger sitting here chatting about it," Lyons replied. "Let's nut up and do it."

"I love when you talk dirty," Blancanales said.

Lyons grumbled something profane and then the three Able Team warriors went EVA. They'd be working in close quarters this time so the trio decided to go in with pistols only. The idea was that they had the element of surprise this time and their enemy wasn't expecting any trouble. Unless the team at the house in St. Tammany was supposed to report to them, and their prisoner they ultimately turned over to the custody of the state police had indicated they'd been left with instructions to await the signal only from Muwanga, this would be a quick hit.

The trio made their way to the door of the waterfront and crouched just outside of it.

"You think it's locked?" Schwarz asked.

"Only one way to find out," Blancanales whispered in return even as he reached for the handle.

Lyons readied his Colt Anaconda and watched as Blancanales tried the handle. It turned smoothly and the door popped from the catch with a barely audible click. Blancanales flashed a cheesy grin broad enough to be seen even in the gloom before he pushed inside. He kept low, the SIG P-229 held at the ready and tracking the darkened room. There was light spilling from under an adjoining door toward the back—probably the same room from which they'd noticed light around the edge of the window.

The soft thump of rock music reached their ears—definitely not the kind of stuff LRA guerrillas would have been listening to. That meant their idea about mercs or soldier-of-fortune wannabes had to be pretty solid. While none of them wanted to do battle with Americans, they also had a higher calling to ensure that they put this arms pipeline down once and for all. If Sudan was to have any chance at all of peace, or Phoenix Force needed the odds stacked in their favor against the large amount of arms being stockpiled there, they had to succeed in closing down the smuggling operation going on right here under their own noses.

Able Team ventured farther into the deep darkness of some kind of large room with a big counter to one side. They cleared their flank and sides and then eventually reached the door. Lyons held up three fingers to signal a countdown, and when he'd counted off he put nearly all of his weight behind a kick at a point just six inches below the door handle. Even though it was a commercial-grade metal door, it proved no match for his speed and strength.

The door whipped open with enough force to nearly dislodge it from its hinges.

Even as he came through the doorway, Lyons got low and moved off to the left—a signal that Blancanales should take the right side. Schwarz came through last, heading straight up the middle with his Beretta 93-R held in front of him in a Weaver's grip. They took in the scene within milliseconds. The man who had answered the door lay against the wall, his blood smeared across parts of it and his body angled against a baseboard in a crumpled heap.

The gunman who shot him, muzzle still smoking, whirled at the noise of Able Team's entrance and leveled his SMG on Schwarz's midsection. Schwarz didn't give the guy an opportunity to follow through. He triggered the Beretta 93-R, which was set for 3-round bursts. A trio of 9 mm Parabellums struck the gunman in the chest with a grouping so tight it created a single hole. The impact lifted the young man off his feet and dumped him into a pile on top of his own victim.

Carl Lyons got off the second volley, a double tap to the head of his opponent. The back of the man's skull disappeared in a grisly display of blood, bone and gray matter that washed the wall behind him. His machine gun sprang from lifeless fingers, and his corpse stood there a moment—stiff and erect—before collapsing to the dusty, cracked linoleum.

The third gunner had found cover behind a long granite countertop supported by a heavy metal base, using the top of the counter to steady his aim as he aligned his sights on Blancanales. Fortunately the Able Team warrior saw the attack coming and managed to evade a maelstrom of hot lead by diving behind an island display of a large, diesel-powered generator. Blancanales's shoulder rolled to a new position, leveled his P-229 and squeezed the trigger. Over long sessions at the range, the pistol had a tendency to create fatigue due to its recoil, but in this short-term scenario the P-229 was regarded as one of the most accurate pistols ever made. A pair of .40 S&W slugs skinned the countertop and literally shot the SMG from the man's hands.

Blancanales followed with a third round that punched through the gunman's upper lip and sent his body reeling into a freestanding cabinet. The cabinet teetered a moment or two, and then unbalanced and collapsed, dumping hundreds of pounds of machine parts onto the deceased.

All three men of Able Team spotted the movement at the same time. The fourth gunner was headed up the stairwell in the back of the massive shop, triggering a burst in their general direction to discourage thoughts of pursuit. Unfortunately for him, the Able Team combatants weren't the types to let that stop them. Lyons kept the Anaconda leveled in the direction the man had disappeared and gestured for Schwarz to take point.

Schwarz flashed him a thumbs-up and then gave chase.

Blancanales took a moment to gather his thoughts, pushing aside the brief realization he'd come very close to getting his head blown off. In moments like this, there wasn't any point in giving such things consideration; that could get a guy killed faster than any terrorist.

Lyons followed after Schwarz a moment later, and Blancanales took the signal he was to hold rear guard. He directed a silent nod of thanks at his friend and the warrior returned the gesture with a quick smile. They had been here too many times before to let just another close encounter shake their resolve. Blancanales had always done his job and he would do at this time; he'd hold the lower floor to prevent any reinforcements from gaining the upper hand while the minds of his comrades were focused on the final target.

Hermann Schwarz felt as if his legs might come off as he took the steps two at a time in pursuit of the final gunman. He knew the importance of taking the guy alive to be sure, but he also didn't plan to die in this place unnecessarily. Even as he chased after the man, Lyons on his heels, Schwarz wondered why their quarry had chosen higher ground instead of making a clean escape out back where he'd have running room. It was almost as if the guy had some mission, something he needed to accomplish no matter what, even if it cost him everything.

Only a few seconds elapsed before Schwarz emerged onto the second-floor landing. The terrorist swung the muzzle of his SMG in Schwarz's direction, but the Able Team commando beat him to the punch. Schwarz aimed high and squeezed the trigger—three rounds left the muzzle. The first pair struck center mass and the third caught him square between the eyes. The gunner triggered a reflexive volley high and right of Schwarz's position even as he collapsed to the floor.

Schwarz holstered his pistol just as Lyons and Blancanales joined him on the second floor. He crossed the distance, gave the deceased a cursory inspection and then turned and shrugged. "I tried to take him alive."

"Don't sweat it," Lyons said. "He didn't give you a choice. None of them gave us a choice."

Blancanales made his way around the dim room but didn't see anything of interest. He then frisked the terrorist Schwarz had killed while his two friends returned to the first floor to check the remainder of the terrorists for intelligence. He didn't find anything and joined his partners a minute later. Schwarz had obviously come up empty, but Lyons seemed to have found a wallet on one of the dead men. He was looking at the driver's license with a puzzled expression.

"What is it, Ironman?" Blancanales inquired.

"This guy's definitely an American citizen. He's carrying military ID."

"Gimme," Schwarz said, snapping his fingers.

Lyons passed it over and Schwarz held it up to the lone lamp that burned on the table nearby while Blancanales meandered off to find the off switch to the stereo blaring music loud enough to give all three of them a headache. By the time he returned, Schwarz was passing the ID back to Lyons.

"It's fake."

"Say what?" Blancanales asked. "How do you know?"

"It's obvious," Schwarz said with a shrug. "That particular ID doesn't have either his unit or his date of birth. I don't know how the hell they've managed to get by with using them."

"Somebody's been sloppy," Lyons said.

"Doesn't really surprise me," Blancanales said. "Even after incidents like the shooting at Fort Hood a few years ago, things still get missed that really shouldn't."

"Well, either way," Lyons said, "we've neutralized their operation here. We should head for Camp Shelby and have the Farm contact a federal task force. Get them in here to secure the place and start digging for any additional intelligence they can find."

"What's the rush?" Schwarz asked.

"Something tells me that Muwanga's bound to hear about this. And even if he doesn't, I'm pretty sure that when he checks in with his team at St. Tammany and doesn't get any answer, he's going to know the show is over. I'd rather be there before that happens."

"Agreed," Blancanales said.

"Well then, let's not stand around here jacking our jaws," Schwarz said as he turned and headed for the exit. "Our chariot awaits."

CHAPTER TWENTY-FOUR

Camp Shelby

Daudi Muwanga watched the activity on the streets with interest as the military policeman waved him through the gates after checking his identification and saluting.

Getting the proper credentials hadn't been that difficult thanks to Scott, who had connections working in PersCom. A military ID card had been easy enough to acquire. A forged birth certificate, just to add a layer of complexity, and a modified pair of Class B utilities acquired from Scott's closet had completed the convincing ensemble.

His narrow escape from the American agents had left Muwanga weary. Still, the thought of his plans finally coming to fruition rejuvenated him. He wondered how things were going in Khartoum. Kamoga was late in reporting status, but he imagined they were busy preparing for their attack on the city. He'd turned on the radio sporadically during his trip, hoping for some news, but aside from a brief on new business concerns in China he'd heard nothing.

There were many who had questioned Muwanga's motives through the years. A number of the members within the LRA, including Lester Bukatem, had said that Muwanga had no real wish to fight for God—that instead he had used the movement to resolve a personal vendetta. But Muwanga didn't care what they thought. He knew where he came from. His father had taught him that ultimately, whether it was a fight for Ugandan liberty or some other call, that there was always a political element at the core—*always.* Groups like the LRA weren't fighting a war for the Lord in the purest sense. They were fighting a political war, and that meant the chances of them producing any results above the purely political were unlikely.

It was this view that had caused him to move away from the movement and start his own. The Lord's Resistance Army didn't stand for religious freedom by the political definition. He chose to represent the common Ugandan, the human being who had to live in fear every day of his life. He fought for the Ugandan who couldn't get ahead, or find a job, or send his children off to school without worrying that it would be for the last time. Muwanga most represented those who had been the victim, or stood to be a victim, of the oppression the civil governments had declared on all Africans. This wasn't the same kind of war they had declared on the SPLA; that was entirely different. They had declared war on the authority establishment because they resented the vile forms of living that clearly violated their religious convictions. But the other war was political, fighting governments bent on making the way of the commoner's life extinct.

Muwanga planned to make sure that his enemy suffered their own fate first.

Within twenty minutes Muwanga arrived at the small building that was the checkpoint for Range Bravo. This was the most remote of all the ranges stretching across the vast lands that made up Camp Shelby. This area had become very useful to them because of its vastness, not to mention the fact that because a good number of the units that operated here were U.S. Army and Air Force reserves, much of the territory remained unoccupied for long stretches of time.

When he reached the front door of the range building, Muwanga looked around and then removed a key from his pocket and put it in the lock. He did another quick check over his shoulder before pushing the door open and moving inside. He closed and secured it behind him, and then waited and listened. The downstairs interior was old, dusty and bare. There were no lights on, and the sun was quickly setting, the crimson light of dusk casting an eerie glow throughout the room.

And then Muwanga heard the voices. They were faint at first, inconsistent, but they were present all the same. Muwanga couldn't tell whose voices, and despite the fact that his team had orders to meet him here, he didn't plan on taking any chances. Muwanga had recently had too many surprises and he planned to be ready for anything.

Muwanga reached inside his jacket and withdrew the compact 9 mm pistol he'd carried right onto the base under the noses of the military police. He quietly ascended the external stairwell at the back of the range building and peered over the top of the second-floor landing. The loftlike room was lit only by the sunlight that streamed through the open-air window. A long table hugged one wall and spread across it were assorted small arms, including M-16 variants, grenade launchers and M-9 pistols.

Muwanga was puzzled at first but then it became clear what was going on when he noticed the men bent over the table and working on weapons with focused precision. Muwanga immediately recognized Pakim and one of his other trusted men. The remainder of the group he'd left at their headquarters location in St. Tammany.

The pair turned upon hearing Muwanga enter.

"Men," Muwanga said as he holstered his pistol. "What is the condition of the inventory?"

"All of the weapons are in excellent shape, sir," Pakim replied.

"Have you arranged for a vehicle to smuggle them off the base?"

"We managed to secure a large van from the motor pool. They will be here within the hour. It was a simple matter of acquiring Scott's signature on the requisition forms."

"Who did you send to procure it?"

"One of the mercenary personnel you hired, the young man named Shamus."

"That is good," Muwanga said with a nod.

Indeed it was. In fact, Chris Shamus had been a U.S. Marine until he'd been ousted for conduct unbecoming during the Iraq war. Men like that had been ripe for the pickings and they had served as a mainstay to shore up Muwanga's team. Most of them were ex-military who'd been deserted by their government, dishonored because they had either been incorrigible or simply unruly. What men like this thirsted for most was combat, but they weren't unwilling to do things—very specific things like posing as enlisted military—if it meant they could feed their families or pocket a little extra cash.

Some worked for vehicles and other toys while others simply enjoyed money. They got off on the thrill of putting one over on the military that had broken them, taken everything by teaching them to kill and then putting them in a situation where they could go to jail or be discharged in shame for doing that job. Muwanga had heard the same story again and again, and he'd learned to specifically target these types of disaffected among America's veterans. In his country, they would have been revered but here they were outcasts and drifters, little more than discard refuse swept under their government's carpet of shame.

"Shamus has proved reliable many times," Muwanga said. "He will be here on time."

"It would seem that perhaps the American colonel is still of value to us," Pakim suggested.

"He's dead," Muwanga said.

"You chose to eliminate him."

Muwanga shrugged as he stepped over to the table and inspected some of the gleaming weapons with a casual eye. "It's of little consequence. He could no longer provide any useful function so I killed him. We'd used him up and since he would not provide any more intelligence that could extend our operations here, I saw him only as a liability."

A buzz commanded their attention and Pakim's companion, a Ugandan Muslim named Joswa Singhal, reached to his belt and withdrew a cell phone. He spoke in short answers and then something went hard in his features. He nodded, muttering, and it looked as if tears had begun to well in his eyes. At last he hung up, replaced the phone and leaned against the table as if he might faint.

"What is it, Joswa?" Muwanga demanded.

Singhal cleared his throat and wiped at his eyes before saying, "That was our contact awaiting us at the port. He has just learned that Lester is dead."

Muwanga sighed and his heart began to thud in his chest. He'd almost expected this kind of news to eventually reach them but he'd hardly thought it would come on the eve of their largest and most important operation to date. The news took him by surprise but it was only half as disconcerting when he considered that in all likelihood his beloved brother-in-law had died alongside of Bukatem.

"Do we know how?"

Singhal shook his head. "He did not have much information. He could only say that he thought it might have been the work of the American special commandos that were sent into the country. He also heard that General Kiir has been arrested and will most likely be executed by the People's Liberation Army."

"This is…terrible news," Pakim said.

"There is more," Singhal continued. "He says that our water-side location has been compromised. The American agents apparently conducted a raid against it and killed every member of the team."

"He is certain of this?" Muwanga said.

Singhal nodded.

"Our plans for this operation must change," Muwanga said. "You will load what we have here in the van when it arrives and head to our alternate location as quickly as possible. I will signal our men in St. Tammany to await our arrival."

"And what if the Americans have discovered that location, as well?" Pakim asked.

Muwanga's face flushed with anger as he replied through clenched teeth, "Then we will destroy them and avenge our brothers. I swear it."

DAWN WAS STILL many hours away when Able Team arrived at Camp Shelby in the sedan Saroyan's motor pool had loaned them. An MP unit escorted them directly to the command post that the DACP had set up in conjunction with the MPs and a DACP special operations squad, the equivalent of a civilian SWAT unit.

The DACP officer in charge was a straitlaced veteran named Terrance Platt. A hulking black man with massive biceps and a barrel chest, he stood as an imposing figure in the center of the large briefing room that took up the center of the CP. Concern was obvious in his eyes. He had one fist leaning on a map of Camp Shelby spread on a table in front of him and the other held a red situation phone against his ear. In the distance, Lyons could make out the traffic from various units that were in the field and obviously patrolling the base in search of the LRA terrorists.

Lyons didn't know what it meant but from Platt's behavior he could guess it wasn't good.

"What's going on?" he demanded as Platt dropped the phone into the cradle.

"Have you located the terrorists?" Schwarz asked.

Platt shook his head. "No, we've been sitting on our butts waiting for you guys to show up. I just got off the phone with the base commander. All he'd tell me is to stand by and wait for assistance from three federal agents who were part of some task force. I'm guessing you're the three?"

"We are," Blancanales said.

"Well la-di-da," Platt replied. "You know what the hell we've been going through for the last three hours? We're supposed to hang around here waiting on you guys while there may be terrorists running around this base with weapons and explosives? Who in the holy hell's in charge of this operation anyway? I got people to answer to, you know, and in my book you guys don't fall anywhere in my chain of command!"

"We're the higher authority on this one," Lyons replied.

"I'm afraid not," Platt said. "In this case, the Department of the Army Civil Police is the highest authority and we answer directly to General Saroyan. The only one with authority to supersede our procedures is the secretary of defense and the White House."

Lyons had reached his limits of tolerance and whipped out his cell phone. "We can get them on the phone if you'd like. I've got them on speed dial, in fact. How about you?"

That seemed to calm Platt a little but he didn't look any too happy about Lyons's flippant answer.

Blancanales adopted a conciliatory tone. "Captain, we can either stand around and have a territorial pissing contest or you can tell us where you're at and we'll go about putting an end to this once and for all."

Platt seemed to consider that and finally nodded. He waved at them to join him around the map. "Based on the information we have so far we're pretty certain they're operating out of one of the ranges."

"That coincides with what we saw at their headquarters," Lyons said.

"We saw a map just like this one," Blancanales explained. "They had circles drawn on all three of those ranges roughly here, here and here. They also had a route marked leading off the post. It ran somewhere through this area."

Platt nodded. "That's South Post Road. We've got several patrols that have already run through that area and we have the exit perimeter manned now. If they try to leave that way they'll have nowhere to go."

"Except for the fact that road runs along all three entrances to the ranges," Schwarz said. "And that's a hell of a lot of territory to cover in a short time. Not to mention they could hide out in that terrain for an indefinite time before we find them. They might even use that to their advantage."

"We've drawn a tight net over this post, gentlemen," Platt said a little defensively. "There's no way in hell these bastards are getting off Camp Shelby without a fight."

"That's exactly what they're hoping for," Blancanales reminded him.

"Is there any significance to the points Mr. Rose pointed out?" Lyons asked.

"I believe those are the locations of the range buildings," Platt said.

"Have you searched them?"

"Not yet. We were following orders to await your arrival. This time of year all three of the ranges are effectively deserted. We have regular patrols go through but they're too large to concern ourselves with the minutiae. The range entrances are gated and the buildings are locked."

"Sir!" a communication specialist called.

"What is it?" Platt asked.

"We just got a report from one of our patrols that he's following a motor pool van. He thinks it may be our subjects."

"Why would we think that?" Platt asked.

"Because he's sharp," Lyons said. "Isn't it strange a van has been requisitioned from the motor pool at this time of morning?"

"Maybe it's for a funeral detail or something. Those are pretty far away some times and the detail has to get up pretty early."

"How many occupants, Specialist?" Lyons asked the comm guy.

The tech held up a hand, talking animatedly into the radio, and then called back, "Just one, sir."

"Only one?" Blancanales echoed. "That's no funeral detail."

Platt just swallowed hard and nodded. "Tell him not to engage that driver."

Lyons fixed him with a resolute gaze. "Now that's our specialty. The breaching of this base by terrorists overrides your procedures, Captain."

"The protocol still stands," Platt said.

"Listen!" Lyons countered. "Your teams are in no way equipped to hold down the perimeter and combat armed terrorists simultaneously. This is what we're trained for and we plan to do our job. I'm authorized by an executive order to utilize whatever force is necessary to neutralize this threat."

"Up to and including shooting anyone who gets in the way," Schwarz added.

Lyons reached to his holster and withdrew the Anaconda, keeping the pistol at his side. Platt hadn't struck him as the squeamish type but Lyons had enough sense to know that in a tense situation like this he could capture more flies with honey. "Now you need to decide whether you're going to help us or hinder us. Right now."

Platt produced a level gaze and obviously saw the mettle in Lyons's countenance. He finally nodded. "Okay. We'll keep back and focus on perimeter security."

"Fine," Lyons said. "You know where we can get a vehicle? A Hummer perhaps? I don't think the sedan we have is going to cut it."

Platt produced a set of keys and handed them to Lyons. "Take my command vehicle. It's parked just outside. And here…take a radio so we can keep in contact with you. We'll have our man keep tabs on him until you can get there. The specialist will guide you to the location once you're en route."

Lyons nodded and then Able Team left the CP and quickly transferred their weapons from the sedan to the DACP command vehicle, a HUM-V. Lyons selected a pair of MP-5Ks for this run. The weapons were especially effective in CQB and would prove much easier to control under the circumstances. Schwarz went with the tried-and-true Fabrique Nationale FNC. A continuing favorite of many Stony Man field members, the FNC operated on the rotating-bolt principle attached to a gas piston rod headed by twin heavy lugs. The weapon was as versatile in the role of an SMG or automatic rifle with its folding, tubular butt, yet it could expend 5.56 mm M193 ammo at a cyclic rate of 700 rounds per minute. Schwarz opted to continue using his M-16 A-/M-203. The over-and-under would provide the additional bang they'd need.

After double-checking their equipment, Able Team climbed into the Hummer with Blancanales behind the wheel and took off in a southeasterly direction. They kept in contact with the radioman, who issued directions per Platt's promise. They rounded the corner of a crossroad just as the van and marked DACP sedan rolled through the intersection. It didn't appear that the driver was concerned about the squad that was tailing him.

"Something's wrong here," Lyons said.

"Either he doesn't have a clue that's a DACP vehicle on his tail or he's playing it cool," Schwarz said from the backseat.

"Well, he can't drive around forever," Lyons replied. "He has to realize that eventually he's going to draw attention. If we don't—"

The trouble seemed to come out of nowhere in the form of a second military van, this one an older-model painted olive-drab. Lyons shouted a warning but there wasn't a whole lot Blancanales could do about it. Something flashed from the passenger window of the van, and the next thing the Able Team warriors knew the front of their vehicle left the roadway and hit the curb on two wheels. A bright ball of flame expanded outside Lyons's window a moment before the vehicle tipped onto the driver's side and ground to a halt, stopped by a light pole stanchion.

"Bail!" Lyons shouted.

They didn't have to hear it twice. Lyons managed to get his head out of Blancanales's thigh in record time, using the A-post on the passenger side to pull himself upright. The door and frame on his side were crumpled, preventing him from opening the door, and although he could have gone through the window Lyons figured it was better to exit through the windshield the old-fashioned way: forcibly. It took several tries before he managed to kick enough of the safety glass out that he could peel it back.

Lyons heard the rounds continue to strike the Hummer even as he squeezed through the windshield frame. He reached inside and assisted Blancanales while simultaneously calling Schwarz's name over the din of the weapons reports. When Blancanales was free, the two hunkered behind the cover of the vehicle, weapons drawn, and looked for any sign of their attackers. Schwarz appeared from practically nowhere and crouched down between them.

"Plan?" Blancanales asked his friends.

"I think they've only seen me," Schwarz said. "Seems like the best option would be me making a mad dash for new cover and drawing their fire."

"Are you smoking dope or something?" Lyons asked through gritted teeth, clenching them tighter as the bullets ricocheted off the pavement and Hummer or just zinged by over their heads. "You won't get ten feet before they cut you down."

Schwarz inclined his head. "I could head for those buildings right there. If I make a run for it, there's a good chance they'll think I'm alone and outnumbered."

"Um, hate to break this to you, Gadgets," Blancanales interjected, "but we are outnumbered."

"There's nothing saying you've got to wait for me to get there before you two do your thing, boys."

Lyons looked at Blancanales, who just shrugged. The Able Team leader chewed his lower lip a moment, and then replied, "All right. I'm doing it against my better judgment, so don't get your ass shot off. We've got enough troubles right now without losing you, too."

Schwarz grinned shyly and said, "Gosh, Ironman...I didn't know you cared."

"Move out!"

Schwarz turned the selector on his M-16 A-4 to 3-round-burst mode and then charged from the relative safety of the Hummer. The chatter of weapons fire, which had dwindled to mostly small bursts or single shots, increased thunderously as soon as Schwarz became visible to the attackers.

Blancanales slapped Lyons on the shoulder and the two men left the cover of the vehicle heading in the other direction.

There were six LRA terrorists in all, lined up in front

of the van and holding M-16 A-2 assault rifles. One terrorist had discarded a rocket launcher at his feet and Lyons knew in an instant he was the one who had taken out the car. It was a miracle Blancanales had managed to keep control of the Hummer as long as he had. Both Able Team warriors opened up simultaneously with their pistols.

The pair of MP-5Ks bucked with fury as Lyons took action. They had managed to take Able Team off guard, and he wasn't happy about that. The warrior's first volley of 9 mm Parabellums took one of the terrorists in the chest and left quarter-size exit wounds. The man staggered against the impact and only the van stopped him from being knocked immediately to the pavement. His eyes rolled upward as he slid to the ground, leaving a gory streak on the shiny silver van.

Blancanales snap-aimed his SIG P-226 and squeezed the trigger twice, which delivered a pair of .40-caliber skull-busters into a second terrorist. The guy's head exploded as his weapon fell from numbed fingers and he dropped to his knees slowly before slumping forward. His head, or what was left of it, smacked wetly on the pavement.

Lyons got on one knee and took out two more terrorists. He grazed the arm of the first one, but the distraction was enough that when the terrorist turned to address his wounded arm, Lyons got him through the neck. The man's head tilted oddly on the axis of his spine and then he collapsed right where he stood. Lyons got the other terrorist out of sheer luck when the man's M-16 A-2 jammed. Lyons shot him twice in the stomach, shredding the man's intestines, which then pushed visibly through the abdominal wounds. The man let out a shout before he dropped to the pavement and began writhing in agony.

As Lyons ducked behind the vehicle and came away with a pair of fresh magazines, Blancanales continued firing at the terrorists.

As soon as Schwarz reached the cover of a nearby building, he lined up the sights of his M-16 A-4 on the nearest target. It was time to start dishing out some of what they'd been taking. He steadied his aim and squeezed the trigger. The 3-round-burst mode of the assault rifle would have been a lot in the hands of lesser men, but Hermann Schwarz felt right at home. He watched as the high-velocity slugs punched through a terrorist's thigh and hip, shattering bone and dropping him to the pavement.

Schwarz followed up with two more bursts, one directed at the remaining terrorist, and the other at movement he noticed behind the wheel. Only one of the rounds he shot at terrorists trying to kill Blancanales and Lyons connected, but the driver took all three in the chest and head, spattering the walls and windows with bloody flesh.

Blancanales and Lyons dropped the last terrorist simultaneously with a sustained dose of heavy fire. All told, the terrorist took four rounds in the chest from Blancanales's pistol and a plethora of lead to stomach and head from Lyons. The terrorist spun, doing a grotesque dance as Blancanales and Lyons hammered him mercilessly. The gunman triggered the M-16 A-2 in his death throes, sending a dozen or so rounds harmlessly into the pavement before he fell flat on his back.

An eerie silence ensued in the aftermath of the heated gun battle. The Able Team warriors held their positions for a couple more minutes, willing to wait out any further wave, but after some time Lyons knew they had taken out any remaining opposition. He gave the all-clear signal to Schwarz, and then he and Blancanales approached the van and the pile of bodies while Schwarz covered them from a distance. Less than a minute passed before they heard distant sirens begin wailing.

Lyons studied the carnage for a moment and then shook his head. Quietly he said, "So much for taking prisoners. These guys aren't pissing around. Do or die seems to be their motto and they're going to make damn sure we don't forget it."

Lyons went to the front passenger door and opened it. A few flies had already begun congregating on the nasty, bloody mess left by Schwarz's handiwork. The strong odor of expended urine and feces, mixed with the sickly sweet smell of fresh blood, was enough to make Lyons want to puke. He'd seen this kind of thing many times before, maybe too many times, but it always seemed a bit different when he viewed the aftermath of the destruction. Even now, after all these years as first a veteran detective with the LAPD and subsequently as part of a team of the best antiterrorist operatives in the world, Lyons still preferred to do his business from a distance. He just never could get into the up-close-and-personal method of killing.

Lyons closed the door. He'd search the body later. His thoughts echoed his earlier sentiments at the start of the missions: he was supposed to be taking a long vacation away from this kind of stuff.

Blancanales's voice intruded on his thoughts. "Here comes the cavalry."

DACP vehicles rounded the corner and came screeching to a halt. As the occupants emerged and spread out, several approaching Able Team with pistols drawn,

Lyons realized the radio had been lost inside the Hummer. He shouted at the DACP officers they were friendly and it took a precious minute or two to get it sorted out. It was a delay that proved costly as one of the radios squelched for attention.

An officer standing near Able Team whipped it out and Platt's voice came on. "Are the federal agents okay?"

"Yes, sir," he replied. "They're here and they're in one piece. Their vehicle's trashed, though."

Lyons gestured for the radio. "Platt, this is Irons. We're going to need a replacement vehicle."

There was a pause before Platt's voice finally came back. "You guys are expensive dates. All right, Irons, take that officer's sedan. He can ride with a partner."

"Do you have a status update?"

"Our man tailing that van indicates it pulled into Range Alpha. He tried to follow but the driver apparently engaged him and he was wounded."

"How bad?" Lyons asked immediately.

"He'll live."

"Where does he think the van's headed?" Blancanales asked, and Lyons relayed the question.

"We're guessing the terrorists are probably holed up in that range building Mr. Rose pointed out," Platt said.

"All right, we're on our way. Again, we need you to keep the perimeter. We'll do the heavy lifting on this one. Irons out."

"Sounds like we got our work cut out for us, boys."

"So it does," Schwarz replied.

CHAPTER TWENTY-FIVE

Hermann "Gadgets" Schwarz wondered if they could have made any more noise coming through the front door. The squeaking of the hinges and the creaking of floorboards under their weight could just as well have been a herd of stampeding elephants. As far as Schwarz was concerned, they had already announced themselves to the enemy, so there was little point in continuing with a soft probe. Except that they wouldn't have heard the barely perceptible shuffle of feet above their heads. There were no voices, no indication of desperate activities, just the faintest hints of activity.

Schwarz had point, so he moved to the right of the interior that was lit solely by the streetlights. He pointed to his eyes and then upward at the ceiling. Lyons and Blancanales nodded in acknowledgment and then Schwarz waved them into positions against the walls that would provide adequate fields of fire. Once they had the room covered, they waited patiently, each wondering what he could expect above them.

Schwarz crossed the room quietly, no longer concerned about where he stepped. He managed to get across the room and edged closer to a door that was just ajar, visible only because of the sliver of light now spilling from it. Whoever awaited them was probably beyond that door, which Schwarz assumed led to the upper level since there seemed no other visible means of getting there.

Schwarz steeled himself, tightened his grip on the pistol and then started to move toward the door. He was about to reach forward and open it when the night outside came alive with flashing red-and-blue strobes, spotlights in the windows and the sounds of car doors slamming. A moment later the heavy pounding of boots slapping the crushed-gravel road and clatter of weaponry echoed through the vast lower floor of the empty range building, and the door that they had left slightly open was kicked inward with such force that Lyons had to jump aside to keep from having it embedded in his shoulder.

The room was suddenly filled with DACP special operations officers, their bodies covered in black fatigues, body armor and load-bearing equipment, weapons held high and at the ready.

"Put 'em down!" one screamed.

"Police officers!" said another. "Drop your weapons! You're under arrest!"

The members of Able Team slowly lowered their weapons as they exchanged furious looks with one another. Lyons opened his mouth to chew them out, but Schwarz shushed him abruptly. The room got silent and there was the faintest sound of something bouncing around inside the wall on the other side of the door. Schwarz realized what it was even before the thing suddenly bounced off the landing and rolled through the small opening in the door.

"Grenade!"

Lyons threw his entire body weight into the two closest DACP officers and used the impetus to force them toward the door. The tactical team members had cloistered together, so taking out the front line also offered some protection for the others. Blancanales went the only place he could: flat on the filthy floor. A cloud of dust rose. The Able Team warrior threw his arms over his head and opened his mouth, preparing for the eventuality the grenade was a flash-bang.

Schwarz dived for a heavy metal table, which also happened to be the only piece of furniture in the room, and overturned it. He threw his body down and away, his feet pointing toward the blast that came a moment later. The floorboards shook with the power of the blast and flame exploded into a funnel shape around the oak table, but it was high and far enough away that Schwarz was protected adequately from the major effects. One of the DACP officers wasn't so lucky. The man's expression went from surprise to anticipation to shock all in the seconds leading up to the blast. The majority of the Army cops had either gone down of their own accord or because of Lyons's fantastic reflexes, but this man hadn't accounted for flying projectiles. A piece of the window frame tore away with the force of the blast, turning a harmless piece of wood into a sharp missile. The officer took the force of the jagged wood square on the center of his forehead. The velocity was too much for the skull to withstand and the wood violated the cranial cavity and lodged in the officer's brain. The man staggered backward and collapsed.

The scene outside went from what seemed like a fairly controlled situation to complete and utter disaster. First there was the sound of breaking glass, followed by loud popping sounds. A moment later the front and rear door windows on the driver's side of one of the police cruisers shattered. Paint bubbled on the door, and superheated shards of metal flew through the interior, scarring the plastic seats and spiderwebbing the rear window.

Lyons saw the damage and his jaw fell open. "They booby-trapped the place!"

Blancanales and Schwarz exchanged a knowing glance and then looked toward the door leading to the upstairs—or what was left of it. The blast from the HE grenade had blown the door off its hinges and scarred the walls. The heat had ignited a small section of the wall where the cheap wallpaper had apparently been peeling and was ignited, but the fire wasn't anything that couldn't be handled by a half-decent fire extinguisher.

Lyons took one last look at the damage done by the terrorists and then got to his feet. "Screw that. If I've got to risk buying the farm, I'd rather go against one round than a hundred."

He then headed for the stairwell. Blancanales and Schwarz joined him and the trio went through the shattered frame and ascended the stairs. Someone was shooting from the upper window, which meant that's where the attention would be focused. They reached the top of the stairs, and Lyons missed the top step. He tripped on the stairs, Schwarz and Blancanales falling on top of him, only their weight keeping him from sliding down the stairs on his stomach.

His misstep saved their lives as the air above their heads suddenly thickened and heated. A millisecond later they were choking on dust and plaster, with wood slivers and pieces of plaster board pelting their faces and hands. Schwarz raised and turned his head toward the wall, only to discover it wasn't there. It had been replaced by a gaping hole, one that would have been large enough to cleanly divide his upper and lower torsos if he hadn't tripped on Lyons.

The men were on their feet and moving into the landing within seconds. Blancanales and Schwarz acquired the same target simultaneously. It wasn't Muwanga but one of his cronies, and he'd tossed aside his expended pistol for an M-16. He was still raising the weapon, but Blancanales and Schwarz had him bested. There was no choice and so they did the necessary thing. The pair triggered their weapons less than a second apart. Schwarz's round punched through the terrorist's chin, shattered his jaw and severed the first and second vertebrae of his spinal column. The LRA terrorist was dead before Blancanales's round took him in the sternum. The impact of bullets tossed his body against the wall, and it collapsed to the floor and rolled twice before coming to a stop.

Lyons spotted a second terrorist in the corner, this one an American. The man was visibly trembling, his hands up in front of his face. He kept looking from Lyons to the other terrorist's body, then back at Lyons. Abruptly his expression changed from fear and shock to hate and rage.

"Don't do it," Lyons told him.

But it seemed the man was no longer hearing him. He let out a bloodcurdling scream and with a speed that was surprising for a man of his years, launched himself out of the corner and charged Lyons. The Able Team warrior would normally have engaged the man in combat, but it was abundantly clear in that fleeting moment that there would be only one way of neutralizing the aggression and Lyons exercised it. He raised his Anaconda and shot the attacker point-blank in the skull. The man's body arched backward, teetered a moment and then he fell to the ground in an almost slow and purposefully deliberate fashion. A suddenly wicked and eerie silence followed, and the three Able Team warriors realized that the shooting had ceased outside. They looked toward the front of the second-floor loft and noticed the casement-style window mounted to the front of the A-frame-like roof was wide open.

Lyons rushed to the window and looked at the scene below. The carnage was unreal. Two huge holes had been torn in the side of the DACP special operations vehicle. Several bodies lay unmoving, some facedown and others upright. They all looked dead.

"Damn it," Lyons said under his breath and then turned to look at his comrades. "We better get down there."

Schwarz led them down the stairs and when they reached the first floor they noticed one lone officer seated just inside the door with his back leaned against the wall. His face was a ghastly pale color, visible even in the poor lighting, and he had his MP-5 cradled in his arms more like a baby than a weapon.

Schwarz stopped and looked down at him. "Get on your feet, man."

The DACP officer glanced up at the sound of the warrior's strong voice but the look in his eyes was devoid of emotion. He'd just seen his friends and colleagues shot down in a heartbeat. But somehow they had missed this one man. That was a case of survivor's guilt that Schwarz could see the cop might never get over. He looked upon the scene with a sinking feeling, and the thing he noticed most was the amount of blood that puddled in the streets.

Sirens wailed in the distance as additional DACP officers were in transit.

"Schwarz, we better go," Lyons told him.

The Able Team warrior looked at his friend, nodded and then crouched in front of the officer. "Look, son, you're going to look back on this someday and it will be easier. I know it doesn't seem like it, but believe me when I say it will get easier. Until then, you've got to stay hard and take it one day at a time. But whatever you do, you can't give up. You hear me?"

The DACP cop stared blankly at him for a while but then finally he nodded. And while Schwarz wasn't comfortable with leaving the guy here on his own, he took solace in the fact that he was getting through—at least it seemed as if he was.

As Able Team headed for their car, Lyons told them, "I think we've gotten most of this group but Muwanga's still unaccounted for."

They were about halfway to their vehicle when a HUM-V screeched to a halt at the curb, and Platt jumped out with three other officers.

"What the hell is going on?" he demanded.

"Maybe you can tell us," Lyons said. "We told you not to attempt apprehension and so you go and do exactly the opposite of what we asked you to."

"I sent these men in here to secure the perimeter," Platt snapped. "But I also gave the tactical officer a standing order that if he saw an opportunity to help neutralize these terrorists that he was free to do so."

"Before this day's over you won't ever give anybody orders again if I have anything to say about it," Lyons said.

"Yeah, and just what the hell is that supposed to mean?"

"Whatever you want it to mean, prick!" Lyons jammed his finger in Platt's chest and said, "Because of your pigheadedness, you've got at least three dead cops over there, and another who's probably going to have to see a shrink for the next two years."

"Go easy, Ironman," Blancanales said, reaching for Lyons's shoulder.

"You stay out of our face, Platt. I see you anywhere near us and you won't be able to get a job policing toilets at Guantanamo Bay. You get me?"

"Is that a threat, Irons?" The radio suddenly squawked with a flurry of traffic. Platt turned to one of the officers and said, "Find out what's going on."

The man reached inside a squad car and yanked the microphone from its holder. "Delta Three, this is Foxtrot Two…repeat your traffic?"

After a pause the officer explained, "That van was spotted by one of our choppers heading down South Post Road. Infrared shows two occupants."

Another voice broke through the transmission before the detective could respond: "Foxtrot Eight. Be advised I have the vehicle in sight. Confirm, we're traveling eastbound on South Post Road. Looks like they're trying to make a break for it."

Schwarz looked at Lyons and said, "Muwanga?"

Lyons nodded, and then Able Team whirled and rushed for their vehicle. Platt started shouting protests, even a few obscenities, but they ignored him. Blancanales got behind the wheel and Lyons took shotgun… literally. The urban soldier jacked the pump on an AS-3 combat shotgun he'd stowed in the front seat, and verified he was loaded with No. 2 and double-aught. Schwarz prepared an MP-5 for himself and then checked the action on an FNC for Blancanales.

"How far is it to Range Charlie?" Schwarz asked.

"Close," Lyons replied, and he directed Schwarz down a utility road that would take them straight to it.

Soon they were speeding south and trying to catch up with Muwanga's vehicle. There was a better than off-side chance that DACP would attempt to stop Muwanga and his men, and there was no way in hell the terrorist leader was going to halt for them. After all, he'd come this far, been so bold as to attempt one more smuggling operation off Camp Shelby. Whatever happened now, they couldn't afford to let him get away.

"We can't afford a repeat of what happened earlier," Schwarz announced suddenly, almost as if he'd been reading Blancanales's mind. "It's do-or-die time, boys."

"Agreed," Lyons growled.

Blancanales punched the shift into overdrive and gunned the accelerator as their first traffic light turned yellow. He wasn't planning to stop for anything if he didn't have to, red light or no, and if they got backed up in traffic he'd get out and jog. He was in complete agreement with Lyons and Schwarz. They couldn't give Muwanga, or whoever it was they were chasing, another opportunity to use those weapons, particularly not against the civilian population. Able Team would have to draw the line here and now.

"There!" Lyons said, pointing out the windshield. There was still only a single DACP squad car following the van and that was one too many. "Think you can take that squad out safely?"

"Piece of cake," Blancanales replied, and he eased into the abandoned oncoming lane.

The officer hadn't chosen to turn on his lights, probably for fear of losing the suspect until he could solicit additional units to help participate in the chase. Blancanales meant to ensure that no further cops got killed today, and he was going to start by saving this dummy's life without him even knowing it. Blancanales stayed in the opposing lane, keeping his vehicle just far enough back that his front grille remained parallel with the fender on the squad car. They continued down the busy drive.

Blancanales waited patiently until his opportunity came.

"Hang tight," he announced, and then he turned into the cop's right fender.

Blancanales dropped his vehicle into a lower gear, and then alternated between accelerator and brake. The cop tried to get out of the maneuver, but in true fashion he spun out and his vehicle broadsided a chain-link fence that twisted up inside his rims and brought him to a spinning halt. As he regained control of the vehicle, Blancanales risked a glance in the DACP cop's direction. He looked surprised but he was certainly unharmed.

Schwarz took the position behind the terrorists' van and the driver immediately increased speed. The vehicles slowed as they rounded steep curves and the more densely populated urban areas became rolling hills as South Post Road curved through saddles and switchbacks.

Suddenly the van veered off the road onto a side road headed for Range Charlie.

"What the hell is he doing?" Lyons said.

"Maybe he's hoping to lose us in the traffic," Schwarz cracked.

"Of course," Blancanales said. "Think about it. They needed someplace they could be secure for a very short time. They probably had to find a way they could house a cache of men and weapons. What better place than a deserted artillery range?"

"How would they have avoided being seen by Department of the Army Civil Police patrols or MP Corps?" Lyons asked. "At least a range master."

"You think someone working here during the summer wouldn't give them a key? Now you're being naive, Ironman. They could have used anything from threats to blackmail to gain access. They might have even coerced Jordan Scott into cooperating with them."

"Well, in a very short time, it won't matter," Lyons said.

Blancanales negotiated the maze of cones and other barricades, some of which looked as if Muwanga had simply driven through, and arrived at the entrance to Range Charlie in short order. The van was parked there but it was empty, the driver's-side door still standing wide open along with the side door. There were obviously more than two inside that van.

Able Team went EVA as soon as Blancanales stopped the sedan and hoofed it from there. The biggest danger from Muwanga's weapons was that he could conceal them just about anywhere, using natural terrain for cover, and use them against Able Team and the accompanying military patrols without exposing his own position.

The trio met their first opposition on the gravel road just beyond the entrance gates, which had been breached by simply cutting the padlocked chain. Two terrorists appeared at the edge of the woods bordering the road and aimed M-16s at them. They unleashed a fusillade of 5.56 mm hell.

Schwarz and Blancanales pressed themselves to the side of the railing, while Lyons went flat, and then all three of them opened up simultaneously. The first terrorist was shocked to see his belly stitched open and his intestines spill out of his stomach. He dropped to his knees and Blancanales ended the transaction with a shot to the gunner's head. The second terrorist took rounds to the chest and a shotgun blast to the belly. The impact lifted him off his feet and dumped him on the ground with a loud thump.

Lyons got to his feet and took up the center position between Schwarz and Blancanales. They continued down the road, which opened onto a large clearing. Dawn had broken about a half hour earlier so they couldn't move under cover of darkness. Rounds began ricocheting off the ground or slapping into the trees or churning dust as they advanced. Able Team fanned out, intent on putting a quick end to the battle. Terrorists had taken up firing positions, some of them from considerable distance, and Able Team had mutually but silently agreed that the key to victory was taking the fight to the enemy.

Blancanales began picking off the terrorists on his left, catching two of them with clean head shots. In some ways, this kind of battle was what he remembered doing in training simulations. What he'd experienced of these terrorists was that they weren't all that bright, seeming more adept at following orders than in taking the initiative. It would prove to be their undoing.

Lyons knew the shotgun would be ineffective against the terrorist at that range, so he left the matter to Blancanales and Schwarz. Besides, he had a matter of his own that needed attending. He abandoned the shotgun for his .44 Anaconda revolver, and then dashed into the woods and headed off in search of Muwanga.

BLANCANALES WENT PRONE, took tight and steady aim with his FNC and squeezed off two successive bursts. A volley of 5.56 mm rounds struck two of the terrorists who were providing covering fire while the remainder made their way over a twelve-foot-high chain-link fence topped by concertina wire. The slugs ripped through their stomachs and chests just as they shot and killed one of the first DACP officers to arrive in his squad car on Able Team's flank. The other officers, armed only with pistols, dived behind the cover of their doors as they realized they were outgunned. Schwarz planned to reverse that misfortune as he found cover behind a large boulder and brought the MP-5 into play. He triggered both weapons simultaneously. The muzzles flashed in concert with the weapons reports as a maelstrom of 9 mm slugs swarmed the terrorist infiltrators.

One terrorist, still halfway down the inside of the fence, took a pair of rounds to the face that split his skull like a machete through a watermelon. Blood and brain matter sprayed the others near him and he dropped from the fence like a paralyzed spider from a wall. Another terrorist took a trio of shots in the chest from Schwarz's MP-5 as he reached the top of the fence and prepared to climb over the concertina. The impact knocked him off his perch and sent him sailing to mossy earth. The terrorist's body bounced once and then rolled to a stop.

Blancanales and Schwarz continued trading shots as they dispatched the terrorists one at a time. The remaining DACP officers, courage invigorated by the support from the Able Team pair, returned fire anew in retaliation for losing one of their own. The dead officer's partner, in a moment of righteous fury, killed a terrorist with a pair of rounds through the neck. The enemy managed to keep one hand on the fence while he used the other to staunch blood spurting from an artery, but eventually he succumbed to the uncontrolled hemorrhaging and released his hold. He was dead before he hit the ground.

The battle continued to rage for another minute until Blancanales took the last terrorist with a double-tap from his FNC. Twin slugs drilled through the terrorist's chest and flipped him onto his back. The guy coughed pink, frothy sputum from the chest wounds, took a few loud gasps and then went still.

Schwarz and Blancanales were on their feet and headed to the nearest security sedan in a heartbeat. Schwarz ordered the officer and his partner to step on it as he and Blancanales climbed into the back. The officers complied and within a minute they were headed deeper into the range.

"Where are you going?" Schwarz inquired of the driver.

"This is a shortcut," his partner answered. "The road curves up here and opens onto the main range. We can intercept them."

Schwarz shut his mouth. Better to trust these guys—this was their territory and they knew it a lot better than he did. True to words, they rounded a sharp bend in the road and, as their convoy of DACP vehicles slowed and was joined by a couple of Hummers filled with MPs, a machine gun opened up on them from somewhere ahead.

"Spread out!" Blancanales ordered the officers.

Daudi Muwanga knew his cause was lost, and he felt personally responsible for the deaths of his warrior brothers.

Muwanga knew there was nothing he could do to bring back the dead, but he could at least ensure that those responsible suffered some casualties of their own. After abandoning the car, Muwanga took the weapons and headed for the pockmarked lands of the artillery range. From one of the shell craters, he could set up small arms in the defilades to fire in every direction and he would be completely out of sight. He took one look at the approaching armor and knew he could set up quickly at minimal risk. The brothers of the Lord's Resistance Army had sworn to protect him, the cause and each other with their lives, and in this they had achieved a major victory.

The attacks from his forces continued, although they were rapidly running out of time and bodies. There wasn't much use Muwanga could see in prolonging the suffering. The weapons were already loaded, so it was just a matter of waiting and watching. He primed the devices and then dropped to his belly on the slope of a crater. Once behind the relative safety of the defilade, Muwanga watched with anticipation as the American military unit came closer.

Muwanga swung the muzzle in the direction of one of the men who was moving along a tree line and shooting down his people as if it was child's play. Muwanga waited until the laser sight locked on to the target and the red lettering on the LCD turned to green and then he squeezed the trigger. The weapon chugged away and sent dozens of 7.62 mm fully jacketed rounds interspersed with tracers in the enemy's direction.

The earth around the approaching Hummers erupted with the impact, sparks emitted from the vehicle as the heavy-caliber rounds deflected the fusillade. Clouds of dust rose and at a lull in the firing, Muwanga watched his enemies scatter for cover. Muwanga changed positions to a fresh machine gun nest set up by Shamus nearby. Smoke still roiled from the red-hot barrel of the first M-60 machine gun even as Muwanga opened up with a fresh volley on his enemies.

CARL LYONS WATCHED helplessly as the terrorists hammered his friends' position.

This was quickly turning into a potential disaster, and Lyons didn't plan to have any more blood on his hands. The thought of the fallen officers at the range building still boiled his blood. He meant to make good on his promise to see Platt drummed out of the DACP service, if possible. He figured his connections could make it happen. Lyons felt a hard knot in his gut at the idea of fallen cops. He'd been an officer with LAPD himself for many years before joining Stony Man, and it still bothered him deeply whenever he heard of a fallen officer. The fact they were Army cops made no difference to Lyons. They were still, many of them, the cream of the crop in Lyons's book. They had practically saved dozens of lives when going up against the crazed Army major who shot up Fort Hood a few years prior and now they were there risking their necks to back up Able Team and make sure that Muwanga and his terrorist goons didn't get escape.

For now, however, he had other concerns that demanded his attention—a distracted soldier could rapidly wind up a dead soldier.

It surprised Lyons as he circumvented the open range field—sticking to the shadows of the wood line so he could come up on the enemy's flank—that he only heard one weapon going. It had been difficult to tell at first but on a closer inspection he realized that it was only one heavy-caliber weapon being fired. In fact, it sounded an awful lot like an M-60 machine gun. Had they actually diminished the terrorists to one lone survivor? It didn't seem possible and yet Lyons knew that if there had been any terrorists left that they would be offering a better resistance than this.

Lyons heard the sound before he saw the shadow that loomed to his right as someone came up on his left flank. Lyons waited until the shadow was large enough, a signal his opponent was in striking distance, and then spun and dropped his weight. Simultaneously he executed a Shotokan foot sweep that caught his unwary stalker at the ankle. The blow toppled the man, who landed on the soft forest floor.

His opponent recovered and rolled from a punch that would certainly have knocked him out cold. The man continued his roll and regained his feet, his dark eyes burning with anger. Lyons also got his footing and took up a ready stance facing his enemy. The man was tall and muscular, with long dark hair and skin. Definitely a Ugandan native, although he could have easily passed as Jamaican with the dreadlocks. Lyons searched the face a moment to verify he wasn't staring at Daudi Muwanga and then readied for the fight.

The man whipped a large combat knife from beneath the camouflage fatigues he wore and charged Lyons with a shout, no doubt an attempt to distract the warrior. Lyons wasn't falling for it and he sidestepped while extending his rock-hard forearm in a clothesline move that caught his opponent just under the chin. The man stumbled but didn't fall, his recovery impressing Lyons enough that the Able Team leader knew he wasn't dealing with a novice. Then again, Lyons was no novice, either, and he was ready for the back slash the man attempted.

Lyons pivoted on his left foot as he swung his right hip around and deflected the slash with a downward block of his right forearm. A moment behind that he followed with a heel-stomp kick that caught the Ugandan terrorist at the back of his left knee and collapsed his strong stance. The terrorist twisted awkwardly, crying out in pain as an audible crack resounded in the air. He'd probably twisted his ankle but it didn't seem to affect him.

This was one tough adversary! The LRA terrorist stepped back and repositioned, waiting for Lyons to approach. Lyons considered going for the Anaconda holstered at his side, but given their proximity he figured there were too many ways such a move could go wrong. If he left even one small opening he might end up with a knife buried in his chest or getting his throat cut, and neither of those were in his plans today.

Lyons went for a feint maneuver and the terrorist fell for it as Lyons purposely targeted the man's uninjured side. The terrorist went to slash at Lyons but made the mistake of overextending just a bit too much. Lyons seized the advantage by changing direction at the last moment and firing a snap kick that caught the terrorist just below the kneecap on his weak leg. The man produced a howl of pain, enough pain that he dropped the blade and Lyons moved in—a relentless offensive would be his only chance to end this quickly. Lyons rocketed a punch that snapped the terrorist's bottom teeth into his uppers. The man's head reeled from the blow and Lyons followed that punch with a knife-hand strike to the throat. The man's shout of pain died into a grotesque gargle of blood as the blow fractured his larynx. Lyons delivered a second kick to the terrorist's solar plexus. Air exploded from the man's lungs as the kick landed with enough force to fracture the sharp end of the sternal process and lacerate the right lung. The man wheezed with the effort of breathing and then collapsed to the ground in a quivering heap. Lyons finished the job by unholstering his Anaconda and pumping a mercy bullet into the guy's skull.

Even as the pistol's thunderous report died out, the machine gun fire continued to echo through the morning air. Lyons realized that whoever was out there wasn't planning to give up without a fight. Time to end it.

Lyons pressed toward his target.

MUWANGA CONTINUED firing the machine gun until it was expended. He switched position back to the first one, which had now cooled a bit, and slapped a new belt into the chamber and snapped it closed. He pressed the stock to his shoulder and took aim on the enemy position.

There was the sudden, unmistakable clicking of a hammer being drawn back, and Muwanga felt the cold barrel of a pistol at the back of his head.

"Put it down," a cold voice ordered.

Muwanga did as instructed.

"Who are you?" Muwanga asked.

"Does it matter?" the man asked.

Muwanga shrugged. "Not really. I guess there was some point in my life where I knew it would end this way for me. I just didn't think it would be this soon."

"People like you usually don't, Muwanga," the man replied.

"You know my name."

"Yeah, but there's some people who know your name

that are wishing they hadn't. You've caused the death of more innocent people today than I care to count."

Behind him, Muwanga could hear the shooting continue as his people fought to maintain control of the situation. The sound of police sirens in the distance began to grind on his nerves. They were already clearly outnumbered. The Americans would only finish what his men had started.

"You are going to kill me," Muwanga said.

"Can you give me a reason not to?"

"I do not wish to give you a reason, American. You must do your duty as I have done mine, to fight for my God and my people."

"You can spare me the speeches," Lyons said.

"There is only one kind of man who will do this—a freedom fighter and a soldier. I am a man who believes that a soldier must fight for his own people. That he must fight for his beliefs and that when it is time to meet his God he should go honorably. This is the only way for a man of a religious fighter, the way of a soldier."

"You're not a soldier, Muwanga. You're a murderer, a fanatic and a nut job. The way to change is peace, never war."

He shrugged. "War is a means to an end, American. But now, if you are going to kill me, and I know you are, I welcome death. In fact, I beg for death. My existence no longer matters because someone will someday replace me. It's inevitable. For now, all I want is death."

When Muwanga reached for the knife on his leg, Lyons granted the terrorist his wish.

EPILOGUE

Stony Man Farm, Virginia

"You did one hell of a job, men," Brognola announced.

"Not that we'd expected any differently," Price added with a smile. She let her gaze rove through the room, scanning the tired faces of the Phoenix Force and Able Team warriors.

"These were unusually difficult circumstances, however," Brognola continued. "We never expected General Kiir would be a traitor to his own people. Or that he would have worked in concert with a man like Lester Bukatem to subvert his own government."

"His motives did seem rather strange to us," Encizo remarked.

"I'm just bloody glad I listened to you, mate," McCarter said. "It was Rafe who actually first suspected there was a traitor among the SPLA ranks. We just didn't think it was that far up."

"Any word on what happened to Kiir?" James asked.

Price nodded. "He was tried and executed by his own army. And it's our understanding that Samir Taha and his brother have been promoted to take over."

"They'll do a good job," Manning said. "They're both top-notch soldiers."

"I'm sure they will," Brognola replied. "There's also no doubt they'll have their work cut out for them. Despite the treaty that separated Sudan into separate entities, there's still a lot of infighting. It's a power grab there, just as it's always been, and the natural fallout from that will be continued strife until the leadership can reestablish a solid infrastructure."

"What about Platt?" asked Lyons, who'd been fuming during much of the debriefing.

"I spoke with the secretary of defense regarding Captain Platt," Brognola said. "That's the most we can do. Stony Man has no authority to dismiss members of another agency, as you know, so I don't know what will be the final determination. According to what I was told, he followed his procedures to the letter."

"He disobeyed an executive order," Lyons protested.

Brognola shrugged and Price said, "There's not a lot we can do about it, Carl. As Hal's already said, we don't have any authority to remove a DACP agency guy from his post. But the secretary did tell us they would conduct a full investigation."

"And despite that, the President was told by Major General Saroyan and Command Sergeant Major Shubin that all three of you deserved medals."

"I think Ironman would rather have his pound of flesh," Schwarz said with a knowing grin.

"Maybe we should just leave this where it's at," Blancanales said with a knowing smile of his own.

Schwarz stuck his tongue out at his friend.

"They did the cleanup at New Orleans," Brognola said, more to change the subject than anything else. "They found a lot of good intelligence that we'll disseminate, redact as necessary and then turn over to the recognized government in Sudan."

"Let's just hope something like this doesn't happen again," McCarter said. "I hate the bloody jungle."

"Hear, hear!" several of his team members chimed in.

Brognola continued. "As I've said, things in Sudan will hopefully stabilize with the treaty between the two territories and the decreased refugee traffic. The American government's also opened up trade negotiations with both sides, including the dispatch of food and medicine."

"Let's hope they can make a go of it," Price added.

"And what about Hansom and Leighton?" Hawkins asked.

"They've both been debriefed and returned to their respective countries," Price said. "I'd imagine that Hansom will be drummed out of the SIS."

"Too bad," McCarter said. "She seemed to have some wits about her."

"There's a better than average chance we haven't seen the last of her. As for Leighton, he'll be reassigned to a somewhat lesser post. He already knew about the LRA operations there, and an informant he had told him about seeing the fuel depot and U.S. armor. That's what generated his investigation and subsequently got him snatched. He made the mistake of reporting his findings to Kiir, thinking the general might actually do something about it."

"But instead, Kiir rolled on him," Manning concluded.

"Right."

"Well, I'd say that's a wrap. You can stand down for now and get some rest. Just don't get too comfy."

"Some new trouble brewing?" Blancanales asked.

"Always." Brognola grinned. "But I'm sure it's nothing you boys can't handle."

* * * * *

TAKE 'EM FREE

2 action-packed novels plus a mystery bonus

NO RISK

NO OBLIGATION TO BUY

James Axler
Outlanders®

DRAGON CITY

**A vengeful enemy plots
a horrifying new assault on humanity.**

A cruel alien race, the Annunaki, has been reborn in a new and
more horrifying form. Enlil, cruelest of them all, is set to revive the
sadistic pantheon that will rule the Earth. Based in his Dragon City,
Enlil plans to create infinite gods—at the cost of humankind. With
the Cerberus team at its lowest ebb, can they possibly stop his
twisted plan?

Available May wherever books are sold.